3.11.2022

Survi

Jo Johnson

For Louise,

Happy Birthday.

I hope you enjoy my novel.

Best wishes

Jo Johnson

x

MYH - Mind Your Head

This edition first published in 2022

Mind Your Head

ISBN (Paperback): 978-1-3999-3532-6

Cover design by Lauren Densham

About the Author

Jo Johnson is a clinical neuropsychologist. She is the author of nine health related publications. She worked within the NHS for two decades before leaving work as an independent practitioner.

Surviving Her is her second novel, and explores themes that, as a psychologist she can write about with conviction and authenticity.

Dedicated to Lucy Funnell – 'It is finished' John 19:30.

1

The Summer Holidays

Nicky, aged nine

'I hate my teacher. I hate Mrs Hobbs because she's a dirty fat liar.'

Nicky's legs are stretched out across his dishevelled bed, his pyjama bottoms too short. Unable to stay still, he jerks his knees up and squeezes his skinny body into a tight ball. Then he rocks forward and back, hitting his head on the inhospitable wall, a little harder each time. The family photographs in brightly coloured frames tremble. But he doesn't care because each bang soothes his tummy, his tangled-up tummy.

Today something disastrous happened. He thrusts his palms into his eye sockets and tries desperately to remember the details. He'd do anything to go back, back to this afternoon, to the time before his dad came home.

He wants to remember exactly what he was doing, because then he could rewind and change it. He could stop it, do as he was told, make it alright.

Today, at exactly six pm, he was at the kitchen table, by the corner with the broken tile, when he heard the electric gates. He stopped what he was doing to pay careful attention. First, the low grumble of the engine crunching up their gravel drive, then the gentle closing of the driver's door and finally the locking ping. His chest released an audible sigh. Dad was home.

'Put that stuff down and put ya bike away,' Dad said, hanging up his long coat. He put down his essential briefcase with a thump and yanked Nicky's cap over his eyes, placing a firm kiss just below his eye. Nicky inhaled his dad's perfume and fresh minty breath.

It's late now but not quite dark, and through his flimsy curtains the swimming pool ladder catches the light. When they moved in, that pool was so deep and so sparkly that he jumped straight in, knees pulled high, holding his nose. It's not blue any more, the sides are green and mouldy.

Nicky tugs at his hair with both hands as he counts, bang, forward and back, bang, forward and back until his limp body runs out of steam and he collapses against his bedroom wall. He sucks in an enormous breath, closes his eyes and goes back to six pm.

Dad's face was hot, towering over him, looking down. There was a cut on his chin where he does the shaving. His head was dipping in a nod, a nod that extended to the outside, like that head gesture could lift his small son into the garden. The battered case was between them. In his picture memory Nicky sees the gold thingy clicking open but dad didn't take anything out.

Nicky chose not to listen. He was doing stuff. But now however hard he tries he can't remember what he kept doing. He can't remember the thing that ruined everything for everyone.

Mum's voice crashes into his mind video. 'Leave the boy alone! He's doing something,' she'd yelled at his dad from the sink.

Nicky buries his face in his hands, not wanting to remember how fast dad was breathing when he shoved his hands into his work pockets on his way to the kettle. Dad flicked on the switch despite the broken lid. The boiling made such a noise that no one could hear what he was saying. He lifted the teddy head off the cookie jar to get a tea bag, then he crashed the lid back down. The teddy is supposed to be full of biscuits not teabags.

Mum did that shaky head thingy when dad dripped brown water near the bin. The mug stayed by the sink. Dad didn't drink his tea, maybe because the sink was too dirty.

'If you don't get your bike in, it'll go rusty. Put it away, Nicky, there's a good boy.' Dad's finger pointed out the window like his son didn't know where to go. The wet splotches smelt of his work.

Nicky knew exactly where his bike was. Poppa says stay within the garden, after all, it's big enough. But going into the crescent makes him feel braver, more grown up. Before he came in, he cycled eleven circuits then discarded his bike half on the pavement, half on the grass, just outside their gates. The front wheel was still spinning.

Nicky's body tightens, he restarts a slow rock to block out dad's face getting redder, his head dripping with sweat; to block out how Nicky tried, he tried to stand up. He was trying to be good for his dad but she took a swig from her glass and then pushed his shoulders down. His bottom was forced back on the chair.

'Give the kid a break he's had a busy day, I'll do it later,' she told his dad, clinking her glass on the table.

Nicky thinks about how his mum looked at him when she spoke to his dad.

His dad had looked at him as well. 'How can a nine-year-old have a busy day? Go to school, eat a sandwich, play on your bike. He'll never learn if you pamper him all the time.'

Nicky looks up at the pictures positioned above his bed. As he remembers balancing on his dad's shoulders to hang the frames, Nicky flings his arms backwards and hits his bedroom wall with the side of his fists. His dad should've known it was the school holidays.

Even though Dad forgot about the holidays, Nicky had tried again to stand up. He wants to learn, to grow up, have a job. He knows without a job, he can't get a house or a wife or a good car with a slippy-back roof.

But Mum had shouted, 'Sit down, I'll do it later.'

He had stayed standing up, jiggled about. If he didn't go to the door, dad would be cross but if he didn't sit down, Mum would be cross. He gets happy more quickly, she's here a lot.

So Nicky had sat back down and carried on, head down, headphones on, doing that thing he wishes he could remember.

Then came the real shouting.

'If you don't put that bike away, I'll put it in Mr Pinkney's skip, then you'll be sorry, won't you?'

Dad was waiting. His chest was going in and out, in and out. He didn't shout very often.

His hands were spread out on the table, waiting. Big hands with nails that are always clean.

The answer was yes. Yes, Nicky would be sorry, he was already sorry, very, very sorry but she was telling him something with her eyes, something he couldn't hear. It was already going wrong. It was already too late.

He tried again.

'Stay exactly where you are, sunshine,' she'd said, grabbing his hood, pulling him back.

Nicky remembers dad's shoulders going down, defeated. His hands rubbing his eyes, his head, the wet sweat went into his hair and made the front bit stand up.

One sock stomped out of the front door but then he changed its mind. Nicky thought it was going to be OK, a usual evening, dad would get changed, he hates feeling dirty. They would eat, he would get his story and fall asleep listening to his dad in the shower.

But, tonight, it wasn't usual. Dad marched back in and pointed his finger near her nose. Then, he screamed at her. He screamed right up to her face. So close, a drip of spit came from his dad's mouth and landed in her hair. 'Tell your kid to put his bike in the shed or I'm telling you, this is *it*.'

Mum put her hands on his shirt and shoved him, she kept pushing with both hands until he was out the door. Then she slammed it, bang!

Nicky startles as he remembers that bang. The window bit at the top wobbled. He thought the glass would smash. Dad's work shoes were still on the mat. He went out in his socks, the blue ones with bright pineapples. When he left, it was silent.

Nicky heard the engine go down their long winding drive, he heard Neil Diamond singing out the car speaker, then the gates opening and slowly shutting. Daddy was gone. Nicky doesn't know how he drove wearing his socks.

The terrace lights outside his room have switched off leaving his bedroom creepy and still. He stops rocking and listens. His mum's sandals are fast padding down the hall. It's twenty-three paces from the lounge to his room.

His heart is stomping and he wipes snotty tears from his face with the back of his hand. He doesn't want his cover getting wet. Then, he scrambles under his bedclothes, hauls the cover over his head and lies completely flat, like a dead boy. He's gone.

Seconds later, his bedroom door flings open, its green knob bangs the wall. Nicky pushes his lips together and holds his breath, hoping she can't see him.

The door closes all by itself, he counts to twenty-three before he breathes out.

Downstairs, her keys jangle as the side door clinks behind her, waving her off. She's gone out again, he knows that. She's gone out and won't be back for hours. She's gone even though she promised Nicky she wouldn't. She's gone even after last time when she begged his dad for forgiveness, promised she'd never leave her boy alone again.

As he thinks about Mrs Hobbs, and her pretty lips spouting lies, the everyday sick feeling seeps out of his tired frame and instead rage fuels his exhausted body. He hurls his duvet onto the floor followed by the stupid baby blankets and leaps out of bed. He jumps up and down on his mattress pounding the wall until the family pictures in their plastic frames lie smashed and unrecognisable all over his sheet.

His teacher promised school holiday fun. She said, 'Whatever you do, boys and girls, you'll have fun.'

'You tell lies, Mrs Hobbs,' Nicky roars as he bangs his forehead on the hard surface. 'I had no fun. My dad went because I left my bike outside. He went in his socks and never came back for his shoes. My daddy left.'

Nicky didn't want this to be *it*. She just had to say sorry, to give his dad his drink. Nicky could've stopped what he was doing and put away his bike. They could have had tea, and story and bed. Nicky is sure it is all his fault and he can't even remember what he was doing.

Nicky knows from now on, everything is going to get a whole lot worse.

Keziah, aged twenty-nine

'I, Keziah Eve Blayton take you, Claus Evan Doerkson...' I hope my guests can't hear the wobble in my voice. After all, I'm Kez, the self-assured one, the good daughter, the mamma bear who stays sober to protect her friends.

'To be my husband, to have and to hold . . . Till death us do part.'

My almost husband flashes me that smile as he repeats the same pattern. That was the smile that made this a done deal at our first drink. It's the smile that crinkles his serious eyes, the smile that lets me in, just me. I alone get to see who he is, who he really is.

'Do you, Keziah, take Claus to be your lawfully wedded husband?' the unkempt religious man splutters as if in a hurry. His dog collar is grubby and he's shaking so much his serious book trembles with each sentence. Thank goodness Ameena and Heidi are behind me. Claus is sufficiently flustered by performance anxiety; a fit of girly sniggering would be the last straw.

'I do.' I do, I do, I do. I suppress the urge to haemorrhage an ABBA song. How on earth did this ordinary girl from a boxy housing estate get this lucky? I catch my mum's eye in the front pew, and for a moment, I wonder. Is she thinking the same thing: that this wasn't what sixteen-year-old Kezzy had in mind? Observing the diamond on my finger and the expensive bracelet, no one would guess this ladylike hand once belonged to a muddy mountain biker who ranted about equality and animal rights. No man was going to imprison her into domestic drudgery. She was destined to be the youngest girl to win the British downhill race.

But that was pre-incident Keziah. That Keziah grew up in a family undefined by tragedy. That Keziah could afford to be selfish. That Keziah could aspire to be whoever she wanted without second guessing what made her parents happy. Mum squeezes dad's hand and for a moment he startles. I've done it! Even if it's just for a few seconds, I've taken away the gaping numbness they suffer every minute of every day. My wonderful mum dabs her eyes with a freshly ironed handkerchief. For once she's crying with happiness.

As if part of a master plan, light from the upper window spotlights my bracelet. The universe is reminding me why this isn't just everything I want, it's also everything I've covenanted to my family.

Despite Claus's promise to stay away last night, at ten to midnight a familiar knock jerked me out of a recurrent dream. I was wearing my oldest dressing gown but without hesitancy I raced to let him in.

'To wear tomorrow,' he said, thrusting a neat box over my mum's threshold with a grin. I yanked him in. 'Sssh,' I whispered, trying not to giggle.

The brown velvet cube was secured with a flimsy white bow. Claus moved from one foot to the other, grinning like a toddler at Christmas. I tentatively tugged at the ribbon.

'Oh, my goodness, you didn't.' I stared open mouthed at intricate silver links underlying sapphire stones.

'I did,' he laughed. I squeezed him so hard he couldn't breathe.

'Put it on then,' he urged, standing me back down.

Taking it out, I glimpsed an engraving. *Forever mine* was etched in italic scrawl.

I fell in love with this bracelet at our first wedding show, then I noticed the hidden price ticket, and hurried away. Claus must've sneaked back to the seller.

The vicar straightens his back and inhales. His eyes are red and watery. 'I pronounce you man and wife.' He closes his exhausted black book, job done.

Yes, Keziah, it's real. You got him, this beautiful, kind man is all yours, for better for worse, for richer, for poorer. Never again will I see my dad's disappointment as I drag some loser over their threshold. My parents were so desperate for me to settle, to bag a good guy, who'd love and protect their precious baby, their only child, their one remaining princess. Their icing will be grandkids, but they'll have to wait a while for that one. Even my beloved Ma and Pa can't have it all in one go.

With throbbing feet and sweat dripping down my front, I slump onto my husband's knee and assault him with a damp kiss. The long tablecloth, once perfectly white, is covered with red stains and crumbs. A couple of wine glasses have passed out alongside the remains of the chocolate cake.

Fingers entwined, we watch my mates prance about whilst my parents laugh at their stupidity. I so want to press pause, slow it all down, savour every moment of my only wedding day. I let my mind wander instead, thinking about what Esther would have made of today. I'm sure none of her boffin friends would be dishevelled and slurring.

Drunk guests or not, today has been everything we planned, right down to the last canapé. I knew instantly we'd found our place when Claus chauffeured me up the bumpy track to this brick barn on the top of a hill. Neither of us were keen on having a soulless reception at a chain hotel. Here the surrounding landscape is mountainous and green. The background slopes in the formal photos can be a small nod to the Kezzy of old.

Then I was gutted: the bloke hosting said the venue's maximum capacity was fifty. I had at least forty on my list. Relatives alone came to over twenty-five, then there were friends from school and university, their partners and a couple of neighbours.

'It's fine, this will be perfect,' Claus told our escort, adding, 'I have only a handful of people to invite anyway.' Before I could question him, they were shaking hands and he was off to pay a deposit.

Our reception is in full swing but Claus has remained here, straight backed at the top table since we finished eating. His fingers are doing their usual tap dance on the table. I know him: he's probably distracted by work even on his wedding day. As a child psychologist, there's always an urgent case, a vulnerable kid arrested, a neglected child left home alone, hungry and dirty. But surely that kid can be someone else's problem for our day.

Before I can check in with my new hubby and make sure he's OK, Tristan wrestles me back onto the dance floor. I give Claus a half-hearted tug to follow but he resists, and I smile to myself; this is definitely not his thing.

'Come on slacker, time to live up to your dancing queen reputation,' Tristan shouts over the music pulling me back to the swell of sweaty bodies and racing hearts. His tie is secured around his head, the tail dangling over his nose. What an idiot!

He twirls me around to 'I Wanna Dance With Somebody'.

Tristan slurs the lyrics out of tune, adding close to my ear, 'I can't believe you didn't marry me.'

'You had your chance,' I remind him, laughing but desperately glad we didn't stay together.

'You claimed to be a militant feminist with no need of a man.'

'Yeah well, deep down I wanted a prince like all the girls.'

'Well, congrats, looks like you got him.' He nods as Claus appears behind me.

Claus' bow tie remains neat and close to his collar. He guides me out of ear shot, his hands on my shoulders until I'm beyond the hub of excited guests. My whole body tingles at his touch as he huddles close to show me a message on his phone.

'Honey, I'm so sorry, the car was booked for later but it's here, I've had a text from the driver.'

'But it's only' – I lift his arm to squint at the Apple watch – 'ten past ten. Can't we ask him to wait?' I try not to sound as upset as I am.

Claus flashes his usual open smile but I can tell he's distracted by the uni lot. Shaun is trying to balance a coin on his nose, and Tristan has sloped back to the bar. When I fell in love with a man twelve years my senior I should've known there would be minor differences.

He pulls his hand back and places it behind my elbow to steer me further from the noisy hub of activity.

'I'm so sorry. I know you're not ready but the driver has another job and, anyway, I can't wait to have my wife all to myself,' he whispers in my ear.

To be fair, I'm desperate to get to the hotel he's booked. I've seen the pictures, it's amazing – but the barn is ours until midnight and full of people I've not seen in years.

'OK, I'll just give Ameena and Heidi the heads up as they've rehearsed an exit routine.' I pull on my big girls pants and give myself a talking to; after all, I've had it all my way so far.

Five minutes later, Claus and I join hands to skip under the canopy of entangled arms. I twist my head this way and that, unwilling to miss a minute. Claus lets me go as we run from the display, everyone clapping and cheering as we disappear. Wishing just another half an hour with them, I steal a last glance at my loved ones – all except one – all in one place.

I can't suppress my giggles as the hotel manager struggles to work out how to use the entry card to open our room. Surely he can't be as tipsy as me.

Oh, my goodness! The room is incredible, absolutely huge; all my mates could share and still have dancing room. It's bigger than my old flat. There's a settee, a writing desk, our own little kitchen area with a coffee machine and mini fridge.

Taking water from the mini bar, Claus perches on the end of the bed and crosses his legs. He's used to luxury but this is seriously the most fabulous place I've ever stayed. I rush about the honeymoon suite, inspecting all the fancy features. A little tipsy, I twirl around, spreading out my arms as I dance. So much space.

Landing on Claus's lap, I snuggle into an unresponsive torso. His arms and legs remain folded.

'What the matter?'

Silence.

'Claus?' I wrap my arms around his neck and push my lips to his cheek. I can smell the extra strong mint he crunched in the taxi.

He reaches behind his neck and pulls my hands down, standing up so I have no choice but to get off. I slip off my shoes, balancing on the edge of the expansive bed, not entirely sure what to do.

'You know what's the matter,' he says looking down at me.

'I don't.'

'Who was he?'

'Who was who?'

'The man you were making out with at *our* wedding.'

He turns his back on me, hands stuffed in front pockets; he marches towards the bathroom but then changes his mind, spins around and comes back. Behind him, the expansive jacuzzi awaits.

'The idiot with the pink shirt and fat belly,' he snaps.

'Oh, you mean Tristan, we were mates at uni.' I smile up at him.

His six-foot frame casts a shadow over the bed as he reaches down for my hand. I hold it higher, ready to be pulled up for a physical apology. Poor Claus, winding himself up for no reason. He stands still, pauses for a moment, suddenly unsure of himself, distracted. I hear voices in the corridor, a female giggle. My hand flops back into my lap; I'm suddenly overwhelmed with exhaustion. My face remains tilted towards my new husband as he runs his fingers through his hair, creating the tousled look I adore. Finally, he looks down and reaches for my hand. Thank goodness, at last. I'm desperate for my honeymoon to start.

I close my eyes, wanting to savour every moment, his hands are softer than the men I've known. My body sighs, ready for his kiss. Instead, his fingers entangle with the intricate links of my bracelet. I twist my wrist so he can easily unfasten it. But, rather the gentle touch of intimacy, my hand drops down at the force of his next gesture. I gasp, my eyes flick open, disbelieving. Claus gives a final wrench and my bracelet snaps in two.

My eyes jerk from my arm to his face. Claus is staring with an expression I haven't seen. His fist is clenched around my bracelet.

As if sleep-walking, his movements slow to a trance. He advances one step at a time to the bathroom. Lifting his closed hand high above his head, he opens it to release my precious gift onto the hard floor. For a small item, there is considerable noise as it bounces across the ceramic tiles. One of the stones rolls towards the bath.

Uncertainty swamps me as I move closer, not knowing what's coming next. Is he ill? What on earth is happening to him?

My eyes widen as he stamps his foot onto the delicate jewellery. Still in slow motion, he twists his shoe around and around, as if to grind a silver powder. Suddenly, as if only just aware of my watching, he looks up. He sees me. He meets my gaze. Momentarily we connect. Then he launches forward and slams the heavy door in my face.

2

The Next Day

Nicky

The next morning, the sun is shining through Nicky's bedroom. The blackout material is still in the Waitrose bag by the front door.

Nicky shivers but can't find his dressing gown. His first thought is about yesterday. Did dad come back or did the *it* he was shouting about mean he wasn't coming back ever? If he wasn't coming back ever, did this mean Nicky no longer had a dad or just that his dad wasn't ever coming back to this house?

Out of his window, a baby squirrel runs around the edge of the pool. Nicky traces its path with his finger on the inside of the glass. The bottom pane has a large crack and he can feel a draft on his hand. If only he knew how to refill the pool with blue glistening water. He closes his eyes and remembers splashing with dad while she sunbathed with her drink and a magazine.

Everything outside looks the same. He wants to open his bedroom door but thoughts warn him. Be careful. As soon as he goes into the hall, he'll know. He'll know for sure if it's going to be OK. He wants to know but he doesn't. With his ear squashed against the cold wood, he can only hear quiet.

The door creaks as he twists the smooth knob. He tries to move, he wants to go to their room but instead he shuts the door so quickly the air blows his hair. Spinning around he leans his full body weight against it, so nothing bad can enter.

Everything is quiet, except Bella who is barking at the birds. Rocking back gently without banging his head, he plucks up courage to try again. This time, he does it, he steps outside his room, slams the door and sprints up the hall. First, he pushes into his parents' bedroom. Nothing is in the four-post bed. The covers are made but dad isn't here. He's not in the spare room either. Creeping out of that room, the room where his dad mostly sleeps even though Nicky's not supposed to know, a flash of inspiration comes. Then he knows. He knows if his dad returned and it's going to be OK, his bike will be back.

Because it's school holidays he has no idea about the time but it's before school. It's probably before breakfast as the dustcart is in their crescent. Pointing his toes to keep his footsteps silent, he studies the lounge, the kitchen and the dining area. What a mess, like a bomb has hit it.

Her legs are hanging over the side of the sofa. Why does she do that? Dad got a corner sofa for when she stays up all night. She's in her day clothes, yesterday's day clothes. The man on the telly is cooking a chicken with a sausage up its bum. Nicky can't think of anyone who would want to eat that. There is no sound coming from the television. Nicky takes the remote from under her face and turns off the screen.

Suppressing a familiar disgust, he bends his face to her mouth. Dribble bubbles from her lips reminding him of something fizzy. Her breath smells of cabbage. He feels sick, not sick like when he's ill. Sick like when he spins around and around on his rope swing. A tuft of her hair stands to attention, hiding her sparkly stud.

She's still as he carefully flattens his palm on her chest and twists an ear to her mouth. The paramedic who came last time said that's how you check if she's alive.

She's alive.

When he shifts her to remove the glass bottle, the remote slips to the floor with a crash. He holds his breath but she doesn't stir. He wipes the red liquid off the side table with the sleeve of his pyjamas and takes the bottle to the kitchen, where he chucks it in the recycling; it clinks the other bottles. By the sink, the fairy liquid is nearly empty so he has to shake it to get some bubbles. The washing up makes him smell grandma and her pink rubber gloves. If only she and Poppa still lived here, the house would smell of cake and he wouldn't feel sick so much.

He washes the glass, being super careful not to smash it. If she wakes up there'll be trouble. Was that what his dad meant yesterday about avoiding the egg shells? When she sleeps in the lounge there's always some trouble.

Today is supposed to be the summer but it's freezing. He finds his dressing gown under his mum's bony bottom but the cord isn't there. Dad says you shouldn't go out in pyjamas but she does even when the dustmen are here.

As he creeps out of the front entrance, a slippery shiver goes from his head to his feet, and he wishes he could tie up his dressing gown. Dad's car is not on the drive. They both love that flash car with its slippy-back roof.

Even though they have the longest driveway in Castlegate he can hear Harry, the driver, shouting to the other man. Nicky wishes he knew his name too. He likes knowing people's names. It makes him feel important.

The gravel hurts his toes as he runs down the drive in his slippers. Today their drive is even longer than on a school day. He tries hard to imagine his bike in the place where it should be, just outside the gate. If it's there, everything will be OK.

He jams his hand on the silver pad to open the monstrous gates. He hates those gates. One day they'll squash him to death like a T-Rex eating fish. He holds his breath and runs to the other side when the gap in the middle is wider than him.

The pavement has chalk from yesterday; through his hedge he had watched two kids from across the road as they scratched their coloured chalks on his pavement. A drawing of a man and a house. The roof is smudged and the man has arms that are too long. Above the door, it says Ollie's house. After the boys went in, Nicky had a go, wishing he had a brother; even a sister might do. His rubbish pictures are still there. He didn't write his name so the neighbours will think Ollie did those too.

The bike is not on the pavement.

He needs to check next door's skip. If he can get his bike out, dad will return. After all, his car is often gone by morning, and sometimes work disappears him for weeks. Yes, he decides, that's it. Dad came back, but left early for the office and will be back for supper. How pleased his dad will be. Nicky grins at the thought of it – the bike exactly where it should be, inside the garage, next to the old wellingtons and dad realising his son isn't pathetic and bad but brave and strong.

Mr and Mrs Pinkney live next door. Mum calls *her* 'the silly cow'. She says that about lots of ladies, the one in the shop, her boss and sometimes even grandma. Mr P, as he told Nicky to call him, is kind and lets Nicky stroke Bella, their dog.

Nicky squats, then crawls on his hands and knees through his hedge hole as the next-door gates are too far to walk. As he squashes through, his dressing gown rides up and the twigs scratch the naked space between his bottoms and the top.

In the middle of the drive is a big yellow skip. The tub is enormous and at first, Nicky's scared he'll die in there because no one has lost him. He would love to be brave like boys at school but he knows he is a weak boy who is always scared. So he is delighted when he finds a plastic chair he can use to climb the skip. The chair gives him enough height to almost peep over the top. He thinks of his bike with cartoon characters on the side and the metal bell he got for Christmas. He can't wait to yank it back home. Swallowing a massive breath as if swimming underwater, he stretches so hard until his arms are straight and hurting but he can see, he can see over the top. There are two lounge chairs, a wheel and loads of brown cardboard. Tillie cat is sleeping on the wheel.

His bike is not there.

Nicky drops back down, scraping his lip on the side of the chair as he lands. The tears take over his eyes and fall down his cheeks and into his mouth. For a moment, he lies back in the damp grass of Mr P's garden, paralysed by a sense of hopelessness. His bike is not in the skip or in the garden. It is not going to be OK. His bike has gone and so has dad. Why was he so stupid?

Eventually the cold gets too much and he crawls like a swimming soldier. He drags himself all the way back on his belly so Mr P won't see him. He doesn't care that his knee gets grazed as he struggles back through the hedge.

When he gets in, his mum is sitting up with the television back on. It's really loud and for a minute he covers his ears with his hands. He sees his reflection in the fancy mirror with gold around the edge. He makes his face into a big smile. He pretends he has found his bike and that everything is a normal day.

‘Shall I make toast for us?’ he asks in his cheerful voice, and gets the butter out anyway.

He counts to an even number while the toast is baking, but it pops up too early so he has to push it back down and start again even though it’ll burn.

Nicky sits with her and eats toast with marmite, well he has marmite, his mum just has butter. Tears are coming down her cheeks. He knows it’s his job to cheer her up, to make her happy but he can’t find his bike and nothing is clean. He clears away their plates, lugs up gran’s hand-knitted blanket and sits next to her on the sofa. It’s harder to fit on a lap these days.

‘It’s just you and me now,’ she says, pushing her face into the back of his hair, but then she’s asleep again and Nicky is all alone.

Keziah

The clock says 7am so I must've eventually fallen asleep. My first sight on my second day married is the narrow back of my newly acquired husband. He's fully dressed in his expensive but crumpled suit, his tan shoes are hanging off the bed. With every out breath, a gentle snore reassures me he's still asleep.

Everything is not alright. The mess in my head is like the aftermath of a robbery: I recognise the rooms are mine but everything is so distorted it appears misshapen, confused. Important things are missing, but I don't know where to look or what to upturn to find them. Everything feels tarnished.

The seagulls squawk their morning greeting, rude and intrusive. Perhaps they're belly laughing at the woman who believed herself worthy of love. Muffled voices seep through the walls, a giggle and the sound of running water. Honeymoon corridor, ecstatic couples lapping up early marital bliss. Defiant tears force their way out. What did I do wrong?

Last night has played over and over, scene by scene, on fast forward, on pause and then rewind. I can't find any answers. After breaking my bracelet, Claus stayed locked in the ensuite. Eventually I knocked, called his name with enforced dignity, then I knocked harder, a pleading tone seeping through. And finally, I collapsed on my knees, weeping and begging for answers, banging with fists, no longer caring about being overheard, snot and tears all over my face.

I got nothing. Silence.

Wearing the complimentary robe, I searched for a communal bathroom and sat on a closed toilet until my feet went numb with cold. My phone was constantly pinging with messages of congratulations, and Ameena calling, asking for the first telling of the honeymoon night. I let it go to voicemail. I couldn't bear the shame of sharing the truth: that my sweet, kind husband wasn't who I thought he was. I had been so furious with Ameena when she kept asking if I was sure. But maybe she was right. Maybe you can't fall in love in a matter of weeks, maybe a six-month engagement is too short. Maybe I'm a complete fool, so desperate to give myself and my parents the happy-ever-after that I've ruined my life and theirs.

In the sweet-smelling bathroom, I waited and waited for Claus to search for me. At 3am, I gave up and retreated back along the dim-lit corridors. I convinced myself he had tried looking for me. Of course, I told myself as I stomped back to our suite, he is waiting. Head in hands by the door, overflowing with remorse for his behaviour, promising never to repeat.

As I flashed the key under the handle, and stepped disoriented into the black space, Claus did not rush to help. Our room was quiet except for the gentle snore of deep contented slumber. He was fully clothed on top of the luxurious cover, sound asleep.

In front of the fairy-lit mirror there was enough light to remove the smudged mess of my wedding make-up. In its dancing reflection, I saw the contents of my suitcase, spilt on the deep carpet. The silky pyjamas, a gift from my bridesmaids, were lying discarded on the top.

Half hoping he'd wake, I ripped off my carefully chosen crimson dress and lobbed it against the wall. Despite the thud, Claus's breathing remained the same: even, undisturbed, exhausted after a busy day. I pulled an exercise vest over my sexy underwear and tried to soothe my racing brain. I couldn't find words to express my confusion, the depths of despair.

In an attempt to stop myself shaking I crept into the cold bed, pulled the covers up to my nose and rolled to the far edge. I watched his right shoulder rise and fall with each breath and wondered whether to leave. Instead, I visualised romantic memories in an attempt to reassure myself that a charming, generous man does not behave like a monster. This is the man who sat on the bath holding my hair, refusing to leave when I was throwing up. This is the man who brings me flowers, buys my family gifts and, when I cry, encourages me to express my true feelings. He's the first to step aside when people push in the queue. He's a child psychologist for goodness sake, a healer, one of the good guys.

My heart reacts as he stirs in the morning light. Claus is not one for a lie-in, routine is to him as breathing is to everyone else. Get up, run, a quick shower before a healthy breakfast.

He turns over to face me. His clothes are heavily creased and his hair unkempt but he's smiling, a quiet, uncertain smile, but definitely a smile. A withheld breath escapes, relief floods my entire system. My Claus is back.

'Can you believe we are married?' is his morning greeting. He inches closer and holds my uncertainty for longer than is comfortable, then he kisses my nose. 'I'm a lucky, lucky man.'

He stretches, gets up and strolls to the bathroom. This time, the door is left open, as his playlist ignites. He alternates between shaving and whistling along to Lionel Ritchie's 'All Night Long'.

Listening to my husband's mellow voice, relief floods me. I'm so glad I didn't do anything rash last night. I was so close to calling Ameena, getting a taxi home.

It dawns on me suddenly how hard yesterday must've been for him with my family and friends dominating the celebrations. After much reflection, he only invited three colleagues, as well as his next-door neighbour and the bloke he occasionally plays tennis with. Claus said he hated standing up in front of people, making a spectacle of himself. He wanted it to be my day, for my friends and family to take centre stage. He added that it didn't matter anyway as apart from me, there aren't really any significant people in his life. In the end only a half empty pew was saved for his cheerleaders.

Knowing how close I am with my mum, it makes me tear up to think about how alone Claus is in the world. His father passed away years ago and his mother lives abroad. She had called to offer congratulations when her confetti-filled invitation had arrived.

'He's a lucky man, Keziah,' she'd said when I answered the phone. Her accent has consolidated after decades in the sun. Before I could respond, she filled the silence. 'We can't afford to come, I wanted you to know first.'

'Oh, don't you worry about that, Claus has been promoted to consultant and I'm earning a good wage. We'll pay for you and L— Simon.' My face flushed as I almost named her second husband.

'That's so sweet of you, Keziah, but we can't possibly accept, you see, Simon is very proud. He would hate to feel indebted to Claus.'

I feel instantly guilty, ashamed. Why didn't I consider his feelings? How would I feel if my own mother couldn't be bothered to come to my wedding? If my own father had died years ago? He put so much work into our wedding day, making sure my family had their happy ending that I didn't stop to think that he might be sacrificing his own feelings.

'Right then, Mrs,' he says when he comes from the shower, 'get your married clothes on. We've got a plane to catch.' Claus waits expectantly with his hand gestured to lever me up from the mattress. My body moves more slowly than expected as I allow him to pull me up. I try to reconnect with my excitement but my mind is hesitant, still unwilling to embrace honeymoon behaviour, still hurt and confused by last night.

Standing together in our painstakingly chosen room, overlooking the sea, everything is so normal. The promenade is busy with couples, hand in hand. So why do I feel like throwing open the window and screaming, 'Is it me?' at the passers-by?

Fifteen minutes later, the room is restored to its impersonal order, our clothes neatly packed, his neater than mine. We slip simultaneously and silently into our casual shoes. We're on our way. The honeymoon night is well and truly over.

Whilst I wait by the door, Claus meticulously checks we haven't left anything.

Clearing away the final few things, a comb, half a packet of polos and a tissue for the bin, his hand stumbles across a small box with a brown lid and a broken seal. He avoids looking up. I can tell he doesn't know what to do. His face flushes as he fiddles with the ribbon. He looks like a little boy who realises he's in big trouble but doesn't know what to do.

'Don't worry, baby,' I say rushing across the room, relieved to be able to comfort him, to be able to finally say something. Snuggling into his body I rest my head on his chest and whisper, 'Whatever it is, we'll work it out.'

He swallows, I hear a small cough before he speaks. Here we go, I tell myself, he'll talk about his embarrassment, the shame of losing his temper. No doubt he was tired, sad about his mum's absence. 'What on earth came over me?' he'll say. 'Maybe someone spiked my drink?'

He breaks out of our embrace and, with a lightness in his tone, says, 'Oh dear, flimsier than we thought.' He throws the box in the bin. 'Less flirting, next time, eh?' He looks at me with expectation and raises his eyebrows into a question.

Surely he didn't just say what I think he did? I wasn't flirting. I was giggly, perhaps. I spoke to loads of people, that's what the bride is supposed to do, isn't it?

I shuffle some responses in my head but my dry lips only manage to mumble, 'Sorry.'

'Oh, don't worry, sweetheart.' He opens his arms and tries to pull me towards him. 'You're one hundred percent forgiven,' he whispers before affectionately nuzzling my neck.

Our honeymoon was truly amazing. Claus had booked a villa nestled in a lush tropical garden facing the ocean. I've never seen such clear water. I sent a few pictures to Ameena with the plunge pool as a backdrop.

'So jealous,' she replied with a picture of Mark asleep on the settee with his mouth wide open, his cap pulled down over his face.

We spent the mornings lounging on comfortable sun beds. I read eight novels. Most evenings we followed the edge of the water with bare feet to a restaurant overlooking the beach. A talented pianist played as we savoured a different fish each evening.

Everything was so perfect.

National Hospital of Neurology

Admission Report

NHS number: 485 777 3496 Gender: *female*

Circumstances surrounding admission:

Admitted by ambulance. Unconscious when paramedics arrived. Circumstances leading to injuries unclear. Police still gathering witness statements and are to be immediately notified if patient regains consciousness.

Condition on admission:

- Severe and complex neurological and physical injuries
- Broken vertebrae in lower spine – no movement from mid chest down
- Skull fracture above right ear and potentially a second one at back of head

Expected outcome:

Injuries most likely incompatible with life. Family advised the next forty-eight hours are crucial but death is the most likely outcome. If recovery, there will be severe and enduring mental and physical disabilities that will not resolve within life span.

Plan:

- Awaiting fmri results
- To discuss DNR (Do not resuscitate) with family.
- To take neuro obs every two hours
- Refer to complex brain injury team
- To discuss with Putney about admission if condition stabilises into low awareness state
- Contact within police – DCI Chris O Leary

Signed:

Dr A. Lutte-Elliott

CONSULTANT IN NEUROREHABILITATION

3

The New Term

Nicky

A barking Bella startles Nicky awake. He notices two things at once. He's very hungry and something sticky is on his face.

The voice of his new alarm is terrifying. He stops it with a bash and the large round object loses balance and falls to the floor. Nicky doesn't care if it smashes.

Dad sent the clock through the post with a letter.

Dear Nicky,

I'm sorry to not be there for your first day back. Your uniform is hanging in the spare room. I'm sending this talking clock to keep you company. It can wake you up for school. I have found a new flat with room for you to stay. At the moment I'm working so hard I won't be able to visit but in a few weeks, Gran will bring you here. I'll see you real soon I promise.

Love, Daddy

The clock did wake him.

Ping. He flicks the switch for his football lamp. He slaps at his face to retrieve the sticky thing. It's a note that's stuck to his face. He remembers now.

It says, 'Dear Nicky, don't forget it's school tomorrow. From Nicky.'

Now it's tomorrow and it's school. He counts to nineteen. Nineteen is a new favourite number. When he gets to nineteen, he can get up. His feet are freezing because the under-floor heating is still broken. The talking clock can't fix things or make breakfast or help with his guided reading. He gives it a hard kick on his way to the hall, the round metal spins away, ending up face down in his ensuite. Nicky hopes the stupid present is dead.

No one sits to eat at the table anymore, they sit on the sofa. He can watch television before school, that's cool. Dad wouldn't like that. When dad was here, he took charge of breakfast. If he left early, he would put butter, strawberry jam and cereal on the table; Nicky would do the toast, she would do the milk. Dad says breakfast is the most important meal of each day.

Now dad's gone, there's nothing on the table and no milk in the fridge.

'Hurry up, Nicky,' she shouts from her bedroom. 'Lou will be here in twenty minutes.'

Nicky stares at his too short trousers, thinking it's not him who isn't ready. Even though he's dragged his socks up high, there's still too much pale leg.

Mum races in with her cardigan half on, half off and plonks herself next to him. She's in her pyjamas. Nicky always puts four bits of toast on his plate, two for him, two for her. She takes a buttery triangle and changes the channel to watch her programme, boring people chatting about news stuff.

The phone in the kitchen rings making them both jump. Usually people ring on her mobile.

'Really!' she shouts chucking her toast on the plate as if it's Nicky doing the phoning. She snatches the handset from its place and sits back down.

'Can't you tell the time, it's his first day for goodness sake,' she snaps.

'It's your dad.' She holds the phone to Nicky's ear, then points the TV remote to make it louder.

'Hello, Dad.'

Nicky balances the plate on his leg to hold the handset, his fingers are sticky from jam.

'Hello, Nicky.'

'Hello, Dad.'

His dad laughs. Nicky imagines his laughing face, eyes screwed-up so you can't see much blue.

'How you doing, son? I'm so sorry I haven't been able to see you. It's a long work trip.'

Nicky thinks he didn't call him son when he lived here.

'OK.'

'I'm calling to wish you a happy first day back at school.'

'OK.'

'Gran and Poppa are going to bring you here, you'll love the flat, it's near the sea, I've got a scooter for you.'

'OK.'

Nicky wonders about his bike, did his dad take that to his flat?

'Alright then, see you next weekend.' Dad laughs again but Nicky can't work out the joke.

'OK.'

Mum can't do any school runs. Most days he'll walk, but for the first few weeks Kerry's mum Lou will lift him. Lou is very nice but he hates Kerry.

Nicky hasn't seen dad since that Saturday when he came for his case. Today he's been gone thirty-six sleeps. Nicky ticked it off last night on the coloured chart under his mattress.

On the Saturday after his bike went, she had woken him when he was still asleep.

'Come on, sleepy head,' she'd said with her hand on his head. That was a good sign, a sign she was having a happy day. She was up before him so she must have slept in her bed. When she sleeps in her bed, it's usually a happier day.

Nicky was pretending to stay asleep so she would keep stroking his hair. Then a hard knock came. Nicky knew it was his dad's knock even though he was knocking on his own door. He flipped back the cover so fast, she nearly fell off his bed. He ran and opened the front door. Dad was in front of him, hands in his pockets. He didn't take off his shoes.

Nicky didn't like dad's eyes, they were big, he could see too much of the blue.

'Hello son, how are you?' Dad was smiling but it wasn't a happy smile

Dad wasn't pleased to see him.

Nicky desperately wanted to blurt out, 'Sorry, I was going to put the bike away,' but before he could, she came.

'Not now, Nicky, go to your room.' She pushed him out the way. Her hand felt hard but she wasn't looking at him, she was dragging an old case by a loop handle. It didn't have wheels like the holiday ones. Dad grasped the loop and dragged it towards him. He couldn't see dad anymore because she stood in the way. Then she slammed the door.

When he heard the whirr of the gates, Nicky collapsed on the floor and sobbed. She found a screwed-up tissue from her pocket.

'Come on, don't cry. You have to be strong. After all, it's just you now. You're the man of the house.'

1 kick, 2 kick, 3 kicks. Come back, dad. 4 kicks, 5 kicks, please come back.

'Nicky, hurry up, you'll be late for school,' Mum screeches from Lou's car.

Mum puts her head back in the driver's window. Her bum is sticking out like a pantomime horse, and she's in her slippers. Mrs Pinkney doesn't like pyjamas in the road, even under cardigans.

Nicky is not stupid. Kerry's mum can't drive with his mum's head in the window.

10 kicks, 11 kicks, please, please, please come back, dad. The wall is hard, his foot hurts but he doesn't care. He's not getting in that car until he's done thirty-six kicks. One kick for each sleep his dad has missed. One kick for each day that's been ruined. One kick for each day he remembered Mrs Hobbs was a liar.

When he's done with punishing the wall, he tugs his school bag behind him, pretending it's his dog. He turns around and waves at the kitchen window so Kerry thinks he's saying goodbye to his dad.

Kerry's ugly pig nose is squashed against the back window. He hates her and pushes his tongue out like Billy's pet snake. Girls stink. One time she tried to kiss him in the back of the car.

Lou is staring out the front windscreen, squeezing the steering wheel.

He creeps up behind his mum. Her talking is fast, she has lots to say to Lou.

'No, not this time.'

'I know, but no going back now.'

'Looking for a flat.'

'Nicky's fine, nothing has changed for him.'

Nicky wants to swing his bag above his head and smack her right in the face. Everything has changed for him and he hates it and he hates her.

'Don't mention anything to Nicky, we've not spoken yet,' she says to Lou whilst he's climbing in next to Kerry.

'God hates divorcing,' Kerry mutters when he's clicking his seatbelt in. The straw from the juice carton is in her tooth gap. He turns his head away from her disgusting sucking. He has no clue what she's on about.

Louise pushes the button to raise her window, his mum pulls her fingers back fast.

Kerry moves towards him, Nicky shuffles towards his door and ignores her.

'My Sunday school teacher said God hates divorcing,' she hisses in his ear

'Who is God?' he asks moving further away. Last term she gave him head lice, Mum had to cover them all in disgusting sauce. Dad had to rub it in his beard. He wasn't best pleased.

'God is a very important person who lives in heaven.' Drops of juice dribble out of her mouth when she talks.

'Oh, what does he hate?' Nicky asks.

'The divorce.'

'What's that?'

'When parents break apart. Everything goes into different houses. My auntie Liz got the divorce. She hates Uncle Neville now. She told my mum he is a terrible human bean.'

'Oh.'

He leans back and closes his eyes; his head hurts, he's exhausted and he's frightened he might throw up.

It's hard to sleep now he's the man in the house. When his dad was here, Nicky's sleep came when dad turned on the water for his shower. Now dad doesn't shower, the sleep won't come. He knows that he needs to be brave as the man of the house but when he can't get to sleep, he gets very scared.

At night, in his bed, he can hear the television but she doesn't come. Brave boys don't need stories, they can read to themselves. Dad used to do his guided reading when she loaded the dishwasher, before she stopped doing things like that. Guided reading tells him he's got a word wrong. If he doesn't know when the words are wrong, he won't learn; if he can't read, he won't get a job. If he doesn't get a job, he'll have no house or a wife.

When the car jolts to a stop outside the school gates, Nicky doesn't know where he is or what he needs to do. All Nicky knows for sure, is that he doesn't want to be the man.

Keziah

I've always loved the first day of the school year, even as a child. It was Esther who cried. It's so frustrating that even on my happiest of days, with a September freshness in the air, a random thought about her brings a lump to my throat and a heartfelt apology.

Newly promoted and married, surely this is it; surely I've made it. But what would Esther think of me now? I hope she'd be proud of how much I've changed. I hope she feels I've made up for what I took.

Marching across the tarmac with amateur confidence, I'm desperately grateful the sun is shining and there's virtually no wind. For my debut performance I want to fling open the classroom door and smile at the carefully dressed mothers with my head held high. I survey the length of the school building and smile; this is where I fit best. The traditional brick is decorated with brightly coloured trees. This was our first joint project, Ameena's logic and my creativity. When we suggested each leaf would be a pupil's hand print, the deputy head looked horrified. Thankfully, she was outvoted and the whole school came together to finish it, each child playing their part, making their mark. I simply love this place. Here I can make a difference, I can change lives forever.

My classroom is accessed from a side entrance which means I can sneak in early and do my prep before anyone notices. With my head down, key in hand, I scurry around the corner only to almost trip over a lone child crouched in a small ball, his back against the wall. He must've been deposited far too early, not even the keen parents are here at this time. Usually I'd sit down, have a few words, make a connection – these unseen kids pull at my heart strings – but today, just as I go to crouch down next to him, I see another teacher walking purposefully towards him. Thank goodness. I can't afford to be distracted today.

Securing the last display poster on the window, I catch my reflection as I reach up. I wish I'd stuck with my chunky belt, but Claus's throwaway comment made me think again.

'Is that what you're wearing for work, sweetheart,' he'd said when I was putting my coat on to leave.

'Yeah, why?'

'Mmm, it looks lovely but I'm wondering if the belt makes it a little clingy in places?'

Not wanting to be late, I unfastened it in a huff and left it on the floor.

The butterflies in my stomach are competing for the Winter Olympics but I brush the chalk off my sleeve, plaster on the face that shouts 'I've totally got this' and gesture for the kids to pour in. I taught this class when they were in Reception so I know most of their families.

Debbie Clay is on the verge of tears as she cuddles Matilda for an inappropriately long time. She's pregnant again but still on her own. For years I thought I'd have kids early like my mum but I have no desire to start that game just yet. If I work hard I reckon I'll get a headteacher post by the time I'm in my mid-thirties. Perhaps then I'll think about kids.

When I look up from Debbie's swollen belly, I catch sight of Jon Barrat and shudder. He hasn't changed much, still a foul-mouthed idiot who thinks personalised plates gives him licence to abandon his car on double yellows. I've hated this man since the first day we met. So how ironic that my very own cupid was Liam Barrat, who is absolutely his daddy's son.

The day I met Claus was a pants day, in a pants week.

A few days before had been the anniversary of the accident. If that wasn't hard enough, the following day, Dylan, the useless bloke I'd been seeing, ditched me for the waitress at The Red Lion.

My students had been unfocused and hard to teach. Liam had already managed to upset four kids and give Harry a nose bleed. I was losing control and could feel the tears pricking at the back of my eyes. The golden rule of teaching is never let the kids see you're losing.

The lunch bell was a massive relief. My head was throbbing.

Before I gave permission for them to get up, Liam sprang up to escape into the playground. His metal chair collided with Kelly's leg as he went, and with a bawling Kelly hanging off my cardigan, the rest of them scrambled for the door.

In an attempt to restore order, I squeezed between the sea of navy jumpers to police the exit, dragging Kelly with me. Unfortunately, she tripped and flew headfirst onto the concrete. This was it, the moment I'd been dreading, the reason I almost didn't apply for teaching – one of my children, catastrophically injured.

Watching a small girl bleeding on the floor, her leg at an awkward angle, took me straight back to the worst moment of my life. My throat tightened and my hands shook.

I wobbled about trying to steady myself and stared helplessly as blood oozed from Kelly's head. The other children crowded around. Sweat was gathering at my hairline and the wooshing in my ears was deafening. Small faces peered up at me, fear in their eyes, as they realised 'Miss' wasn't up to the job.

To stop myself fainting, I grabbed onto the door frame. The last thing I heard was Liam shouting, 'Get a teacher, Miss Blayton's dying.'

And then *he* came. As if by magic, in rushed a broad-shouldered knight with a battered case, a long coat and a bow tie. He discarded his bag, scooped up Kelly, a fireman cradling a limp body out of a blazing house.

As he brushed past me, the stranger mouthed, 'Worse than it looks.'

I couldn't quite place his accent as he calmly reassured Kelly. 'Don't you worry, little lady, your teacher is just here and you're going to be as good as new.' He sounded suitably deep and heroic, precise but not too posh. He gently unfolded her onto a chair, stemming the bleeding with a spotted scarlet handkerchief, then removed an old-fashioned hat to reveal thick blonde hair with a floppy fringe, grabbed another chair and gestured to me.

'And how are you, quite a shock for you as well?' he said, leaning down.

On a cold chair too small for my frame, my senses came back in a rush. Whilst I was swooning, a man had entered my classroom without a visitor pass. A sackable offence. Before I dipped back into a panic, I managed to gasp, 'Please tell me you're not from Ofsted or social services?'

'No, I'm the clinical psychologist, here to assess Billie Jenkins. Dr Claus Doerkson,' he said, shaking my hand.

Fortunately, Kerry was fine, order was restored, and at the end of the day, with every child gone, the tables wiped and the displays ready for the following day, I locked my classroom with a sigh of relief.

When I turned around, there he was, his smile revealing straight, white teeth.

‘Hello again. I do hope you don’t mind. The head teacher said I could come back and make sure you were OK.’

Did I mind?

As we sipped orange juice in the beer garden down the road, he told me he wasn’t a fan of alcohol, especially in the working week.

‘Vulnerable children don’t deserve errors from disinterested adults,’ he explained, waving his arms about to add clarity.

‘A child,’ he added, ‘must be the main character in an adult’s life not a disposable extra.’

I nodded enthusiastically, hoping I didn’t look like a moron. I can’t resist a passionate man. I checked his shoes, they were polished with no dirt on the heels, an interesting shade of dark brown.

Tasteful clean shoes, tick.

I was less sure of his overall look – a silk scarf that took forever to unravel, an old- fashioned waistcoat and *that* hat; a combination of Dr who and an old-fashioned spy – but something about it made me smile.

And I checked his nails: manicured, short and clean.

Tick.

And finally, I read the star shaped metal badge on his lapel: ‘Be kind’.

Tick, tick, tick.

Not only an irresistible man with clean clothes and a sensitive soul, but an intelligent, irresistible one with clean, if quirky, clothes and a sensitive soul.

I resisted the temptation to text Ameena to say, ‘I’ve found the father of my future children.’

Standing by my desk, watching the children pour into my classroom, I relive the memory before straightening my back like my first cycling coach insisted. I smile broadly and prepare to begin my first day as Mrs Keziah Doerkson, Head of key stage one.

4

At the Flat

Nicky

'Come on, my poppet,' Grandma's voice booms into the kitchen through the speaker on the gate.

'It's best if you meet grandma outside today,' Mum told him before the buzzer went.

His grandparents don't press the buzzer. They have keys because his house used to be theirs. Dad moved here when Nicky arrived in his mum's tummy. She was living in a flat that was too small for a boy. Now dad is in a flat too small for a boy and his grandparents are living in a bungalow controlled by traffic wardens.

Nicky knows not to leave Mum alone when she's having a bad day. He knows she's having a bad day, because he's leaving her alone but he doesn't know what to do. When dad was man of the house he decided.

'Sorry, son, we're going to cancel cos it's a bad day for your mum,' dad would say, putting a hand on Nicky's head and scrambling up his hair.

Nicky has been up most of the night. He knows he's the man. He needs to decide but he doesn't know how. He's tried everything. He counted to 974 which is his highest good number. He prayed to the God Father Riley said is listening, and he made eggs on toast just how she likes it. Nicky's head hurts and so does his chest which is probably where his heart got broken. That's what his new favourite teacher said, anyway. Having lost all confidence in Mrs Hobbs he's picked a new favourite teacher. This one is younger with a ponytail and nice teeth. She tells the truth and laughs a lot, even when he's being weird.

His grandma's voice bursts back into the kitchen. 'Come on, Nicky, love. Just open the gates and we'll be waiting. Poppa is sitting in the car, he has crisps, the green packet you like, the cheese ones.'

Nicky jiggles from one foot to the other. He knows mum is crying even though she has her back to him and is pretending to watch the birds. He grabs the bottle of wine by the chair and shoves it in his bag before his mum turns around. He has left one of his love notes under the cushion.

'Bye,' he shouts as he sprints off. He can't look back. He doesn't want to see her face. After he closes the door, he does forty-three quick kicks. He can't believe he is going to see his dad again after forty-three days.

Running down the drive, the gravel crunches and the juice in the bottle makes a whooshing sound. He hopes it hasn't leaked onto his school books. He high fives the square metal button. The gates start whirring.

Outside, near his curb, Grandma stands with her arms wide open. The intimidating gates stop him for a minute but then he charges straight into her, knocking her backwards. Nicky inhales her comforting smell, flowers and cake and lavender.

'Oh my boy, my lovely boy,' she whispers over and over as she kisses his hair and then his cheeks. 'I've missed you so much, my favourite grandson,' she says.

Nicky knows he's her only grandson.

Nicky doesn't stop holding her until the gates have clicked shut. He won't look behind him and he squeezes his eyes shut until his grandma puts him in the car.

He tries to not think about his mum. He tries to not hear her crying or see her face. He tries not to remember about his bike and how it's all his fault this family is smashed up. He hopes Poppa doesn't know it was him that made dad go.

He's left his mummy a flask filled with coffee and some tissues by her chair. She says she's going to watch a film and she doesn't want boys in the way. He feels reassured that his notes make her happy. He writes her a note every day before school. One time, he wrote a whole story but usually it's just a sentence like, *I love you* or *I miss you* or *I won't leave you.*

Nicky feels beside himself with pleasure as he sees his Poppa in the passenger seat His white stick is poking into the back.

'Here you go, sailor.' He thrusts an orange carton and a penguin biscuit through the gap in the middle. 'That'll keep you happy for the journey.'

Nicky feels sad for his Poppa as he can't drive anymore. Poppa says it's a sodding nuisance especially as grandma is not a good driver. His poppa used to be a pilot in the olden days.

'What's your mummy doing today?' Grandma twists around to speak to Nicky as she fastens her seatbelt

'Having a rest day.'

'Having a rest day!'

Nicky can't tell grandma she is grammatically incorrect. They are doing this in English. What grandma needs to say is, 'Why is she having a rest day?'

'She's a bit tired,' he answers the question she forgot to ask.

As Nicky unpacks his music and puts on his headphones he remembers last Christmas when he shouldn't have got a music player.

'He's nine, Lisa, it's not good for young children to be listening to loud music,' dad had said

'All the kids have them,' his mummy answered as Nicky unwrapped his present.

Dad didn't answer, he just grabbed his mug from the table and went outside in his naked feet.

'That's it, you put your headphones on Nicky, it's quite a way to your dad's,' Poppa says in a loud voice and looks at him in the lipstick mirror. Nicky knows Poppa can't hear or see very well so he doesn't mind his shouting.

They drive away and Nicky doesn't let his head look back. Instead, he looks over Mr Pinkney's white fence. The loaded skip has gone. Mummy said they shouldn't have a skip in his garden because they are a private road. Nicky loves Mr Pinkney. The other day Nicky realised that if he stood on his windowsill and peered up high he could see over Mr Pinkney's hedge and into the bedroom. When his bedroom is dark and he's all alone, he closes his eyes and imagines Mr Pinkney and his dog sitting in bed reading the newspaper. It makes him less afraid.

Grandma holds the steering wheel but looks at Poppa.

'Can you believe her? That woman's unbelievable, bed in the middle of the day. She's lucky she hasn't had to work for the last decade like everyone else.'

'Well, to be fair, she's working now.'

'Whose fault is that? If she didn't spend so much at the off-licence, she wouldn't have to work. And anyway, when she was at home, she barely lifted a finger. Every week without fail I cleaned that house from top to bottom and you kept the garden pristine. Goodness knows what the Pinkneys must think now. The state of that terrace, anyone would think it is social housing.'

Grandma thinks Nicky's headphones block their chatting. It goes quiet and he can hear the birds.

'Gerald, did you hear me?' Grandma isn't looking at the road, she's poking Poppa but he's not listening.

'Yes, Ursula, yes, I did but what can I say? It takes two to tango, our boy can't be completely innocent.'

'I'm sorry,' Grandma says to him. Nicky knows she is not sorry. 'You're his father, how can it be his fault? He's earning a fortune but in a one bedroom flat. She's living the life of Riley in millionaire's parade and drinking his income. I told you it was a terrible idea letting them have that house, now she's got our home and we're all living like paupers.'

'Hardly! And anyway, he walked away,' Poppa says back

Nicky wants to say, 'I saw him walk away wearing his socks,' but he says nothing. He knows grandma doesn't like rude boys who interrupt.

'He had no choice, she told him to go.' Grandma grips tight on the steering wheel and leans nearer the window like she can't see either.

'You've said that to me plenty of times in thirty years. I'm still here.' Poppa laughs but Nicky doesn't find it funny.

Poppa goes quiet, he turns around with his thumb up. His mouth says, you OK? He doesn't speak as Nicky has headphones on.

Nicky nods his head and puts his thumb up.

Grandma starts stalking again

‘You’re different, Gerald, our son is a sensitive boy, always has been, like our Nicky. He worshipped the ground that woman walked on but, a man can only stand so much.’

Poppa turns the radio on. Nicky’s headphones slip down behind grandma’s seat with a clonk.

‘You alright, poppet?’ she turns around to see what the clonking was.

‘I’m OK.’

‘Are you hungry?’

‘No.’

She gives Nicky a green packet. He opens the crisps but doesn’t eat any. His tummy feels bad and his head hurts. He looks out of the window. The road is big and busy. He counts seventeen fast cars and feels a little better. Seventeen is a good number.

He’s asked his mum three times if they are getting the divorce like Kerry’s uncle.

‘Ask your dad,’ is all she says.

Suddenly Poppa is rolling down his window and pointing. ‘Over there, Ursula, I see him.’

‘Look who it is, Nicky,’ grandma shouts.

Nicky looks out of the front and sees a long line of cars along the edge of a very long road.

Poppa is shouting to dad even though he’s not in the car.

‘We’re just looking for parking, son,’ he says.

Nicky’s feeling terrible but the counting isn’t helping. He pushes clenched fists into his cheeks and does some gentle rocking.

‘Look, Nicky, it’s dad, he’s up there.’ Poppa points to the biggest building in the road. It’s blue with hundreds of windows. The windows have fences. Some fences are painted in different colours.

Poppa turns around and taps on Nicky's knee but Nicky doesn't want to see. What if his dad is still angry about the bike? His dad doesn't like ungrateful kids and he doesn't like irresponsible boys.

'Nicky,' Grandma shouts, 'wake up, darling, and look out the window, Daddy's waving.'

The car stops and Nicky thumps his head on the back of her seat.

'Watch what you're doing, woman!' Poppa shouts.

'Can you see him?' Grandma asks.

'Yes,' Nicky replies politely. What he wants to say is that he's not blind.

'That's his flat, he's waving from his flat.'

Poppa gets out the car. He is speaking fast and moving like the day he took Nicky to the zoo on his birthday. He opens Nicky's door and bows like he's a servant. He's having great fun.

'Come on, out you get, bet you can't wait to see your dad.'

Nicky can wait. His tummy is still bubbling and gurgling like he's very hungry but he's not. His head hurts by his ears. *Thump, thump, thump.*

Then his dad comes. He's rushing with his hands in his pockets at the front of him. His shirt is his soft one with squares but his belly is smaller. His hair is much longer and hanging in his eyes.

'Here he is!' Nan rushes across to hug her son, who looks at Nicky over his shoulder and winks.

After he escapes from grandma, dad swoops down and lifts Nicky high above his head, then pulls him down to hug and spin him around. His face scratches, he's not done any shaving and he smells unlike himself.

When he lands back down, Nicky feels dizzy and his feet wobble. Dad crouches down, holds Nicky's arms and looks in his eyes. Nicky is glad his dad's eyes are still blue like his.

'How's my Nicky Noo?'

'OK.'

Nicky tries hard to look happy, he tries a smile but he's really not feeling at all well. His tummy gurgles and his throat makes a horrible noise.

Dad sees it coming. He runs with his small boy in his arms until his messy blonde head is in the hedge. Sick pours out of Nicky's mouth and all over his dad's black trousers. A green bit that Nicky thinks is a pea lands on his shoelace.

Keziah

Unbelievable – it's week two already. So far, so good. It's been such a delight reconnecting with the kids. Even Liam is more focused.

We're halfway through our first topic, the Romans. It's been stressful having responsibility for the whole key stage but get me, I facilitated the staff meeting on Friday and everyone nodded along when I outlined my ideas for the new curriculum. I was so worried the other teachers would miss my predecessor, maybe doubt my competence given I'm not much older than some, but the team have been really supportive.

The only downside is I'm putting in heaps of extra hours. I couldn't have got through this first fortnight without Claus's support. He has been so patient, and as I've been so busy he does all the cooking. I've never felt so looked after. I feel so sorry for Ameena; Mark is totally useless. If he gets home for dinner she's grateful.

Beyoncé is playing on the car radio. Feeling pretty on top myself, I sing along to 'Love on Top', and smile at Claus.

Travelling together means ten extra minutes in bed and I can't deny Claus's heated seats are rather nice now the mornings are getting chilly.

I turn up the radio for more car dancing, but Claus leans over and turns it down. 'Tone it down a bit, hun, after all you're almost thirty,' he says, raising his eyebrows with a smile.

Too true. Whilst I feel eighteen, in under six months I'll no longer be in my twenties. Ameena and Heidi are already planning the 'do' for the grand entrance into my third decade.

The thought of Ameena tightens my chest and speeds my breathing. I've got myself in a horrid pickle. Unless I feign illness, by seven pm I'm going to be outed once and for all. As we rushed out of assembly last Friday morning, Ameena suggested a get-together for this evening.

'Come on, it's been ages, let's do something Monday,' Ameena begged. 'I get the fact hubby likes you to himself on a weekend but surely he can't mind a school night?'

'He'll be fine, it's me, I'm shattered all the time.'

'Well, let's keep it small and I promise you'll be back with Prince Charming before becoming a pumpkin.'

'Sure,' I agreed with reticence, but then felt guilty and added, 'Do you want to come to ours after work and we can go together?'

All weekend I've been stressing. Why? Why did I say that? I've tried to change the plan, meet at hers or even Heidi's, but she's not taking the bait. I know she wants to see my new place as much as I want to avoid it.

Ameena and I met at teacher training eight years ago. The induction lecture was in mid flow when the door burst open. Everyone turned to stare at the late student. Without a hint of embarrassment, in sauntered an Amazonian beauty wearing bright orange dungarees and a matching headscarf. The remaining spare seat was next to me and we hit it off immediately. That lecture was the first of many we giggled our way through. We shared the same taste in music, fancied the same blokes and until I met Claus we agreed on almost everything.

When we were both appointed at Chertsey Street Primary, we found a local flat share and it made sense to also double up on transport. Claus' and my marital home is in the opposite direction, only by a few miles, but it means I either get a lift with Claus or I take my own car. Somehow, so far,

I've managed to avoid any of my close friends seeing the house. I've asked to meet at the old flat, lying I missed it, which I do a bit though it wouldn't be the same anyway as Mark's there now. If Claus takes me in, I then stay late to avoid accepting a lift home from Ameena. Most people would love showing off but she's struggling to make ends meet. Maybe a little part of me feels a bit awkward or embarrassed; but if I'm being truthful, perhaps the house still feels more his than ours.

Claus slows as we turn into Chertsey Street. Streams of identically dressed children, carrying flappy bookbags, race towards the main gate. The resilient ones clutch their own kits, the pampered ones get mum to carry their stuff until secondary school.

Claus unfastens his seat belt and pulls me in for a hug and a lingering kiss. I almost close the door but then remember.

'Hey babe, don't forget I'll be rushing out after work. Heidi's cooking so I won't need food.'

'Lovely,' he says, giving my hand one last squeeze.

As always, he does a quick beep to remind me to wave, before carefully reversing and driving off. Off to do good work. Clinical psychologist is not his job, it's his vocation. On our first date he said he'd wanted to help kids since he was a teenager. I'm not sure when his dad died but I know it devastated him. He's talked a bit about the rejection he felt when his mum moved abroad whilst he was still at university but mostly he clams up when I ask about his history.

That's one of the reasons for the instant click between us. Of course, I fancied him rotten but early loss changes you, it gives a sense of purpose and urgency that others lack.

I catch two kids from my class giggling over the fence. No doubt they spotted me kissing Claus. Jack nudges Daniel and they both run off.

‘What you blushing about Mrs P?’ Ameena interrupts my train of thought. No doubt she was watching too.

She links her arm through mine as we walk in the main entrance. As always, she looks effortlessly stylish in navy three-quarter-length trousers and a simple top. With such a short waist I would look like an Oompa Loompa in that.

‘Are you still on for our girls’ night in?’ Ameena asks, with two kids hanging off the back of her jacket.

‘Try and stop me,’ I say, focusing on the fun and not the fear of her judging my palace.

By the time the bell rings for close of day I’m ready to cancel, but then Ameena bounds up behind me so I stay quiet.

‘My car’s over there, get in and I’ll lock up,’ she says, chucking her keys to me.

Ameena’s car stinks. There are sweet wrappers on the floor and an empty can. I’m now driving a top-of-the-range Mini with a soft top, it’s on the same credit arrangement as Claus’. Both our cars get a weekly valet, which makes me feel way too grown up.

Ameena slips on some flats to drive and starts up the car. She looks across at me. ‘I’ve missed you, Kez, maybe we should go together every day, it would only be ten minutes extra time.’

It’s great to have a catch-up now we are living apart but I suspect Claus will be disappointed if I went back to car sharing. He likes to drop and collect me when possible. He’s such a worrier, always checking the internet so I can avoid accident hot spots. If I’m five minutes late he’s on the phone. He’s set up the hands free so I can answer whilst driving. I shouldn’t moan, it’s great to feel so cherished. My old boyfriends wouldn’t notice if I was missing for a week.

‘Maybe. I’ll chat to Claus,’ I say, watching Liam by the school fence.

‘Really?’ She raises her eyebrows as if I’ve confessed an arranged marriage. ‘Does he realise it’s no longer 1950, women are allowed to think for themselves now, you know?’

Internally, I search for a suitable response. Claus wonders if she’s a bit jealous. With him being older we can afford luxuries they can’t. Instead, I change the subject. ‘Did you get hold of Guy’s social worker?’ I ask.

‘Yes, that was the start of a nightmare afternoon . . .’

We chat so much that before I realise we’re at the bottom of our hill. My hands won’t stay still and I can feel a familiar warmth spreading under my chin. I direct her into the narrowing lane and we pause whilst a smart Audi TT inches past.

‘Blimey, Kez, these houses are amazing.’ She stares open-mouthed at the two properties on her side of the road, craning her neck to see further back.

My heart is beating hard inside my jacket, a present from Claus for completing my first week. She says nothing as we pull up outside the wide gates. I lean out of the window to alert the opening mechanism and slowly the gates pull back.

‘Park there.’ I point, as if our drive doesn’t have room for seven vehicles. As I head for the door, Ameena stays by the car to call Heidi to check timings.

I pause before touching the key pad. Pull yourself together, Keziah. There has to be some downsides of living like a princess.

Claus opens the door before I can push in the security code. He’s wearing an apron my mum got him for his birthday, a muscular man in swim trunks grins at me. Claus does not match his expression. An instant cloud descends over his face when he sees I'm not alone.

'What's cooking?' I inhale the smell of well-cooked meat

'Roast lamb with all the trimmings.'

'Wow, nice, you having friends over?' I'm secretly pleased. He rarely goes out and I can't recall him inviting people around.

'No, it's our evening meal.'

'But I told you I was off out this evening.'

'Not to eat?'

'Oh Claus, I'm so sorry, I thought I mentioned dinner, never mind, you enjoy and save me some for tomorrow?'

'If that's what you want,' he says as Ameena arrives at the door.

'Nice body,' Ameena laughs, pointing at his apron. Claus doesn't.

'Hello, good to see you.' He manages a front of house smile but I can tell he's irritated.

'Wow,' Ameena gasps as she steps inside, mesmerised by the huge twisty staircase.

'Yeah, I know. It's awesome isn't it? Claus helped the architect design it, didn't you?' I say in an attempt to drag Claus into the conversation.

He nods but doesn't comment and instead steps aside to let us pass. 'Help yourself to a drink, Ameena,' he says before retreating to his kitchen.

Usually he loves showing off his home, explaining how he designed the layout of the renovations, pointing out the historic features and choosing the guest's favourite tipple from his personal mini bar. Everyone loves the spectacular stairs.

‘You go in the lounge,’ I tell my friend but then remember ours is the kind of house where you have to escort or they’ll sit in the wrong reception room. In the flat I shared with Ameena and Heidi, the lounge was the one with the sofa.

Ameena spreads herself out on the corner suite.

‘Here, make yourself comfy,’ I say, handing her the TV remote. ‘The cloakroom is by the front entrance when you want to change. I’ll be back in a minute’

‘Get you, Mrs – since when did we talk about cloakrooms?’ Ameena laughs, giving me a friendly kick with her socked foot as I walk off smiling.

Moving her shoes to the rack by the door, I go in search of Claus who is no longer in the kitchen. His comic apron is discarded on the table.

I find him lying on our bed watching the television with the sound switched off.

‘What were you laughing about?’ he asks.

‘When?’

‘Just now.’

‘Oh, Ameena was teasing me about sounding posh.’ I lean over him for a kiss but he doesn’t respond. ‘What’s the matter?’

‘Nothing.’

‘Claus, there’s clearly something wrong. I’m sorry if you forgot I was out this evening.’

‘Oh. Claus, I’m sorry you forgot.’ He mimics my voice in a way that makes me sound childish, pathetic.

Shock runs through me. I turn my back to leave. I won’t be spoken to like that. As I try and close the bedroom door, Claus is right behind me. He wraps his arms around me from behind and pulls me back to himself with an intensity I crave.

'Keziah, forgive me, it's been a long day.'

My body softens into his, relieved that we've resolved the misunderstanding. I allow him a few more minutes and then disentangle myself to get changed.

Boy, have I missed my mates, I think, stepping over a mass of discarded shoes and bags. Six of them are chatting in different tangles. Ameena and I take a chair at opposite ends of the crowded table, the only seats left.

'I'm still owed a blow-by-blow account of the honeymoon,' Heidi demands, pulling out the chair next to her. As a single mum, she often hosts.

Pulling my phone out to show off my holiday photos, I see Claus has sent a couple of texts.

I'm so sorry, I just love you too much.

I hope you are there? How was the traffic? What time might you be home?

I can't bear the thought of an evening without you. Have fun, I'm going to do some reports. Poor old me, eh?

Did you get my texts, wondered if you've arrived?

Initially, I feel irritated, given how grumpy he was earlier, but then I soften. I smile to myself, revelling in the knowledge I'm the only one with someone elsewhere pining for me. I bet Ameena's Mark hasn't given a second thought to being home alone.

'Come on,' Heidi nags. 'I thought I was getting photos.'

Just as I go to show her, another text pops up on the home screen.

Love you SO much darling, see if you can get back by ten, it's a school night, ha ha.

I look at my watch. It's 8.15. I do hope he's joking. I tell the girls I'll Whatsapp them the best pictures rather than waste time now. I switch my phone off and engage with the girly nonsense I've been craving for a fortnight.

The evening flies by, we chat, over eat and finally collapse on the floor with a third bottle of wine to watch a film.

When I pop to the toilet I sneak a peek at my phone. I have three missed calls. My heart starts pounding, why on earth did I switch it off? My mind races through the possibilities. Has something happened to my parents? Has my dad forgotten where he lives again? Did I forget to lock the classroom door?

Thankfully, the messages are from Claus so he must be alright and he's left a voicemail. Why on earth didn't he call on the landline if it was urgent? He spent ten minutes carefully writing down the contact numbers before we came out.

'Keziah, where are you, it's late, you've missed the news. I'm waiting. I do hope you haven't been drinking, it's a weekday.' I can feel the swell of irritation pushing out the panic. For goodness sake, he's not my father.

Later, as Ameena drives me home, I think of Claus stressing at home. Not many people understand, but once you've suffered a family tragedy, you're always close to high alert. I'm the same if anyone is later than expected. For years after Esther was killed, I'd phone my mum five times if she even went to the supermarket. I was so terrified something bad would happen.

As we drive into an area of better signal, some more WhatsApp messages appear. They are all much the same, telling me he is missing me, describing what he's up to, enquiring what I want in my packed lunch tomorrow.

I can see Ameena looking to my lap.

'Sorry,' I say, feeling rude

'No worries, how come so many messages?'

'Not sure, for some reason my phone's having a moment and producing heaps of old messages.'

My tone doesn't convince me either.

5

Out Late

Nicky

'Come on then, son,' dad says as they trudge their way down nine floors. The lift in his block of flats is still broken. Nicky thinks 'son' might be the label you get when you become a man in your own house.

Dad picks up their rucksack and chucks it over his shoulder with a loud huff. He offers Nicky an open pack of polos and they both take one to refill their lost energy. Nicky is pleased to see the sick patches have gone from his dads' trousers, and he has new brown shoes. They're much the same as the pair he left on the mat but with thicker laces and black bottoms.

Despite his dad's advice, Nicky keeps his school bag close to his chest. The bag is heavy and he wishes he could leave it at the flat or in the car, but he can't. He's very glad his bag has three separate compartments because the number three has become his favourite one, he's sure it's the right number to keep his people safe. In the most spacious bit, there is his exercise book. Tucked within the lined pages is a certificate he got for good listening when John Eagle came to talk to his class about a monster called Grendel. No one has seen his certificate yet, he can't wait to show it to his parents and then Mr Pinkney.

The bag has a zipped pocket where he keeps his three favourite pencils and a spare rubber.

On Monday, Mrs Hobbs is expecting a story in his own words about Grendel. The trouble is, Nicky is terrified of monsters. At night when he's alone and scared, monsters are all he can think about. He is not sure how Grendel looked but he knows he was strong and murderous and probably had fangs with blood on and had a bad mother.

The closer they get to the sea, the more worried Nicky feels. He's heard people say the sea contains many monsters.

'How's school?' dad asks

'OK.'

'How's mum?'

'OK.' Nicky tries not to think about mum's sad face as she scrubbed the dirty brass pot. He overheard gran say his mother was a bad one. If that's true, will he grow up to be a bad one?

'Do you have other words?' Dad asks whilst he's still thinking about Grendel and his mother and his writing and the monsters.

'Sorry.'

His dad laughs.

'I mean have you any words other than "OK"?'

He doesn't know what words his dad would like. Does he want Nicky to tell him about the bike? Or did he take the bike? Is he wanting Nicky to say sorry or ask him about it before he gives it back?

Before Nicky can work anything out, dad dumps the rucksack on the pavement and pulls his son down the beach towards the sea. Nicky refuses to leave his bag when it's full of important things. He can't wait to show his dad the certificate over lunch; he's keeping it for a surprise.

The sea has things floating in it but they make a gravelly sandcastle with a discarded bucket. It's dirty and the handle has snapped off but it does the job.

'Let's get chips, and a donut,' his dad says when they get too cold to carry on.

Hand in hand they jog along the promenade passing shops that sell buckets, and donuts, and ice cream. Children wave from a train, tooting as it drives past. Nicky is glad he's almost grown up and no longer has to endure such things.

There are empty deck chairs on the sand but one holds a lady snuggled in a duffel coat, her body hanging low in stripy material. She's trying to keep a cap from blowing off which Nicky finds hilarious. Suddenly, he's laughing so much he has to lean forward with his arms across his belly. He doesn't want his sides splitting with laughter. Kerry told him that's an actual thing and her dad is a doctor.

They burst into a café smelling of chips, a bell sounds as the door blows shut behind them. A lady with curly hair rushes out of the kitchen wiping her hands on a mucky apron. She gives them the best table, by the window and they watch the screeching seagulls swooping down at an old couple on a bench.

Nicky clutches his bag to his chest in case anyone is tempted to steal it.

Dad nods at him. 'What treasure you got in there, little man?'

The bag makes a rude noise as it opens and they laugh at exactly the same time. Nicky can feel a big grin spreading on his face as he reaches for his book and closes his fingers on the certificate. He likes the smoothness of the cream card.

‘It’s my . . .’ His chest tightens as he remembers. He remembers her crying, he remembers all the tissues and the bad days. Why on earth did he think it was right to show his dad before her? She had asked him who he loved most and Nicky had reassured her. It’s her he loves, her he needs, her he wants to keep safe and love forever.

He counts in his head and taps his feet a few times until the feeling reduces to a simmer.

‘Err . . . a book,’ Nicky tells dad, hoping he didn’t spot the gold-edged card with his son’s name written in swirly black ink. Instead he pulls out the dog-eared exercise book.

‘I’ve got to write about a monster called Grendel who gets killed by a hero called Beowulf, but then his evil mother comes back and starts killing people too. He might even still be alive living in a swamp.’ Nicky can hardly breathe as he gabbles on hoping his dad can’t hear his thoughts.

They enjoy what his dad calls man to man chatting over their chips and finish their meal with donuts and a beer. Well, he has blackcurrant squash.

By the time they’ve walked back, climbed all the stairs and taken off their coats and bags, it’s getting late.

Dad puts two cans of coke on the table. It’s only a small one but big enough to fit a stool on either side. As his dad leans over him with a plate of custard creams, Nicky feels his dad’s warm arm against his shoulder. A heavy and strong arm to keep him safe from the monsters. He can smell his dad’s perfume and is glad he’s here, him and his dad together.

Dad looks at his watch. ‘We need to get going soon, I promised your mum we wouldn’t be too late,’ he says, blowing his nose

Nicky takes tiny sips and eats his biscuits super slow. They’re his best biscuits and he could easily shove in three at once and gobble them like a greedy monster.

‘Come on, you’ve had twenty extra minutes already, use the toilet, matey, then we need to go,’ Dad says, snatching the plate before Nicky can lick up the crumbs with his finger.

Nicky counts ten paces to the hall. He’s glad of an even number as apart from three, he prefers the even ones. This is such a small place. Nicky takes a sneaky look at his dad’s room through an open door. There isn’t a wardrobe, just one set of drawers with a photo of his only son sellotaped above. The covers are tidy and he can’t see any pillows. Nicky wishes he could stay a night.

The bathroom has a bath not long enough for a dad. There’s a shower curtain around the tub but no shower. Squeezed in the small space is a toilet and a sink. It’s all brown and ugly. Dad has his electric tooth brush in a jar that used to hold grandma’s jam. Whilst washing his hands for a third time, Nicky spots his dad approaching in the mirror. There’s no place to hide secrets in this flat.

‘To keep mine company.’ His dad drops a smaller toothbrush in the jar. It’s super cool and has batteries to make it move.

‘Come on, you’ll soon be back.’ Dad puts his arms over his son for a hug. They both stare into the mirror. Nicky wishes he was taller.

They stand, staring at themselves in the reflection whilst Nicky jabbers away about Bella and Mr P and Grendel and Mrs Hobbs and Kerry, anything he can think of to keep his dad standing there for as long as ever.

Then, something happens that stuns Nicky into silence. He cannot believe what he is seeing. He’s never seen anything like it before. He’s so confused that he slips out of his father’s grip to spin around for a better look.

And when he looks up at his dad, not in the reflection, but for real, he sees he was right all along. There in his own bathroom, the tall man who is his father, has tears dripping off his chin. His dad is crying, properly crying like he does, with snot and sniffing. He's never seen him cry, he didn't even know men did that.

Nicky reaches into his front pocket.

'Here you go,' he says, holding a hand up to his dad's face

He always has a tissue in his pocket for the crying.

Keziah

'Bye Mum, bye Dad,' I say for the fourth time. Claus grabs my hand and presses it to his mouth for a kiss before we walk on. Turning around one last time I give a final wave. From their front doorstep, Dad is on tiptoe, waving very enthusiastically without a pause. Mum just blows me a kiss.

They won't move until they see the car disappear into the distance.

So many years have passed, yet I bet there are people who march past these identical plots and stop by the one with the faded slats and chipped paint to whisper, 'That's the family who lost their daughter,' before sauntering back to their untainted lives. What a stupid expression. If Esther was lost, we'd still be looking. Sometimes I find myself still desperately looking.

Now we're nearly back to the car I can cry.

'I'm sorry,' he says as he helps me to settle in the passenger seat like I'm the vulnerable child. A deep sense of calm descends as he shifts his arms to pull me into the warmth of him.

Other people make me feel guilty for being sad, like I should be over it by now. They say stupid things like, *She's in a better place*, *She'd be so proud of you*, *She's looking d*own. I just want to scream, *Shut up*, *you didn't know her and have no idea where she's gone or how I'm feeling*.

Claus is the only person who listens, really listens to understand. The day she died a massive boulder landed in our front room. A rock so gigantic, it takes up the entire space with just inches each side. It blocks floor to ceiling. Time doesn't heal. The boulder is still there, dominant, ugly, immovable.

Our family discovered ways to squeeze around it, maybe my life got bigger and I've changed but the boulder hasn't shrunk. Sometimes music plays despite the boulder and some days I can even laugh and drink champagne but the boulder is still there; heavy, stuck.

Claus stays quiet and simply rubs my back when I sob. He tells me I shouldn't feel guilty, that it wasn't my fault even though deep in my heart I'll always know it was, that I killed her.

I was dreading Esther's birthday, I always do. This morning, though, thanks to my husband, I've glimpsed our pre-accident family sitting around the dining table chatting and laughing as we looked at the photographs he'd collated as a gift to my parents. Esther on a donkey at Camber sands, the two of us hand in hand at the school fete and finally the flowers at her funeral. He must've searched the memory box under the bed, the one I've kept for years; it's stuffed with mementos of all my special moments.

Fortunately, dad is increasingly oblivious. In some ways his dementia has saved him. The emptiness in his eyes has replaced the acute heartache that stole him for such a long time. He is now constantly in the present. He laughs how he used to and scoffs his food like there's no tomorrow. The weight gain makes him look much like the father of our childhood, round faced with a belly to match.

I was gutted when Esther's birthday clashed with Claus's important work do. Mum told me not to worry, to live our life, that they'd be fine. Of course, I know they are not fine on any day, let alone this one.

When he found out Mike was retiring, Claus couldn't stop grinning. He arrived home with a bottle of wine. He'd even left his tie at the office. This is what he's been waiting for. He'd hoped to become head of department in Oxford but something went wrong and an external candidate was appointed. He hasn't shared many of the details but I know that he was gutted, that it flattened him. He ended up taking a few months off and didn't return to the post.

He'd only been living here in Shropshire for a few months when I met him. I know he missed his old home and colleagues but had felt he had no choice but to move on. At his initial interview Mike made it clear he had an eye on retiring and that Claus could be his natural successor. It was the compensation he felt he deserved, so he upped sticks and relocated.

Mike's retirement is the first departmental thing Claus has organised. He feels it's his chance to impress before the advert goes out for his replacement. We talked endlessly about where we'd host it, and eventually we settled on Casalingo's, a shared favourite. The food is consistently great and the staff are attentive without being annoying. Claus showed an excitement I hadn't seen before, and I couldn't wait to be shown off as part of the package. But then Mike announced his date. He wanted to go out on the day he'd started work forty years ago even though he wouldn't officially leave for six months.

He wanted his leaving bash on Esther's birthday.

When Claus told me, he was so kind. I was amazed he knew the date, I'd only told him a couple of times. 'Please don't think I forgotten what this day means for your family,' he said. 'I promise we'll find a way of making it special for everyone.'

And boy, has he kept his promise.

At breakfast, he presented me with a plain silver necklace with two letters entwined, a K and an E. He'd had it made in the bespoke jewellers in market street. Then we came here, to the childhood home my parents will never leave even though the stairs are too steep and they can't afford to update anything. For them, their home will always be where Esther lived. Her bedroom is suspended in time, untouched.

Claus has been so generous; my parents will have no idea that he's hosting such a pivotal evening tonight.

He waits patiently whilst I regain my composure, then he gently removes his hand from mine and starts the car. As we drive away, I don't want to watch. The overwhelming sense of loss and sadness I feel when leaving makes no sense. Instead I distract myself by faffing about with the contents of the passenger side door. There's a child's beanie hat, handknitted with a cute bobble; somewhere there'll be a sad kid just realising he's left a favourite hat in his psychologist's car. Claus's car is so neat and clean. Other than the hat, there's only a traditional map book like my dad has, still pristine, protected by sticky-back plastic. Most of my friends can't even use a map, we're all so tech dependent. The rebellious crinkles in the plastic take me back to primary school. There are a few shopping receipts tucked in the cover, work expenses yet to be claimed. Often Claus doesn't bother. The top one is a fuel station in Guildford, Surrey, which must be from a trainee as even the out-of-catchment visits only go as far as the Midlands.

'Hey Mrs D, don't you go messing up my systems,' Claus laughs, taking the book and tidying it into his side pocket. He rests his hand on my knee and speeds up. It'll be a rush to get ready but today I've fallen in love all over again.

As the car pulls smoothly up the long winding hill to Casalingo's, my hands are jumping about all over the shop. In the end Claus reaches over and pats my hand. I'm glad it's still light enough to see the hills. Right now, I'd do anything to escape into those slopes, to feel the breeze in my hair, to smell the outdoors. It's so beautifully rural out here, we could easily be in a remote village in Italy.

'It'll be fine, try and stay calm.'

The waft of garlic as we open the restaurant door takes me right back to our early dates when we came here often. The obligatory Vespa statues in the far corner in front of the open kitchen. A dark-haired chef I don't recognise is stretching the dough for this evening's pizza. I squeeze Claus's hand. We did it, this is just perfect.

We have booked the entire restaurant so it's one long table in an intimate room. Unfortunately, the only two empty seats are at opposite ends of the table. We should have left more time but Claus insisted we shouldn't make my parents feel second best. The one next to Mike has obviously been saved for Claus, and an older lady attempts a move to make space for me, but her friend yanks her back, and then looks embarrassed when she sees me staring. Claus doesn't attempt to resolve the situation. I'm beginning to feel out of place. A quick scan of the table reveals a diverse range of female outfits but they're all colourful, casual. My cocktail dress feels a bit formal.

'It's fine, we don't need to sit together, do we Claus?' I say, releasing my hand from the tight grip of his.

Claus takes the seat not far from the door. He shakes Mike's hand and offers a peck on the cheek for the woman on his other side. A few couples are scattered within the noisy group but mostly people have separated into mature and less so. I breathe in to squeeze behind the row of filled seats to reach the remaining empty chair at the younger end. My face is a deeper crimson than the velvet seats.

The youngest-looking girl wearing a beautiful dress pulls out a chair for me to join her. The two people sitting opposite are obviously a couple. His arm is casually slung around the back of her chair. They obviously all know each other very well.

'Thanks,' I offer, but it's left hanging as they carry on their conversation.

'I'm so glad I've finished my training now, it's fab having your evenings free,' the girl next to me says. Her bright cerise dress perfectly complements her dark skin.

'I envy you. Sometimes I'm not sure I'll make it,' the ginger-haired girl sitting opposite me laughs, with her mouth wide open.

'You will and it's worth it when you get there.' The man who is slightly older moves his arm to give his girlfriend a reassuring squeeze

I can feel tears welling up. Sitting here I feel like a Reception pupil. I try desperately to make eye contact with Claus but he's not playing.

'I've just realised we've been chatting about business and haven't even introduced ourselves or asked about you, how rude,' the man opposite says. 'I'm Ricardo Bruce, this is Harriet, my partner, and . . .'

'I'm Clara,' the girl next to me finishes his sentence. 'I've just qualified but Ricardo's been qualified . . .'

'. . . five years nearly,' he says.

I reckon the age gap between him and Harriet is not far off ours, that makes me feel a bit better.

'Don't worry, I'm a gate crasher. Am I the only non-psychologist?' I ask.

'No, you've just ended up down the junior end.' He nods to the middle end of the table. 'No doubt you know that's Mike Rogers, he's been around for decades. The two ladies there, Sal and Kate are admin staff, the man in the bright orange shirt next to Claus is Sal's husband. Mary, the woman to his left, is a social worker on the mental health team. What do you do?'

'I'm a primary school teacher, although sometimes I feel like one of the kids.'

'Imposter syndrome.' Clara throws her head back as she laughs and the others all nod.

I notice Claus look up, having been deep in debate with the woman next to him. He looks very serious.

'What?' I ask, feeling stupid.

'Feeling too young or incompetent in adult life! We all feel it.'

'Yeah totally,' Harriet agrees

'Wow, I thought psychologists are all sane and secure.'

'You can't be serious, they're the most messed up of all.' Ricardo loves flashing his perfect teeth, veneers surely. I wouldn't have put him with Harriet, who seems very organic. I bet she's a vegan.

'Yes, not everyone is as professional as your husband.' Clara nods towards the other end of the table. As she helps herself to more wine I catch Claus looking and put my hand over my glass. I hope he didn't hear his name and think I'm gossiping.

'How long you guys been married?' Harriet asks.

'Only a few of months, it's been a bit of a whirlwind,' I confess. Claus is still watching when the waiter comes to clear away the first course. I smile but he looks away. I can see the social worker trying to get his full attention.

'Keziah?'

I feel my neck flush as Ricardo is waiting expectantly. He's obviously asked a question.

'Gosh I'm so sorry, what were you saying?'

'That Claus is the clear front runner for head of department.'

'Yes, I'm sure he'd be great.' Claus warned me about discussing anything personal, and gave me a few ideas of relevant topics I could raise. He's so thoughtful like that, my previous boyfriends wouldn't have given a second thought to me at a work social.

Claus strolls behind Ricardo's chair, presumably off to the toilets.

'You chaps alright down this end?' He smiles his professional smile, though doesn't single me out. It must be hard for him blending work and home, especially when he is feeling pressured to make it a good evening.

Clara brings back her attention to me.

'How is Claus these days?' her tone has changed.

'Fine, I think, enjoying married life, I hope.'

I catch a sideways look to her partner but he flushes red and looks down to the floor.

'So terrible what happened in Oxford,' she goes on. 'I was so shocked when Ricardo told me.' Ricardo is definitely trying to communicate something; he catches her hand and brings it closer to him, but she doesn't seem to notice.

'I just can't imagine,' she goes on, staring at me for a response. 'I mean how do you get over something like that?' They all nod, with those forced empathic faces that people use when I share what happened with Esther.

'Yes, I know he felt hurt, it sounded very unfair.' I smile tentatively, desperately searching for a topic to change the subject. Claus would hate me chatting to his young colleagues about his feelings.

Clara takes in a deep breath and I'm certain that Ricardo gives her a gentle nudge with his elbow. I have no idea what's going on for them. Perhaps she's like Ameena and gets a bit gobby when she's had a drink.

'I'd be so hurt. I mean, what must it be like for someone like us to be accused of neglect or actually doing harm. It's unthinkable. As psychologists our identities are so entangled with being healers, rescuers of vulnerable people. I just can't imagine.' Hattie offers an imperceptible nod as Clara natters on, expressing feelings of sympathy that don't quite reach her eyes.

This time, I'm absolutely certain. Ricardo gives her a definite shove in the ribs whilst maintaining appropriate eye contact with me. Hattie is ripping small snowflakes of white paper off her serviette and discarding them under the table. I watch her hands gaining speed in her lap, her bracelet jangling in time to the rhythm.

I feel the heat moving up my neck, the sweat gathering around my collar. What are they talking about? Surely, they can't just mean missing out on a job. You wouldn't describe that as an accusation or as unthinkable.

We only spoke briefly on an early date, when I didn't know him well enough to probe, but he hinted that the situation resulted in some sort of personal breakdown. I did think his reaction to missing out on a job seemed a bit excessive. But, hey, who am I to judge, being judged negatively makes you a bit crazy, I know.

I turn to Hattie who is looking at me with equal interest, her perfectly arched eyebrows slightly raised.

'I can totally understand why he needed a new start. It's awful when things happen and you know people are gossiping but they go quiet when you enter a room.'

'Yes, that was exactly it,' I say.

He told me he moved up here because there were no promotions in Oxfordshire. What wife knows less than her husband's junior colleagues. Maybe he got the sack or got accused of a misdemeanour. My head races off down some dark avenues. Was he accused of a sexual assault? I suppose that would be something you wouldn't want to headline in your tinder profile or share on a first date.

As if he knows, Claus offers me a smile as he heads back to his seat, and raises his eyebrows, not an enthusiastic gesture but the first hint of connection. I want to make an excuse to leave my place and ask him outright. Getting my husband to talk about his history is like getting blood from a stone. He says, 'The past is passed, the present is a gift and we need to learn to stay here, now.' That's one of the many irritating -ology phrases he uses to escape tricky conversations.

I'm still searching for a way to ask more when a waitress leans over my head.

'Dessert menu?' she offers, dealing four sheets of paper onto the table.

'Marvellous,' Ricardo says rather too cheerily as he thrusts one under his partner's nose. 'I've been told their puddings are divine,' he adds as the waitress hovers with her pad and pencil

Whilst Harriet and Clara shout out their orders, Claus appears behind Ricardo, looking intently at his back, distracted, tired perhaps.

I'm so pleased when he beckons me over.

'Excuse me,' I squeeze behind Hattie to escape. 'Sorry, so sorry.'

I bound up to Claus, proud to have survived the evening so far, knowing no one.

'They're a great crowd, aren't . . .'

He cups my elbow and gently but deliberately moves me away from the table.

'Sweetheart, I'm so sorry, but do you mind if we leave a bit early. I have a rotten headache and it's so very dull at my end?'

I can see the tension written behind his eyes. I suspect he'll end up with a migraine. He puts too much pressure on himself.

'Of course, no worries,' I laugh, 'you've saved me from committing a sugar overdose.'

Harriet passes over my coat when I apologise that we have to rush off, my cheeks flushing as I tell them my husband feels unwell.

'Great to chat to you, Keziah,' she shouts and the others nod and smile in agreement. Claus offers a playful salute to the table as we leave.

'See you all tomorrow, team,' he smiles affectionately as we manoeuvre out of the restaurant door and into the bitterly cold night.

As we walk to the car, Claus plods along at the pace of a snail. Head down, like a child who has lost his favourite ball in a deep lake. When he sees me staring, he fumbles for his hanky and wipes his eyes before the emerging tears give him away.

'As soon as I saw her, I knew what she was up to,' he confides, reaching to hold my hand.

'What? Who?'

'Mary, that social worker. She wasn't even on the guest list. She wangled an invite from Mike and then set about ingratiating herself. On and on, all evening, "Interdisciplinary departments, that's the way forward," she kept saying, fluttering those ridiculous lashes at him. It's happening again, Keziah, I know it. I'll end up on the scrap heap and she'll jump unashamedly into Mike's position.'

I'm still folding my coat into the car when he manoeuvres out of the car park, narrowly missing a wooden post. Careless driving is so unlike Claus.

'I'm so sorry, I know how much you wanted this evening to go in your favour.'

He rests his hand on my knee.

'Don't apologise, you were perfect.'

I watch as his thoughts entangle him. His eyebrows sag, his body shrinks, his energy runs away. What a day. Now is definitely not the time to ask about his cupboard skeletons.

Defeated, I pull my collar up and lean my head against the window. I feel so sad for my gentle husband who tries so hard to impress. I know it shouldn't be about me but, I feel such a fool. What do those people know that has infused their good cheer with awkwardness? How come they know something so important and life changing but I don't. It's not like trainees would be his confidants, surely. They must know about this dark secret because everyone knows. Everyone, except me.

National Hospital of Neurology

Three-Month Review

NHS number: 485 777 3496 Gender: *female*

Current diagnosis:

- Low awareness state
- Occasional eye blinking
- Mother reports orientation to voice when calls name.

Injuries sustained:

- Severe and complex neurological and physical injuries
- Broken vertebrae in lower spine – no movement from mid chest down
- Skull fracture above right ear and occipital region

Progress to date:

Minimal. Multidisciplinary involvement but no obvious evidence patient is aware

Family situation:

Family intelligent and supportive, mother continues to visit daily, no sign of father so far

Plan:

- Putney currently have no coma beds
- Manage family expectations – low chance of full recovery
- DNR in place and signed
- Contact within police – DCI Chris O Leary

Signed:

Dr A. Lutte-Elliott

CONSULTANT IN NEUROREHABILITATION

6

The Man About the House

Nicky

'Mum, I'm coming, don't worry. Hang on, please hang on, mum, Nicky is here now,' Nicky shouts knowing she can't possibly hear anything.

Nicky runs around to the back of his house; his face is covered in snot and tears but for once he can't care. He knew he shouldn't have gone to visit his dad. He knows he shouldn't have enjoyed himself and forgotten her. He knew something bad would happen.

Stupid boy, stupid boy, stupid boy, he repeats as he searches for a piece of wood. He needs a log that's big enough to smash glass but light enough to lug to the door.

He is out of breath as he searches through the bonfire dad promised he'd light before the end of the summer. They were supposed to have a night camp with fire and toasted marshmallows. Right in the middle of the pile under a broken scooter he finds the perfect piece of wood to smash the cat flap. He turns back for his award. He was holding it ready to make her day but now it's dropped on the grass. He shoves it into his back pocket.

He uses the lump of wood like a cricket bat, bash, bash, bash. He ignores the hurt in his hands. Finally, he prizes the plastic out with his fingers and creates enough space. Lying on his belly he tucks his arms as close to his body as he can and like a seal, wiggles himself through the hole.

He's in. There is no time to deal with the blood dripping down his leg, that'll have to wait. He checks the all-important certificate is still in his pocket. If he can save her, she'll love that.

He can't believe he didn't come in the house straight away. Stupid boy, stupid, selfish boy. He knows he should've come in like he was told, but he wanted to hear his dad's car until it had gone all the way away.

Because he is so irresponsible and childish he sat on the curb for ages, listening to the sound of Neil Diamond floating away, hoping Bella would bring Mr P for a chat. Now she'll die and everyone will hate him – dad, Mr P and all the kids at school. If only he'd checked her through the window when he first got back like a good person would've done, like his daddy always did when he got home.

Nicky crashes through the utility room knocking over the washing powder on his way; blue snow tips all over the floor. He hurtles down the hall and into the second lounge where he saw her from the terrace.

The monster is still there. He can't see his face because his shovel-like hands are around her neck. He can only see the outline of the massive head behind hers. The grotesque beast has hair around his face. He knows it's Grendel. Nicky feels the warmth of his pee but can't stop. He has to be brave, he has to rescue his precious mum. He's the man of the house, after all.

For a moment, Nicky watches from the door. She hasn't seen him but is making quiet groaning noises. Grendel is holding his hand on the back of her head pushing it against his face. The monster is so tall, the top of his bushy fur is touching the light shade. Nicky knows he can't be weak any longer. He pulls in a big breath and runs with full force towards his mum, ready to save.

He pulls his leg back as far as he can, the line of blood from his knee has reached his sock. He kicks the monster's leg with full force and then punches every part of him at the same time. The monster's body is hard but Nicky keeps going, kicking, punching with all he has.

'Get off, get off her,' he screams at the top of his small voice.

It works. The monster lets go.

'Ouch!' shouts a boom-boom voice at Nicky. 'What do you think you're doing, you crazy little blighter.'

Mum jumps backwards; she's free but Nicky carries on kicking and punching. He wishes he had a dagger to plunge into the monster's side.

In she comes behind her boy. He knows she's going to pick him up and carry him to safety. They can run next door and call the police. Dad will come back and be so grateful Nicky rescued her.

But then she grabs his arms from behind and holds him back so he can't fight the monster.

'Nicky, stop,' she commands.

She pulls her son around to face her and gets down on one knee. She looks him in the eyes. He sees she has lipstick around her mouth like she's been eating jam toast. Her breath smells of drink.

'Nicky, calm down, it's Paul. Paul from the phone,' she says.

Paul stands up. Nicky is facing his big belly, it is hanging down so you can't see his zip. His teacher said only ladies can have a baby.

'Cor, you're a feisty little midget, aren't you?' Paul says, brushing dirt off his trousers.

Nicky hangs his head.

Mum takes Nicky's hand and stands next to him. They lean against the back of the sofa. Nicky is exhausted. Tears come but he wants to keep holding hands so he lets them run into his mouth and down his chin.

'You best go,' she tells Paul from the phone.

Paul pulls his jacket from the floor. Nicky was treading on it when he tried to kill him.

'Please tell me that isn't pee all over his trousers,' Paul says with his face scrunched up in an ugly ball. Nicky is repulsed by the size of Paul's flabby ears. The end bits hang longer than any ears he's seen and wobble when he speaks. In his right ear he has a silver skull.

Nicky wrenches his hand out of her grasp and runs past his parents' room, past the room his dad used to sleep in and past the guest room. He runs at his bedroom door so it opens but heads straight into his ensuite. He climbs into the shower and turns on the water. It's cold. Without undressing he sits in the shower tray. He counts through all the numbers until the door slams. Now he can find a safe number and stop.

Fastening the buttons on her shirt, his mum reaches into the bathroom and tugs him out. She wraps him in a thick white towel until he stops shivering. As she dries his back, she speaks quietly.

'Paul off the phone, came to do some jobs.' She tries to get closer for a cuddle but he pulls away. She stinks of that monster.

She hangs his wet trousers over the heated towel rail. He sees the cream square sticking out of his back pocket.

‘I got this for my story,’ he tells her, handing it over with a small smile.

She carefully unfolds the certificate.

‘I didn’t show dad, I wanted you to see first.’

‘Oh Nicky, it’s crumpled and wet, I could’ve put that on the wall.’

Keziah

Hearing the gates buzz, I launch my ipad onto the oak side table and grab my novel. I gulp some deep breaths. Calm down.

I haven't heard his car door yet, hopefully he's on a call, he usually is. My heart is pumping as if it was me in the video. I'd be mortified if anyone saw me bouncing up and down with each virtual decline. Watching a female biking champ performing on those hills is my guilty pleasure, me in the saddle, riding free. I can't explain, but going back there is the best therapy after a stressful teaching day. But it feels private, just for me, so by the time the front door slams shut, I'm slouched into a corner with my book.

His coat still on, Claus leans over the back of the settee and plants a lingering kiss on my mouth.

'Hello Mrs, I've missed you enormously,' he says, extending the last word so it sounds more important than the others.

He's only been away two nights but it feels longer. A large box of Lindt chocolates land in my lap.

'I stopped for fuel and thought you might fancy these,' he says.

They're the salted caramel ones I love. He didn't get those at the garage, they only sell the plain ones. He'll have driven the long way around to pick up my faves.

I reach up to pull him down, closer, longing for more. It's lovely to have him home and such a relief that he seems brighter, nearer his usual self.

'Oooh you're all wet. Is it raining?'

‘Chucking it down. The wipers were struggling to keep up. I’m shattered. I used to be able to drive all day and still be bright-eyed, now I struggle with a four-hour drive.’

‘I thought this conference was in Manchester?’

‘It was, yes. I meant generally. Generally I can’t do the long trips so well,’ Claus explains, distracted by the drips seeping down his old-fashioned case. ‘How was your day?’ he asks, fingers tight around the brown leather handle, now restless to get upstairs and change, retrieve himself from work mode.

‘You know, the usual. Liam is improving in response to your guidelines but still such hard work especially when he teams with Billie. I could’ve throttled both of them this afternoon.’

Claus pauses, searching for the exact phrase. Unlike me he’s never hasty with what he says.

‘It’s hard the work you do. I couldn’t teach those tricky kids all day. Believe in your magic, I do,’ he says, letting go of his bag to massage my shoulders. I lean back, closing my eyes. His strong hands push into my tight muscles. I don’t want him to stop.

‘You can’t underestimate the good you’re doing, it’ll take time, maybe more time than you have,’ he says.

His hands drop back, for a moment he’s still, thoughtful. I wait for more wisdom. It doesn’t come. He can never hover for long.

‘Why don’t we get a take-out? I think we both deserve a treat,’ he asks, before rushing upstairs to wash away the bad stories. Stories from his messed-up kids, all broken and neglected because nobody cares. He won’t relax until his routine is complete. Taking his case, his psychometric tests and the children’s files, he retreats to the spare room. On my first visit, he gave me a peep – I could see an extensive double bed and a pale metal cabinet but he snapped the door shut without letting me in. He keeps all his work stuff there, his cases are highly confidential.

Each day, after work, he showers in that ensuite and when I hear the key turn to lock the door, I know he's ready to return, be home.

I'm still longing for the right moment to have the Oxford chat. Since Mike's meal I've thought of little else. I'm ashamed to say I googled my husband's name to see if there was information on the internet. I could feel my cheeks flushing as I typed, embarrassed, guilty. There was nothing. Then I felt stupid, bad for poking about like a suspicious neurotic.

'Just ask,' Ameena would say. And if it was her, she would ask. I daren't tell her what those trainees said, she's such a nosey blighter. She wouldn't understand why I wouldn't challenge him. Ameena has had a straightforward life, sometimes she's naïve. Everyone is black or white, right or wrong, guilty or innocent. After Esther died, I discovered shades of grey.

Claus was so down after the retirement do; I've never known him like that. Everyone at work had told him he was the obvious choice, cheered him on. After the meal, I tried to cheer him up, reassure him he'd get the job. Of course, he would. Everything about him shouts leader, top of the pile. But Claus was right. The managers from the wider NHS Trust have decided to restructure the children's mental health services. Claus assures me he will keep his post but the lead job will go to a non-psychologist, most likely a social worker. I'd be furious. He's just down, dejected.

He's been so out of sorts the last fortnight. He's always slept an occasional night in the spare room, when he's preparing for a conference or has an early start but his insomnia has been so bad, he's been sleeping there several nights a week. I usually sleep like a log but he's been worrying me. Do psychologists get depressed? Ameena was telling me about a friend of Mark's who killed himself, there was no buil- up apart from an issue with his ex. He was also an insomniac. The night before Claus went away, I was half awake and I'm sure he was on the phone but then I heard the car engine. My bedside clock shined 3am. He finds a night drive helpful, says it helps him solve problems. By the morning, he was showered and packed for his trip. He said it was most likely the car radio I heard.

When Claus joins me, his hair is still wet and I have to push away my desire. 'I've ordered a curry to be delivered at seven, we can have a fun evening and an early night.' He grins, placing himself next to me on the plump sofa.

I reach out for his hand. 'You seem brighter?'

'I am, a night away has given me perspective. Work doesn't matter, does it? It's just a job. Now I have you, everything's perfect. It's about us. Our future. As long as there's us, nothing else matters.'

Despite his cheery tone, his head flops down, somewhat defeated. He studies his restless hands and looks sideways at me from under enviably long lashes.

'I know what I'm like and I'm sorry. It's really not what I want to be like, it's not what you deserve. It's not you, honestly, it's not. I've just been feeling a little inadequate.'

Claus sits up straight and leans his head back, he closes his eyes. When he opens them, his lower lashes are brimming with tears. He's so gentle in nature. I still remember him cradling Kerry into school. He's so different to the other professionals. I love watching him when he comes into my class. He kneels down, lower his voice and speaks so quietly to the children who are struggling.

'It's the legacy of boarding school, I think. All the popular lads were sporty and loud but I was a late developer, weedy. I lacked confidence. The others teased me,' Claus tells me, still somewhat distracted.

I study my husband's broad shoulders and thick blond stubble that if left for two days becomes a beard. It's hard to imagine anything other.

'It sounds awful,' I say.

He squeezes my hands and continues. 'It was very lonely, but within months of being there, I was nearly six foot with a morning shadow to be proud of. I was suddenly quite popular with the girls.'

He flashes me a wider smile and I snuggle deeper into him. He tightens his arms around me.

'I'm sorry, I'll try harder to be the man you deserve,' Claus says, kissing me lightly on the lips. 'I know I'm a bit intense at times. I want to be the best husband, to know you're safe. I dread you being hurt again. Sometimes I get a bit carried away.'

'We'll be OK,' I reassure him, knowing we will.

There's a pause, while Claus strokes my hair. 'Perhaps it's time to start our family,' he finally says.

I pull back slightly. Looking up, I try not to seem horrified. Claus and I still haven't explicitly discussed the right time to start a family. I know he loves kids and would make an amazing dad, I've seen him with Heidi's little ones. When I found out he was ten years my senior, I worried he might have kids, that would've been a deal breaker for me. I want to start a family at the same time as my partner, for it to be the first of everything for both of us. It's odd to think that given the age gap, Claus could be the father of a teenager when I still feel like a teen, immature, not quite ready to grow up. I shake that thought away. It can go in one of those locked boxes in my head.

'Oh, Claus, kids are everything, the icing, but not yet, we've not been married for six months and I'm loving work and anyway, we don't know if I can fall pregnant, there are no guarantees.'

He hesitates. I can see his mind whirring, wanting to say the right thing.

'Maybe that's why we need to start trying.'

I so don't want to disappoint him. He clearly wants kids way sooner than me. My parents would love it. It's so tempting, a way to make them happy, to give them joy but I don't want it. I just don't.

After a longer pause I continue. 'I need more time, a lot more time. Can we revisit in a year or so please?'

Claus starts to speak 'The thing is I've already . . .' But then snaps his mouth shut and smiles, resigned.

As if deliberately configured, the buzzer rings. A male voice speaks. 'Cottage Tandoori for Mr Doerkson.'

Before I settle down to sleep I wonder whether tonight might be a good time to clear the air about the Oxford puzzle. Claus is frowning intently at his text book. The title is 'Training the Impulsive Child'. No wonder he can't sleep.

I reach out for his hand to test the waters. Do I ask?

Besides, what can be so sad that it's noteworthy by his junior colleagues but not worth telling your wife? I can't help but worry that maybe he doesn't trust me, thinks I'm too immature to be burdened by anything serious.

I take a deep breath, I need to know.

'Claus, can I ask you something?'

‘Of course, anything, sweetheart,’ he says, closing his book and placing it on his bedside table. He turns to give me his full attention.

‘Ricardo and Clara were talking about a sad thing that happened before you took up this post, I had no idea what they were on about?’

Claus pauses. His body stiffens and quickly turns away from me, stares at the monochrome photograph on the opposite wall.

After a pause, he flips back the corner of the duvet and gets up. His movements are slow as he moves around to my side, his hands deep in the pockets of his pyjama bottoms, head down. For a minute I think he’s going to sit next to me to talk more but instead he looks out of the window with his back to me.

Without turning back around, he speaks to the view outside.

‘She must have been talking about a sad case in Oxford I would rather forget. It was a professional matter. Nothing for you to worry about, water under the bridge. And, surely, we’ve both done enough emotional talking tonight, haven’t we?’

Before I can agree, he comes back to me, kisses my cheek and takes my mug.

‘I’m thirsty, do you want anything from downstairs?’ he says, before making a hasty retreat for the bedroom door.

7

In the Newspaper

Nicky

He's been awake since the early hours. That wasn't in the plan. Today, he needs to be alert like the rabbit caught in dad's headlights. Today, he can't be tired, he needs wide open eyes. Today, he's going to fix his broken family. He broke it so he has to fix it. Today will be the end of twos. Tonight, they'll be restored to a three.

His tummy is so tangled up he can't swallow his toast. So he bins it and searches for his plan. He unwraps the scroll he's been keeping inside an empty kitchen roll so it wouldn't get crumpled like his award.

He's been working on this plan since he was shortlisted. He waited for a time his parents were close together, then he told them. Outside on the pavement when his dad took his bag from his mum, he announced his story had been shortlisted for a prize and Dr John Eagle was coming for the presentation and the newspaper were coming and everything. As he finished speaking, he watched them. It worked. They looked at each other and they beamed megawatt smiles and then they hugged him together. Mr P and his grandparents were also delighted but they are not invited to the ceremony. That's only for his family of three.

He smooths out his plan. He took a piece of paper from his dad's case last time he visited. It's the stuff his department use for important legal reports. After the hug on the pavement, Nicky wrote the title in black capital letters.

THE PLAN.

There are nineteen tasks to be achieved, he joined a few items together to make the right number.

His mum will look wonderful and his dad will be overtaken with love. They'll refill the pool and then go on holiday. Then, the laughter will return. That's what he misses most. Laughter. Laughter in his house, laughter coming out of his mum when she's not drunk and laughter coming out of him.

'Hurry up, Nick, if you don't get a wiggle on we won't be there in time,' Mum shouts down the hall. For once she's ready before him.

The first three items on the list got done yesterday. He ironed his clothes and polished his shoes but first he ironed her best dress. The velvet one with the miniscule blue flowers. He pressed each corner making sure he didn't burn the material, just like dad showed him. When he finished ironing every inch, he draped the floaty magic on a hanger. He climbed up on the wooden trunk to hang it on the wardrobe door. When it was hanging, he thought about his parents dancing. Dad loves that soft dress, he says it makes her eyes shine. He can't wait to see dad's face when he walks into the hall and spots his wife, all dressed up and pretty. Then she'll remember he mends all the stuff, makes tea and cleans the bath on a Saturday. He can't wait for them to fall back in love and for dad to come home.

Mrs Hobbs said he has a good chance in the story competition. His parents will hold hands as he reads, they'll look into each other's eyes as their son is crowned the winner.

He can't wait. If he wins he'll get another certificate. He regrets screwing the last one into a tight ball and lobbing it down the toilet.

When he stands up from fastening his laces, he's horrified to glimpse his mother in jeans and a scruffy T-shirt.

'I ironed your dress,' he demands.

'Thanks mate,' she says. 'I'll save it for when I go out.'

At least she smells good and her hair has been done at the hairdressers. That's eight and nine on the plan. Dad hates it when she goes out with a bed head, he feels it's undignified.

She's done her eyelashes like spider's legs, there's black pen written under her eyes and thick creamy stuff on her cheeks. It makes her look not herself. He doesn't like it at all and is not sure what his dad will think. He pushes those thoughts out of his head whilst he scrubs at his hands until they hurt.

He ticks some other things off the list. Smart trousers, tick. Clean face, tick. Breath mints for dad, tick.

The final four can't happen until after. Item sixteen, dad leaves car at school and drives us three back home. Item seventeen, supper. He doesn't mind who cooks. Eighteen. Dad showers. Nineteen. Goodnight kisses. He sleeps tight and his parents go to their own bedroom to watch films.

All he has left to do before leaving for the ceremony is put the pages in the plastic thingy.

Then he's ready.

His grandma typed his story on her computer and they printed it out together. He has been practising reading with Bella. Every day after school Mr P meets him outside the gate with a can of something. Mr P said he must stand to project his voice from the stage. When Bella wiggles her ears, she can hear and if not, he has to speak more loudly. He's not good at that, his voice is too squeaky.

He hasn't read it to his parents as he doesn't want to spoil the surprise.

Nicky finds the plastic thing and slides the papers in. Poppa calls it a slippery fish. He uses them to do his accounts. Nicky thinks he might like to be an accountant. When he mentioned that to his grandparents, they both laughed and said, 'You are certainly good at counting.'

By the time they arrive, the school hall is full of chairs and adults. Nicky searches for dad. He isn't here.

'Hello, do take a seat, there are lots at the front,' one of the big kids says with a microphone from the stage.

Lou's bright turban stands high above the other heads in the front row. She's waving and pointing at two seats next to her.

Mum grabs his hand and pulls him towards Kerry's family. He likes Lou but he wants to save space at the back so dad can easily see them when he arrives. On the front row, there's only one space at the wrong end, next to the wall. He tugs his mum's hand. Not there, please not there, he pleads with his eyes but she doesn't listen.

Mum squeezes in front of Kerry's parents to sit by the wall. Lou is next to her, then Kerry with two ugly gaps in her teeth, then Kerry's dad, the chinacologist who's never at home, then one spare seat for his dad. How can his parents hold hands with all those people in between?

Mrs Hobbs rushes over. She's wiping her bright red face with a tissue. 'Hello Nicky, we were wondering where you'd got to. Come with me, have you got your story?'

Nicky looks from his mum to his teacher. He wants to wait.

'Go on, Nicky.' Mum nods her head to the stage.

Nicky follows Mrs Hobbs onto the stage, where the other three children are already, shuffling paper in their hands. A man in grey trousers is kneeling below the stage with a great big camera on a necklace. He keeps looking through and pointing it to the stage but he's not taking any photos.

Mr Martin, the head teacher walks behind the four children, hands behind his back. He looks like he might topple over. Nicky still can't see his dad but he sees the teacher he loves, sitting with her legs crossed. She gives him a little wave but he looks away. Dad promised he'd be here for the whole assembly and stay for a chat at the end. It's a shame mum isn't looking as pretty as he likes but her hair is nice and her perfume smells of flowers.

'Try not to wobble about Nicky, and speak up,' Mr Martin whispers behind Nicky's head. He doesn't speak to any of the others. Mr Eagle puts his thumbs up and smiles.

Nicky has looked into every seat. Mum and Lou are chatting, their heads bobbing up and down at the same time. Kerry's dad sits arms folded, chin down. Maybe he's asleep. Kerry says chinacologists have to work many nights in the hospital.

Nicky is not going to read his story if his dad isn't here.

122, 123, where are you dad? 124, 125 . . .

'Good morning, Parents, carers and children.' Mr Martin stands behind his wooden stand and reads from his papers. 'I'm very pleased to introduce Dr John Eagle, a longstanding friend of the school to celebrate a morning of Beowulf . . .'

I44, 145, please come dad, 146.

A door opens right at the back. The few people clustered in front of it turn around. Miss Underwood lifts the velvet curtain to the side to let him in.

Nicky's dad has come.

Nicky watches his dad sit on his own in the middle of three seats.

I'm so sorry you have to sit on your own. I'm sorry I didn't save your seat, I'm sorry I left my bike out, I'm sorry . . .

'Nicky, start us off with your fabulous account of this Anglo-Saxon tale.'

Nicky is very hot. He sees a million eyes. As he stares, the bodies disappear and he can only see eyes, more eyes, monster eyes.

'Nicky, please start reading when you're ready,' Mr Martin repeats.

Nicky tries to stay still. He takes in a big breath through his nostrils so he can do a loud voice.

'There was a king who loved his people. Every time he had a party in his great hall, someone disappeared. The king followed the blood trail and realised an evil monster called Grendel was doing the killings so he needed a warrior to kill it. Beowulf was the greatest warrior . . .'

The words on his page are blurring into one, his hands are shaking. He feels very strange. He tries counting but his numbers muddle into a dream. *188, 179, 185* . . . Everywhere he looks he sees monster eyes staring back at him.

'Nicky, Nicky?'

'He doesn't need you fussing, give him some air.' His dad's voice is in the dream.

‘I think we need an ambulance, he’s fallen on his arm,’ Mrs Hobbs says.

‘Excuse me, I’m a doctor, can I see?’

When Nicky opens his eyes, his parents have their heads close together. They are staring down at their boy. He knows it’s all going to be OK, his family are back together even though the velvet dress is still hanging on the wardrobe and they didn’t sit together. His arm is agony but his heart is back in its right place.

Kerry’s dad is looking at his shoulder, Nicky tries hard to be brave even though his arm is so sore. No one needs him snivelling and ruining the love.

‘Smile,’ the man in the grey trousers is here. Nicky pushes his chin forward and forces his mouth into a Cheshire Cat grin. A massive camera flashes a light in Nicky’s eyes.

‘Seriously!’ Dad pushes the man back and Nicky feels a swell of pride.

After Kerry’s dad has pronounced that his arm is just bruised, dad lifts him off the hard floor into his arms and pulls him close. Nicky leans in to his chest and listens to his beating heart. As he is carried towards the car park, he makes sure mum is following.

Nicky holds tight to dad’s neck.

‘What’s that bruise on your cheek?’ Dad asks looking at the side of his mummy’s face.

Nicky didn’t see a bruise at breakfast but now he can see a red line, maybe a scratch near her eye and a blue circle on her cheek.

‘I fell in the garden,’ she tells him.

‘Did you?’ Nicky asks.

His arm is painful, his mouth is dry and he feels too big to be carried but, for the first time in ages Nicky has a genuine smile plastered on his face. His plan is working. A plan keeps everyone on track. Obviously, he didn't plan to faint and nearly break his neck but their family is a three again and they're are speeding towards his mum's car. He visualises the paper but can't work out what number they're up to. Dad's car is nowhere to be seen. They can go home and have supper, just as they should.

Before he can decide on his choice of pudding, dad plonks him down next to mum's car. She fumbles in her leather handbag and finds her keys. But instead of handing them to her husband, she gets in the car and starts the engine. Dad opens the back door and gives his son an unwanted hand into the back. The door is shut and his mum doesn't even say goodbye. She jerks the car forward leaving his dad with his hands in his pockets, still in the school car park.

'Sit round, and put your seat belt on,' she snaps. 'Don't you think you've caused enough drama.'

The next morning Nicky is up before her. He needs some paracetamol for his arm but it's in the high cupboard in the medical box. He hopes it isn't broken as he can't lift it over his head.

The gate buzzer sounds making him wobble on the kitchen stool.

'Morning, Lisa.' It's Mr P's voice. 'I've popped a copy of the *Herald* into the box, Nicky looks great on the photo. Hope he's OK, send our love.'

The stool falls over as Nicky jumps down, grabs the key and races out towards the gate. He smacks his palm on the metal. Even before the gates widen he's through and unlocking the box.

The newspaper is in a roll but when he opens it, there he is. On the front page, there's a photo of him at school. Him sitting against the stage with his dad, Kerry's dad and Mr Martin on the side.

The thick letters at the top say 'Disaster on History Day'.

Nicky sits on the curb and follows the words with his finger. He skips some big words but can read the fourth line.

Nicky, aged nine was reading his prize-winning story at an Anglo-Saxon celebration day, when he became unwell. Gasps from the audience punctuated his slow-motion fall from the stage. Nicky sustained a broken arm and suspected concussion but is recovering at home in the care of his mother.

When Mrs Pinkney looks out of her bedroom window she spots Nicky in bare feet and pyjamas, newspaper rolled up under his arm like an old man. His head is down as it always is and he's muttering to himself as he always does. She closes her curtains, she can't bear to watch any longer.

Keziah

Claus left this morning for a three-day conference. He was gutted when I pointed out the clash with my first half term.

When we got married, I didn't realise he'd be away so much. He has a quarterly conference, regular out-of-county school visits, and now he's joined a monthly supervision group that rotates around different locations. Each time he disappears, it takes me a few days to adjust; I miss him but have to admit it's fab having me time, no pressure to please or eat at the right time. No worries if I run late, just me, chill time, friends, family and a few more glasses of wine. Besides, working away seems to do him good. On his return, his shoulders are always less hunched and the bags under his eyes less obvious. The added bonus is he usually comes home feeling very amorous.

Today, I'm going to indulge in a few more chapters of my Jodi Picoult novel, do a dash around with the hoover and then dress up for a late lunch with my mates. I've not seen them for weeks. All I seem to do these days is work and be married. I'm getting stupidly unfit, have hardly seen the olds and can't remember the last girly weekend I went on.

Before Claus went, his embossed leather notebook came out for the umpteenth time to check mobile numbers for my parents and Ameena.

'Just in case I need to get hold of you,' he said, kissing me yet again, then a final hug.

I told him I was lunching with friends then spending the evening with mum. I said I might even stay over, like old times and take her and dad out for breakfast to the garden centre they like.

‘Which friends?’ Claus wanted to know. Then, ‘Will you or won’t you stay over at your parents?’

‘I don’t know until I get there, it depends how much they irritate me, whether I have a glass or two, I’ll decide when I’m there.’

‘But how will I know where you are?’

‘I’ll text you.’

‘But I don’t want you driving even after one glass, the roads between here and there are hideous on a Saturday night, it’s probably best if you come home.’

‘OK darling,’ I told him. Sometimes it’s easier to smile, agree and then do as I please.

Just an hour before I meet Ameena, so I pop in my ear buds and allow myself a boogie to My Chemical Romance as I hoover. I didn’t tell Claus I’ve given Sue, the cleaner, the week off so I’ll have to do an hour a day so it isn’t a slob’s palace on his return.

I love a dance but haven’t done anything in ages. Note to self, lighten up Keziah Blayton, I tell my housewife persona. I wiggle about, manoeuvring between the bed and the side tables hoping the old bloke in the next garden doesn’t look up. He seems to be there all the time, on his hands and knees, ignoring his wife issuing instructions from the upstairs window.

Dusting the photograph of my family, I’m struck by how normal we were. I give Esther a quick kiss, bless her. I can’t pinpoint exactly when it was taken, definitely one of our yearly caravan trips to Scotland.

Each year my mum would book a slot at the holiday park’s photo studio, basically an odd couple in a shed. In the morning, she’d nip out to get her hair done in one of the other shabby sheds. Then, we’d all troop off, despite mine and my dad’s complaints and have our picture taken. Us four. Two little girls in matching outfits growing older each year, a smiling father with my mum's elbow poked sharply in his ribs.

After she died, there was never four, only three. We have few family photographs from after. The empty chair was too painful, the resulting portrait would have been asymmetrical, wrong.

For six months, I wore the thick wool coat I was wearing when we found her. I have no idea how overheating in that filthy thing helped but, somehow it did. I felt safer with it on. In the end my parents gave up making rules about when and where it could stay on. I wore it in school, in bed, at meals and then, one day, I guess I stopped.

This photograph, now faded, has followed me wherever I've gone. It came on international bike tours, it sat on my desk at university, on the narrow windowsill at the flat and now, here, on my marital bedside. The cheap plastic frame looks out of place in our hotel-like suite but I can't interfere with it in any way. Perfect families are always made of four. After Esther went, I became an 'only'. But three in a family wasn't enough.

Remembering she will never be someone's wife, never have children or grow old still makes me panic. I perch on the edge of my bed, give myself the moment I need before pulling myself together. I can't believe how far I've come. It's still hard to forgive my younger self. Claus says we all have a past self who did things that weren't ideal. He says that's how we have to think about it, it wasn't us now, but us then. He has helped me heal in so many ways.

Wiping away the tears, with my dressing gown collar, I shove the hoover under my side of bed and do a few hip moves as I swivel to Claus's side, though I can feel the mood is lost.

On his bedside, there are no family photos, no tooth picks or magazines – just the Dickens novel he's reading and his alarm clock. No phones allowed in the bedroom. Under his side table are three piles of books neatly stacked in size order. Trying to be as unusually thorough as my husband, I sit on the thick pile carpet to dust each one and have a sneaky rest. However many years pass, mourning remains exhausting. I lean against the bed and pull the hefty books between my legs.

'Attachment Disorders' is written across a black and white image of a mother breastfeeding her child. Don't fancy that. A couple of history books are on the bottom, one about Oxford and another about Queen Victoria. I can't stand non-fiction.

On the bottom of the second pile is an older book. Missing the dust cover, it's a sombre dark book with gold writing. Without the title it might be mistaken for a religious text: 'Overcoming Shame and Guilt'.

Trying to recreate the piles exactly as they were, I notice a page at an awkward angle. He'll be distraught about a ruined paragraph. To Claus, using turned corners as bookmarks is blasphemy.

I open the book to the right page, and find the bookmark is a narrow strip of newspaper.

Only one column. A black and white picture of a young girl at the top, her features blurred by the ancient fold. She has long hair with a headband. Esther and I had matching ones. Hers was blue and white striped, mine red. We'd fought over the colour choice. Well, I'd taken red and she accepted the only other.

Thick bold letters shout the headline. School Girl Mowed Down.

Yesterday whilst out walking with her family, an eleven-year-old girl was hit by a car on the Spitfield Road in Portsmouth. She was rushed to the Queen Alexandra hospital but her injuries are thought to be incompatible with life. In a tribute, her family said: 'She was a beautiful, kind, loving and genuine girl with a heart of gold. She would do anything to make you smile. She brought happiness and joy to the life of everyone she met.'

Bricklayer Bernard Wilson was driving and saw the incident unfold. In a statement to our reporter, he said: 'One minute she was holding another child's hand, playing about by the Spitfield sign and the next, she was in front of that sporty car. It happened so fast, I couldn't work out how it could happen.' The girl can't yet be named. The car driver, in his teens, is being questioned by the police.

Just under the photo is a date in tiny writing at the bottom of the page, the month has been torn but it looks like the year was 1988.

Folding the flimsy paper, I do some basic maths. Why has Claus kept an article from three decades ago? Perhaps, it's a client, or a relative? I don't even know if he has cousins. Could it have something to do with Oxford? Perhaps it's just a forgotten book mark from the previous owner. My mother uses coupons she cuts from supermarket flyers.

The crash of a bird headbutting our window jolts me back; I'm now rudely late for my friends. I throw the books back together as best I can and fly out the door.

8

Milestone Birthdays

Nicky

Happy birthday to you

Happy birthday to you

Nicky waits patiently whilst his dad takes an enormous intake of breath to continue his song.

Happy birthday dear Nicky

Happy birthday to you.

'Thanks, Dad.'

'So, how are you then?'

Nicky desperately wants to tell him how he is. He wants to tell his dad, he misses him so bad, he cries every night. He wants to tell him that his mum goes out most evenings despite what she promised, that she drinks so much she wets herself, and that sometimes she forgets she even has a son. He knows it's his job now, to keep her safe and well. He wants to tell his dad that he he's trying, really trying. He wants to tell him he hides her keys and cleans the house but however much he tries, she gets worse and that he knows it's his fault and he's sorry. Most of all he wants to tell him about yesterday. That yesterday when the teacher with the long hair and straight teeth asked him what makes him laugh, he had nothing to say.

He had nothing to say because he doesn't get any laughter. There's absolutely nothing in his life that is funny.

Nicky's mum has put the phone on speaker so they can both listen.

'I'm fine. Thank you for asking,' Nicky replies, trying to sound grown up, like a ten-year-old.

'At least your birthday fell on an inset day. I know your mum has some plans?'

'Yes, we're going to the Italian restaurant for pizza, the one you like,' Nicky says, wishing he was going bowling like Ollie. But it doesn't matter as he has no friends to invite and he does enjoy the restaurant. The waiter with the twisty moustache always gives him a balloon and a sweet.

'Well, I'll collect you late afternoon. We'll watch an episode of something and then have the best supper. Pick anything you fancy?'

'Errrrm, but, dad, you can only cook spaghetti Bolognese and cheese on toast.'

'Go on, what do you want? I'll make sure you have it, choose anything, anything at all.'

'Mac cheese with bacon.'

'Consider it done. I've also got the best surprise coming for you.'

'What surprise?'

'If I tell you, it won't be a surprise, but it's a good surprise, in fact it's a really good surprise. I can't wait to see your face.'

Mum snatches her phone back

'Can you collect him at 1.30, please? I've taken a day off work and I have plans too, you know.'

Nicky thinks that's strange as she's been off work all week.

Nicky opens the presents his mum got him. Now that he's man of this house, he knows he has to grow up. So he asked for aftershave and blue socks with pineapples. Some of his mum's other presents are good and he smiles at her as she talks, but it's hard to listen. All he can think about is his surprise. Could it be new headphones or even a radio like grandma's, the red one with the silver aerial poking out of the top?

When he hears Bella yapping next door, he knows straightaway what his surprise is. His dad knows he loves that scruffy old dog. His dad has got him a dog. It'll be amazing. When his mum goes out, he won't be frightened as he'll have his dog. When he gets home and it's cold and silent, his dog will come bounding up, wagging his tail.

Ideally, he'd choose one of those great big ones with a bottle around his neck but he knows he will only get a small one. Nicky starts to think about names for his dog. Maybe Bruce sounds nice or Baggyface or Gerald after his grandad. He could put a sign on the gate saying 'beware of the dog' so everyone will be scared to burgle him and he won't have to worry anymore.

Nicky collects his birthday gifts, he puts his new films in the rack by the television and hides the scratchy jumper under the cushion. Later he'll hide it in his wardrobe. The wardrobe is his safe place where no one can get to him. There, he feels less small; there, he pretends he is doing well in his roles as grown up and care taker. When the door is closed, he wraps himself inside a blanket and closes his eyes. There, he feels safe and warm.

Whilst he is eating his toast with the television on, his mum shouts into her phone.

‘Not today, it’s his birthday, I promised.’

Nicky shoves a cream egg into his mouth, glad he’s allowed chocolate for breakfast on his special day.

‘Well OK, but not until 12 at least,’ his mum whispers.

‘To his dad’s.’

‘No, not overnight.’

‘Grow up, Paul,’ she says before throwing her phone onto the table. Nicky watches the black rectangle slide across the surface.

He knew it would be Paul from the phone. He’s been here all week, every day when he gets back from school. He’s here. He lies back in the armchair with his boots on the coffee table. His dad would hate that.

Nicky hides in his cupboard most nights, but he can still hear the shouting and screaming.

One night, Mr Pinkney pressed the buzzer knocked and said, ‘Are you alright, Lisa?’ but Paul said, ‘Poke ya nose in someone else’s house.’ He added some swearing which Nicky found very unnecessary. Mr Pinkney doesn’t poke his nose. He has very good manners.

In the end they don’t go out to the restaurant. His mum remembers they have pizza in the freezer so they share a pepperoni one and eat some chocolate cake. His mum can’t remember where she left the candles but Nicky tells her it doesn’t matter, he’s not a child anymore.

Paul turns up half an hour before his dad arrives. As soon as he barges through the door, Nicky seeks respite on his favourite curb to wait, the place by the gurgling drain where the curb dips down. It’s a little cold under his bottom but he doesn’t care as he’s going to get his dog. He’s decided to call his dog Bruce, even if it’s a girl.

In the end he can't wait any longer so he brushes the dirt off his trousers and races to the entrance to their crescent. Luckily, before he gets to the end of the road, dad's car skids to a stop. With his hand still on the wheel, dad throws open the passenger door. His dad has got the music ready but it's Nicky's job to hit the play button. With matching cheesy grins, father and son drive away with windows wide open.

Neil Diamond starts singing. When he gets to 'Sweet Caroline' he and his dad sing at the tops of their voices. It's their song and it's Nicky's all-time favourite. It was the song his parents played when they drove him home from hospital the day he was born.

Nicky turns the music up and up, until his dad puts his hands over his ears. Nicky is glad his dad only let's go of the wheel for a few seconds. It would be very sad if they had a crash and both died on his birthday.

Dad turns the music down and winks at Nicky.

'I've got such a good surprise for you, young man,' he reminds him. 'Tonight, we are going to have a feast.'

When they arrive at the flat, the lift is still out of order. Hand in hand they climb all the way up singing 'Sweet Caroline' even though Nicky's daddy is panting and keeps stopping to catch his breath.

On the outside of the front door is a long silver banner saying 'Birthday Boy'. Balloons are hanging from the balcony, flying out into the air. A handmade poster for the wall says 'Happy birthday, Nicky'.

In the middle of the side table with the wonky leg there's a massive cake. It's the best cake Nicky has ever, ever had. It's covered with his best sweets, flakes, smarties and chocolate biscuits. Nicky pushes his finger through a small gap in the side, then wrenches it back loaded with chocolate icing. His dad laughs when Nicky shoves it in his mouth and makes an exaggerated sucking noise.

'It's great isn't it. My new friend made it, you'll love her too.'

'Can I have a slice?'

'Well, maybe we should light the candles later.'

'Let's do it now.'

'Well, I've got another surprise for you. It'll go nicely with the cake, make it better.'

'OK, is it ice cream?'

'Not exactly but I promise you'll love it.'

His dad gives him a large square parcel which Nicky gives a quick shake. It's quiet so it's not alive. It's too small for a bike. Dad gets a beer for himself and a coke for Nicky. The present is on his lap. He can't wait to open it but first he has to count to the right number to ensure he'll like it.

'Go on then, open it,' dad says. He puts his arm across Nicky's back to stop him fidgeting.

The wrapping is tight. Nicky wonders what can be inside. He knows his dog is a surprise and that his dad's friend is bringing it later. He can't decide if that'll be Pete from work or Brian from his old footie team. If his dog is coming a bit later, maybe this present is a bowl and a sleeping basket.

When the paper falls open, it's a fabulous Lego set. It's a pirate one that he wanted for Christmas. He's very pleased and gives his dad a big hug. If he wasn't getting his dog the Lego would be amazing.

'We can build it at the weekend when you come,' dad says.

'It's a good present,' Nicky says and makes a smile on his face.

Dad keeps looking out of the window, he gets up and looks at the balloons, then sits down, then gets up again. He puts the kettle on but doesn't make tea and then he puts the kettle on again.

At last, the doorbell plays 'Jingle Bells' even though it's not Christmas.

Dad jumps up with a big grin on his face. 'It's the surprise!' he says.

Nicky stays in his seat and wraps his arms around himself as he counts in time to his body, back, forward, back, forward. He can hear. The door is close to everything. He's so excited but the voice is not Brian or Pete. It's the sound of a girl.

The lounge door opens.

'Hello,' his dad says.

'Hello,' a lady says.

'Come on in.'

Nicky thinks his dad's voice sounds a bit funny.

Dad ushers the lady into the room carrying a parcel wrapped in silver foil. It smells nice.

'Nicky, this is Nancy, she's made you macaroni cheese.' His dad touches the lady on her shoulder and smiles at her face.

Nicky looks at the lady, she smells nice. She has a leather jacket like Mrs Pinkney when she goes to the pub. He thinks he's seen her somewhere before but he's not sure where.

The lady says, 'Happy birthday, Nicky,' like she knows him, but she doesn't.

His dad follows her into the kitchen like she's not a stranger. Nicky stands behind them both and watches. She carefully lowers the parcel onto the work top and then hangs her coat over the chair.

Nicky can't wait any longer.

'Where's my dog?' he blurts out.

'What dog?'

'My birthday dog.'

Both his dad and the lady laugh. 'I'm not sure where we'd keep a dog in a flat.'

Before Nicky has time to wipe the tears pushing over his lower lashes, his dad says, 'Close your eyes and smell your wonderful birthday food.'

His dad slowly lifts the foil like there's something in there he doesn't want to climb out.

'Mmmmmm – take a sniff of that, Nicky.' He gives the lady another smile.

Nicky gets closer but all he can smell is her. It's the same smell his dad smelt of on History day.

'What do you say Nicky, homemade macaroni cheese, just like you asked for.'

'Where's the bacon?'

'Nicky,' his dad snaps, going red in the face. 'That is SO rude.'

'Where's my big surprise?' Nicky says.

'Oh, champ, It's Nancy. Nancy is your birthday surprise. She made your cake and your macaroni.'

Nicky wiggles free from his dad's restraint. The silver-covered dish falls off the table with a loud smash. Angry tears cascade as he races down the concrete steps, shouting at the top of his voice, 'Liar, liar!'

Keziah

'Happy birthday, dear Keziah,' Claus sings for the final time this morning as he reticently leaves the bedroom. His card is simple, but inside he's written, 'To my beloved, the love of my life. Thank you for marrying me.'

Just in case I've forgotten, he's scribbled at the bottom, 'Dinner date 7.30pm @ Casalingo's'.

This time last year we'd been on a handful of dates. The drink after disaster day doesn't count but the following week Claus took me to Casalingo's. The staff clearly knew him well. They look happily surprised when he had a woman in tow. I took that to be a good sign, a sign he didn't wine and dine a different girl each week. We tried the cinema but quickly realised that wasn't his thing so we settled into romantic hill walks and serious chats about love, loss and our hopes for the future. Waking up to a chocolate croissant and a glass of champagne on my thirtieth was right up there.

However happy I feel, birthdays will always have a bitter edge. The worst one was when I made nineteen. For the first time I was older than my sister would ever be.

Esther, I'm so sorry. Am I doing OK? I stopped the biking, couldn't risk another kid dying. I worked hard for you, went to university. And now, Esther, I've made them happy with the perfect son-in-law. You'd love him. He went to Oxford, super clever and geeky!

Determined to have a great day, for Esther if not for me I put on an everyday drab skirt and a high neck blouse. Then, with a racing heart, I grab my purple mini dress from the wardrobe, wrap it into a towel and shove it right at the bottom of my workbag. I kiss my husband goodbye and leave for work.

I did try. I even waited for a Sunday morning. He'd been on his run and was enjoying his weekend treat of croissant and a smidgeon of butter. I told him whilst I couldn't wait to celebrate at our swanky restaurant, I would love a few hours with my girly friends and to pop in on my parents.

He didn't respond immediately which is always a good sign but then he got up, switched on the kettle and said, 'Let's do this year differently, go to work as we'll need your holiday for summer trips, you can chat on the phone to your friends or see them another day. We can enjoy a grown-up meal in the evening.'

There are some battles that are not worth fighting, both at home and in the classroom.

In the end, Ameena persuaded me to party in the day. She planned it all. Claus makes home visits in the area so we're going out in her car. I didn't lie, I just omitted to reveal my birthday fell on an inset day that only involved key stage two.

We meet the usual crowd in a bar close to our old flat. Claus only sends texts at first break and lunchtime. I count fourteen before we order lunch. It used to make me feel special but sometimes it's a bit suffocating.

Walking into the restaurant to a sea of faces, my happy mood returns.

'Happy birthday to you

happy birthday to you

happy birthday dear Keziah.

happy birthday to you.'

The waitress places a beautiful mermaid cake in front of me. It has turquoise hair and a long blue tail circling the cake.

'Wow, thanks, Heidi. You're so talented.'

She comes over and wraps her arms around me.

'You're worth it, happy birthday, girl,' she laughs. 'We've missed you,' she adds.

'Ameena said you're out with the old man this evening,' Tristan shouts across the table. I can tell he's had one too many already, and I'm not the only one: the women on the next table look up and raise an eyebrow. 'Sorry,' I mouth to the one facing me. She looks away without a response.

Watching my friends muck about and get louder, I can see Claus's view. They are being inconsiderate of other guests and for a lunchtime we are dominating the room. Maybe I'm outgrowing this bunch.

The clock chimes three pm. My schedule is so tight I might as well be Cinderella but if we leave now, I'll have heaps of time to arrive home, have a bath, indulge in a bit of crap TV and be looking gloriously mature when my husband arrives home after six pm.

I nudge Ameena. 'I have to go,' I say, feeling more flustered than I'd like.

We don't chat much as we drive back to school; apart from work we seem to have less and less in common these days.

'What are you like?' Ameena throws her head back in an exaggerated laugh as I use her back seat to scramble back into my grown-up clothes. What would the school governors make of that?

She drives off without a backward glance leaving me struggling in the rain to find my own car keys. Claus is right, she can be quite selfish. It wouldn't surprise me if she's off back to the bar. Unexplained tears gather under my lids as I search my messy rucksack for the keys. I love my birthday, yet I've lied to my husband to escape with friends who feel increasingly distant.

Even my car feels surprisingly alien. I named her Bessie like my old one but because it gets cleaned each week, she doesn't even smell like mine. I hardly drive her and struggle to remember where high beam is or how to switch off the heated seat pads. Claus loves to be my chauffeur. 'Nothing is too much trouble for my girl,' is his daily mantra. Guilty feelings push the tears over the edge.

Pushing down on the accelerator an unusual noise shouts for my attention. I ignore it. Every few miles, I slow down but the troubling noise is still there, it sounds like metal, a churning sound. Please tell me I haven't driven over something. Pulling into a layby I get out. It's starting to get dark and panic comes from nowhere, filling my chest, rising in my throat. I don't want to drive up the steep incline to our house. The road is so remote, it would terrify me to be stranded alone and in the dark on that final stretch.

After Esther died, full blown panic attacks were a relentless enemy for a good few years. My first one was that night. It was hammering down with rain and I was complaining, I was good at that in those days. I was furious with her for making me late for ride night. I didn't care that it was me who'd made dad late. Me who'd kept her waiting. Me who'd made her late.

Rain is hammering on the windscreen now, making it harder to drive. My chest is heaving. I can't inhale sufficient air to calm down, keep myself in check. The red numbers on the clock are like a time bomb.

'Pull yourself together, Keziah,' I snap at myself, twisting the key to restart the engine. I pull off slowly, relieved the Mini garage Claus uses is on my way home. It's not quite five pm. I have plenty of time to get the car checked, calm myself down and get into my glad rags before he swans in.

The garage forecourt is bright and obviously open – what a relief. There's a solitary car at the pumps but if I squeeze past I can park right outside the showroom and offices. I swerve Bessie and deliberately block the exit. I offer the steering wheel a gentle tap of thanks. The clock's numbers reassure me. As long as I can find a bloke to give the car a quick once over, I'll be home and dry. Before my breathing can return completely to baseline, all the outside lights go off. I spot a nerdy lad in overalls heading over to turn off the inside lights.

Abandoning my bag on the front seat, I scramble towards the automatic doors and fly through waving my hands about like a mad woman. I rush over to the back office where he's putting away a file, backlit by the only remaining light and rap my knuckles on the door before bursting in.

'So sorry, but don't lock up, there's a problem with my car, and I need to get home and I haven't got much time.'

He sighs wearily, but says, 'Gimme five to lock up out the back.'

Outside, I daren't sit in my car in case he thinks I've given up and runs in the other direction. Instead I retrieve my hat and gloves and lean on the bonnet with my eyes fixed on the offices.

Come on, come on, I plead, stamping my feet to keep warm. At least the rain has calmed to a drizzle. My time widow is rapidly shrinking. If Claus gets home first he'll have the stronger position. I can see him now, ready to pounce, having heard the gates, arms folded, eyes on the clock. Unspoken questions.

When the garage chap finally appears, he's carrying a long black bag. Hoorah, tools.

Without speaking, he slings his bag on the floor and opens the driver's door and plonks himself down, one leg stuck out of the car. His badge says Adrian.

He turns on the engine and pauses. 'Nope, can't hear anything. Open the bonnet, I'll have a look but don't have time to fix anything.'

He closes the bonnet and then strolls around the car checking each tyre. At the back wheel, he bends further and removes something, straightens up, wipes his hands on a cloth and puts them back in his pockets.

'Can't find anything obvious, maybe book it in for a service next week just to make sure,' Adrian suggests.

I expect him to walk away but he doesn't. His face flushes red under the light, a clash for his auburn hair.

He opens his mouth to speak but then stops, and reaches into his pocket and brings out a small black box. It's perhaps a battery as it has two silver buttons on the upside. He opens his hand and offers it to me.

'Mrs Doerkson, have you put this on the car?'

'No, what is it?'

He speaks to his shoes, an awkward young man desperate to escape. 'A car tracker.'

'Why would the garage want to do that?'

'They wouldn't.'

'Well, I can tell you, we purchased the car here, as far as I know my husband only uses this garage.'

'Yeah, the car came from here but that device didn't, it's a fancy tracker you can buy on the internet. None of my business and it wouldn't be what's making a noise but thought you should know.' He looks as if he's about to turn to go, then stops and asks, 'Who has access to your car apart from you?'

'Only my husband.'

He pauses.

‘Talk to your husband then.’

I get back in my car, my hands are trembling and I don’t know what to do. Adrian stays by the car and when I’ve fastened my seatbelt, he slowly closes my door from the outside.

With only a small gap left to speak through he pauses.

‘Be careful,’ he whispers.

National Hospital of Neurology

Six-month Review

NHS number: 485 777 3496 Gender: *female*

Current diagnosis:

Increased awareness noted by all professionals, recovery potential dramatically increased

Injuries sustained:

- Severe and complex neurological and physical injuries
- Broken vertebrae in lower spine – no movement from mid chest down
- Skull fracture above right ear and occipital region

Progress to date:

- Remarkable progress, presumably related to younger age
- Speech and language therapist reporting attempts to speak

Family situation:

- Mother still visiting
- Yesterday a young boy brought to visit by social worker

Plan:

- Daily physio, speech therapy and occupational therapy
- Referral to psychology for behavioural management
- Referral to psychiatry for assessment and medication
- Sedate at night as wakes up disoriented and distressed

Signed:

Dr.A. Lutte-Elliott

CONSULTANT IN NEUROREHABILITATION

9

Shattered Trust

Nicky

Before leaving his dad's, flat Nicky made a solid commitment to silence on the journey home. No music, no chat, no singing and certainly no 'Sweet Caroline'. He refused to answer his dad's questions and left his cake in the car. He was very brave all the way home. He wanted to cry and shout and give up, but instead he counted. He used all his best numbers but refused to allow bad thoughts to burgle his mind.

On arriving in his crescent, he grabbed his bag and ran through the gates before his dad could turn off the engine. He knew he wouldn't dare follow. By the time he stomped into his kitchen, his tears refused to stop. Everything that he'd suppressed in the car came out.

His mum was watching a movie about soldiers with Paul. Even though his heart was hurting Nicky felt pleased when his mum got up and ran after him like he was little. Nicky sobbed for a good half an hour, face down, shoes and coat still on. Mum said he could have anything he wanted as it was his birthday, biscuits, ice cream and even a new bike but he wanted nothing.

Mum sat on the side of his bed and stroked his hair which he liked but by the time he wiped his face and turned over, she was on her phone. Paul had crashed in twice to ask her to 'leave it' and come back to the film. But she'd stayed and lay down next to him, staring up at the glow stars on the ceiling. Nicky remembered lying in exactly this place as his dad clambered about trying to stick the plastic pieces on the ceiling. Nicky gave instructions. The sun, moon and stars all had to be in their exact places to represent the drawings in Nicky's favourite solar system book.

'So, what's all this about then?' his mother asked, clutching his clammy hand in her own. Nicky noticed there wasn't much difference in the length of their bodies, his feet went down almost as far as hers. He was pleased he was finally growing up.

Nicky turned on his side and mum copied him which made him smile, not a big happy grin but a little smile flickered on his lips for a brief moment. He stared into her eyes, looking for her. Her make-up is smudged and there is hair in between her eyebrows where it used to be smooth.

'What's broken your heart, baby boy?' she whispered in a sing song voice he hadn't heard for a long while. 'What's so bad, it's ruined your birthday joy? Is daddy ill? Has poppa died?'

Nicky hadn't thought about Poppa dying which made him feel bad. He didn't have any words to explain about the dog and the food and her, that woman. Mum was waiting, waiting for Nicky to tell.

'Dad brought a lady home.'

'Is that it?' Mum let out a big sigh and sprung up which made Nicky topple nearer the wall. As she stomped away, without looking back, she said, 'For goodness sake, I thought something bad had happened.'

With her hand on the door knob, she muttered, 'People move on, it's inevitable, unpack your bag and get into your pyjamas.'

Then she went, letting the door bang shut.

The clock says ten pm. Nicky is sitting on his bed. He should be fast asleep but he feels so sad. His rocking gets faster and his head hurts but he can't stop. He turns up his cassette player so Neil can sing louder than his bad thoughts.

Then, BANG, his door crashes opens up and the monster marches in with something in his hand. He launches the slipper like a cricket ball. The hard-plastic sole hits Nicky in the face, by his ear. It's his dad's slipper.

'Will you stop that racket,' Paul yells before slamming back out.

Then there's the shouting.

Nicky climbs into his wardrobe, but he can still hear it.

'Get that kid a snot rag and a cork,' Paul shouts, 'or I'll shut him up once and for all.'

Then more shouting and another crash. Nicky pulls his pillow over his face but he can still hear even with the wardrobe door closed.

He must've fallen asleep as when he opens his eyes, his pyjama bottoms are soaked and the door is being opened from the outside. An unfamiliar hand with a silver ring, tugs the rebellious door until it's wide open. Nicky clutches his cushion tight and peers over the top.

His eyes take time to adjust to the light. Shiny black shoes. Standing over him is someone dressed entirely in black. She kneels down and tentatively peels the pillow from his face but doesn't take it away. Her hair is wrapped in a bun like Mrs Hobbs.

'Hello Nicky, my name is Natalie. You don't have to be scared anymore.'

She pulls him out by his hand and sits next to him on his bed.

'I'm a police officer. One of the neighbours heard a lot of shouting from his garden.'

Nicky is worried she knows he's been hiding his mum's keys. After all, it's stealing, isn't it.

'How are you?' Natalie asks him.

'OK.'

'You can say if you're not OK,' she says

Nicky doesn't answer so she gives him some more questions.

'Do your mum and dad fight a lot?'

'My dad left because I left my bike out,' he blurts out

'Ah, so the man with your mum in the kitchen, who's he?'

'Paul from the phone.'

'Did she meet him on the phone? Or do you mean the internet?'

'No, she met him at the garage, he sells petrol.'

'Oh, I see.'

'Does Paul get angry with you?'

Nicky stares at his curtain. The top bit has come off the rail and is hanging down at the corner. His mum said Paul would fix it.

'It's OK, Nicky, you can tell me the truth,' Natalie says.

Silence.

Natalie takes Nicky into his kitchen to get a drink. He sees a short man with no hair talking to his mum. She has her head in her hands and her nose is bleeding.

'I don't care what happens to him,' she says. 'All I care about is my little boy.'

Nicky thinks about that while he sips his juice. Natalie stands with him.

Then another policeman walks from the hall with Paul. Paul has got handcuffs on.

Nicky and his mum watch from the door. It's very dark and Nicky shivers; his mum puts her arm around his shoulders. There are two police cars parked in the drive. He has no idea how they knew the code to the gate.

'Sorry,' his mum says and strokes his back. But Nicky doesn't mind. Paul going to prison is the best birthday present ever.

Paul gets his head pushed into the back of the car and the two men get in the front.

Natalie has the other car. Before she drives away, she comes back to the door.

'Nicky,' she says, giving him a white card. 'This is a number you can call if you feel scared.' Natalie doesn't say goodbye to his mum, which he thinks is a bit rude really. His grandma says manners don't cost anything.

Nicky's mum goes to bed but he feels wide awake even though it's the middle of the night.

Before he goes to his room, He locks the front door, then, the side door and hides the keys under the teabags in the teddy jar. Now she can't run off to the garage if she gets up.

He pads down the hall in his new slippers that grandma sent in the post. They have warm fluff inside and a rabbit on the front. He pops into his mum's bedroom. She's fast asleep, still in her clothes. He peels off her shoes and tugs the heavy duvet up to her chin. He takes one last cuddle. He carefully carries her glass to the sink in case she wakes and breaks it.

It's already light and the birds are singing. When he checks the kitchen clock he realises it's no longer his birthday.

Keziah

'Good evening, Signora Doerkson.'

Ludo takes our coats, offers Claus a firm hand shake and me a professional peck on the cheek. 'Happy Birthday, young lady.'

We have our usual table at Casalingo's, the one in the room Ludo calls the snug. There're only two tables out here and we like to sit by the big window overlooking the steeply inclined gardens, and the twisting single-track road that leads down into the valley. In the early-evening light you can see the fancy statues that cascade water into a central pond. I inhale the blend of culinary flavours and desperately search for my birthday mood, pushing everything else to the back of my mind. I want to have the best evening. This is the only time I'll be thirty, an intimate evening with my newish husband. Fairy lights decorate the ceiling, the lights are dimmed and it's peaceful.

Claus reaches across the table for my hand, no doubt seeing something isn't quite right, he's quick to pick up on an atmosphere.

'Shame it's too dark to get the view,' he observes, interrupting the flow of memories. I force a smile but it's my happy teacher face. The face that hides a myriad of grown up feelings that can't be revealed.

Nothing to do with the garage, privately fitted. Ask your husband are the tapes on loop in my head. The image of Adrian shifting from one foot to another doesn't help.

Yes, Keziah, ask your husband. Ask him what happened in Oxford. Ask him why he's tracking you. And whilst you're at it, ask yourself. Why are you scared to ask these questions?

Ask yourself how big a price you're prepared to pay for ruining your family's life, for being responsible for your sister's death.

In my head, two angry fighters stare each other down in a boxing ring. One punches defensive thoughts like, What are you thinking? Where's your loyalty? The trust you promised at the altar? Remember your history, the men who treated you like a slave, who put their mates and the football first.

But the other boxer punches back. He's suffocating you, why are you tolerating this? Of course, he put a tracker on your car. I'm devastated by guilt and shame for entertaining such nonsense.

With my happy teacher face on, we manage a lovely evening – until coffee.

Claus opens his wallet and my heart sinks.

'Please, Claus, not now,' I plead. 'It's my birthday.' He gives a half-smile. I know he's trying to rein himself in but he unfolds the increasingly crumpled sheet of paper. It's thick with faint lines, the stationary of a private consultant.

'There's only a couple of extras,' he reassures, flattening it between us like we are planning the menu for a celebration, a project we both need to review, a task that requires mutual input and agreement.

Sadly, I know exactly where this is going. Oh Claus, you're going to regret this as much as me.

'Go on, then.' I resign myself to the process.

He smoothens out the A4 sheet, the texture of the pink blotting paper I used to steal from Esther's desk. I loved watching an inkblot explode from pinprick to massive blot. My husband's finger inches down from the top, I can see him mentally working through each listed event. His carefully filed nail points to item five.

‘So, just take me through this again. You dated Tristan in 2010 for eleven months, I’ve written it here. *Tristan Blake – March to January 2010.*’

‘Yes,’ I affirm with a sarcasm that’s lost on him.

‘But Ameena said something about a Valentine’s dinner with him back in the day.’

‘I don’t know Claus, maybe it was celebrated early, maybe I was a few weeks out . . .’

‘So, was it until end of January or mid-February?’

‘I honestly don’t know. I’m sorry, it’s my birthday, why are you doing this?’

I watch his face as he struggles to pull himself back, take some breaths, but I can see I’ve lost him.

I notice Giorgio and Lummi chatting in the corner. She leans in but keeps a distance that’s professional. No one would know they’re a couple. It’s unusually quiet tonight, usually they’re run off their feet, paying careful attention to subtle gestures that request service, drinks that need topping up, plates to clear.

With the confidence that comes from a public space, I launch.

‘No, Claus. Stop it.’ I push the paper back towards him and move my chair back from the table.

He looks horrified; scared almost, or perhaps furious. I’ve never been so bold. He folds away his paper and puts his pen back in his pocket without amending my history log. But when I check his face, I see it. He’s already reached the place of no return. The Claus I know and love, the one that is generous, kind and open, that Claus has gone. And I don’t much care for this one; in fact, maybe I despise him. This man has hollow eyes, deep lines on his forehead and an expression I can only describe as a grimace, like he is being tortured from within.

I want to run home, to my old bedroom with pop stars on the wall. I want to put on my old woollen coat and hide under my covers. I want my mum and my sister and the smells that make me feel clean and safe.

'Please, Claus, I'm your wife, not your child.' I soften my voice, one last try, but with a determination not to turn into that powerless mute mouse I'm worried I've become.

His arms remain folded across his chest, a head teacher willing to exclude a rotten kid.

I should leave it, ask Giorgio to call an Uber, see if with some space he can calm himself down. This has never happened in public before.

But I don't leave it, I can't. I have to speak.

'Whilst we're talking honestly, please tell me you didn't put a tracker on my car?'

He stares at the white cloth. Silent.

In this moment, I know. I know without a doubt he installed a tracker, to track my car, my movements, to monitor me.

I don't wait for a reply. Wiping my sticky hands, I place the serviette on the table and stand up, using my palms to steady myself. The coke glass stumbles over and vomits its last few drops. Thank goodness, I declined the wine, I'm stone cold sober.

'I can't do this, Claus, you need help.'

As I turn away from our table, Claus stands and grabs my arm but Giorgio intercepts. 'Here's the bill, Sir.'

I've never heard him use that tone.

Taking the opportunity, I rush out of the rear exit, and speed walk into the car park, realising almost immediately that I've left my coat, and with it my phone.

All I can think is, I need to get away, I need to get away.

The glow of the restaurant is fading as I race down the hill, my strappy sandals flapping on the uneven track. Unable to see where the ditch meets the road, my foot slips and I yelp. Bending over to catch my breath, I feel the familiar panic beginning to rise. I count to four and hold for four before a steady exhale like the school counsellor showed me. It's so dark, all I can see is the glow of my linen trousers.

I need to get away. I know this can't be right. In my heart, I've known for a long time, maybe even since our wedding night. Surely my parents wouldn't want me to be unhappy, frightened?

As my breathing steadies, I hear the low rumble of an engine, the space around me becomes clear in the headlights. The car stops, a door slams and heavy footsteps approach.

'Keziah, you can't leave, I'm coming, please wait.'

I run. My ankle twists so I kick off the stupid sandals and sprint down the hill, praying there are no idiots speeding on this one-way track. If this ends badly, it will kill my mum and dad. All I can see is Esther's limp coat on the road, her head twisted on the curb, exactly where that boy racer smashed her. Blood streaming from her, onto the road, the paramedics pumping, pumping, but both eyes staring, accusing. If it wasn't for you, I'd be alive.

My husband's voice is louder, he's so close, his breath is on my neck. My legs freeze, my chest hurts. I'm defeated.

Claus grabs from behind and pulls me back. There's no escape. I fall into his arms to be guided like a floppy doll, empty, immobile.

10

The Little Room

Nicky

With his chin resting in his hands, Nicky waits on his usual curb. The gurgle in the drain is especially loud and for a minute he wonders if there's something sinister down there. That thought shifts him to further along. He hasn't seen his dad since his birthday. He's still deciding whether to forgive him but his mum said it's hard luck, as she can't wait any longer.

She left earlier this morning. She is working away for two days including a night. Mrs Hobbs said it was OK to miss school for one day as his mum didn't have childcare. Just this once, she said. When she went his mum was wearing her new lipstick, the pink one. Nicky stared for some time before deciding she was very pretty.

As if he's been watching, Mr Pinkney arrives on the curb with Bella.

'Alright, fella?' Mr P asks. 'Bella was wagging her tail like she wanted one of your stories.'

Mr P forgets Nicky is quite old now and actually the man of his house.

Before Nicky can think of something intelligent to say, Mr P has sat down next to him. 'Alright if I wait with ya?' he asks, stroking Bella, who sits between them. 'I'd like a word with ya dad.'

Nicky can't think which word would make sense on its own. When he asks, Mr P taps the side of his nose. 'Mind your own business, young man.' He laughs.

Nicky hears Neil Diamond before he hears the car.

When the car parks, Mr P needs a push from behind to get up. Nicky can't hear what the two men are saying as the music is still singing. He's determined to stay put on his curb for as long as possible, he wants his dad to know he hasn't forgiven him. Mr P says his word and walks away. He doesn't even say goodbye.

'Hey champ, good to see you.' His dad picks up his bag and throws it into the boot.

Nicky drags his feet and makes his dad wait for as long as possible, and when he gets in the car he puts down his head and counts. His dad doesn't comment but instead presses the triangle. A new song starts to play.

Nicky recognises it as 'Sweet Caroline' instantly but refuses to be lulled into giving in. Squeezing his knees together he refuses to give into their jiggling. His dad must know how angry he is, his dad needs to know he's not forgiven.

Much to his annoyance, Nicky's dad seems unaware of his protest. Instead, he taps his fingers against the steering wheel and hums along with the music. Nicky looks out of his own window but there's only road. He leans his head on the glass and closes his eyes. He mustn't cry.

He remembers when they used to swim with the windows open so they could hear the music floating out from inside the house. His mummy didn't like it, it gave her a headache but they did it anyway. He can almost feel the sunshine on his face as his dad lifted him high into the air. He knows his dad is very handsome and his mum is very beautiful and that if he tries hard enough he can fix their broken family. He's been searching for his bike and he sprays his clothes with her perfume so his dad will remember the good times.

Nicky's dad turns up the music.

Nicky speeds up his counting. He knows this song so well. He knows the next line and he wants to open his eyes and stare and his dad. His body can't suppress the urge to move but he's supposed to be asleep.

Nicky's dad is singing and bashing his steering wheel. He doesn't seem to care his son is sleeping. Nicky's hands move to the rhythm despite being anchored under his bottom. The music keeps playing and then the chorus comes back. He so wants to stay furious.

Words erupt out of Nicky without his permission. He sings at the top of his voice –

Sweet Caroline.

His hands bash his legs, his feet jiggle about and he sings with his dad. Their song. His dad opens the windows even though it's freezing. The cold rushes in but Nicky doesn't care. The wind is loud and his hair is going mental but he's singing with his dad. They sing and sing and sing all the way to the flat.

By the time his dad opens the boot, Nicky notices his happiness is back and the counting has stopped.

The flat is unusually tidy and his bed is made. There are some new curtains with ties that keep them away from the window. The tiny settee and chair have been covered in new material with matching cushions and curtains. The room smells of grandmas.

Nicky follows the smell into the kitchen. The surfaces are wiped clean and there are no wine glasses or crisps left on the sides. Nicky can feel the heat of the oven and peers into the square window. He can smell cheese. A dark oven dish is overflowing with bubbling sauce.

'Mac cheese?' Nicky asks his dad hopefully.

'Yep.'

'Is she here?' Nicky can feel the anxiety rising his stomach.

'No, it's father and son time.'

Nicky does a silly dance and punches the air. Dad doesn't join in.

'She put bacon in your mac cheese which is more than you deserve. You were very rude,' his dad snaps

Nicky forces a smile, fearing his dad might stay cross and remember the bike and history day.

'There's a good boy, go and put your bag on the bed, then we'll stuff our faces.'

As soon as he turns away Nicky takes the smile off his face. This whole flat could fit into his bedroom and ensuite. The bed is not much wider than his but his dad has added a chair and a new chest of drawers. He sniffs the plant whilst wondering why his dad has flowers in his room. After all, that's what girls do.

The mac cheese is amazing and they eat it all. Nicky is cross that he likes it so much. He's cross that he came here. He's cross he gave into the music. He needs to tell his dad that Paul has gone away, that it's safe for him to come home, that his mum is pretty again, that she smells nice now.

'She sure can cook, can't she?' his dad says with a huge stupid grin.

Turning around, Nicky pretends he is looking out of the window so he doesn't have to smile back. He wonders if he could learn to cook so Nancy won't be needed.

‘How’s your mum?’ Nicky knows his dad is changing his subject

‘Paul’s gone.’

‘Has he?’

Nicky watches his dad’s eyes.

‘Yep, the police took him away. They put handcuffs on him. One of them sat in the back cos he’s proper bad.’ He takes an extra breath before he finishes. ‘They thought he might kill someone.’

‘But how’s your mum?’

‘Yes, she’s very nice. She’s putting lipstick on and polishing the house. Yesterday she did all the washing in one day. Do you want to smell how clean my clothes are?’

Before he can unzip his hoodie so his dad can have a closer smell, his dad smiles and stands to clear the table. Nicky can tell his dad is pleased his mum is back on the market.

He watches his dad as he fills the washing up bowl with water and shakes in the liquid. He’s glad his dad doesn’t know what’s really been happening since Paul left. Their house is filthy, grandma would be so horrified she’d be forced to put on her gold rubber gloves and clean. His mum has slept for days, he makes sure she has a flask before he leaves for school. He’s doing his best to keep the house tidy and he’s done some shopping. He asked the nice teacher if he could help her with playground duty rather than do art club. He can’t get his uniform covered in paint as the washing machine is broken. He doesn’t play in the trees like the other boys but that’s OK as they don’t like him anyway.

Nicky has had an amazing night with his dad. They watch three episodes of the professionals, an old programme his dad loves. They swig stacks of Pepsi with donuts and finish up with a hot chocolate and marshmallows.

'Go do your teeth and then I can turn off all the lights,' his dad says when they are both in their pyjamas. At home, he has to turn off all the lights. Sometimes he has to run out in the dark and close the porch. That's terrifying.

His dad's bathroom is a tiny room. Dad says it's what's called a communal one and that not everyone has a bathroom in their bedroom.

When he pulls the string, the light makes a loud noise and he jumps back. A spider runs along the windowsill. He quite likes spiders.

He looks for his toothbrush, it's with dads but the jar isn't there. The toothbrushes are in a china cup with round holes in the top. There is also a dish for the soap that has matching fish and a folded-up flannel. They're all the same, white with blue. Matchy matchy, Nicky thinks.

His stomach lurches and his chest hurts when he sees it. He sees something that revolts him, something so vile he wonders if he might throw up. The vile thing is right there, for anyone to see, right in the middle of the white fragile pot with the stupid holes and the stupid fish. He sets off the counting and rocks a bit. He snatches the thing out of the pot. It's cold in his hand. He squeezes it so hard in his clenched fist that it hurts him. Then he takes the plastic stalk, one end in each hand and he pulls his hands down as hard as he can so it bends in the middle. He pushes and pushes until his face feels hot and his head sweats. Finally, he feels the pleasure of the snap. He now has two smaller bits of plastic to dispose of.

He looks down the toilet but wonders if it might get stuck.

'Nicky,' his dad shouts from the bedroom.

He'll be under the duvet waiting for his son, waiting to cuddle up together, his teddy between them for a warm night's sleep.

'Nearly finished,' he calls back, flushing the toilet for sound effects.

The bath edge is cold under his feet but if he climbs up, he can reach the miniature rectangular window. He manages to balance; his long toes grip the edge as he reaches across the bath. The window is open, just a crack. Nicky thinks if he puts one foot either side of the tub, he can do it.

'Just finishing my wash,' Nicky shouts to his dad.

Nicky wobbles, clutching the plastic in his hand whilst forcing the window open a bit more. Clutching the bottom of the frame he moves the metal arm to widen the space.

He pushes his fist through the gap and then opens it wide to release the smashed-up brush. He doesn't hear it bash at the bottom, it's too far.

Goodbye, stupid pink toothbrush, Nicky screams inside his head. I hope you die on the pavement and never come back.

When he climbs down, he has a wee but before he pulls up his PJ's he dips the fluffy pink flannel in the toilet bowl before placing it exactly where he found it.

'That'll learn her,' he thinks.

He cleans his teeth until he reaches a happy, safe number and returns his brush to sit next to his father's. Two blue brushes sitting in the pot.

Nicky climbs into the narrow bed and snuggles up to his dad. Just two, that's enough, he thinks as he closes his eyes for sleep.

Keziah

This room is on the darkest side of the house with the smallest of windows. The space is no bigger than a prison cell and the smell is damp trainers. My gut tells me the time before I hear the familiar knock. I know exactly how the next ten minutes will play out.

Lying here, staring up at a ceiling that's crying out for a lick of paint, I'm beyond exhausted. I didn't realise it was possible to be this tired and still get up every morning to face demanding small people. But I did it. I survived a week as a woman who left her marriage.

The walls are covered in faded posters and the wallpaper is brown over the door and window frames, but this space is a memorial to my dead sister, a shrine. My dad insisted it wasn't to be touched. My room, the biggest of the three, with the most natural light, was slowly dismantled. Esther's stayed frozen in time.

A well-thumbed biology book remains on the shelf and her revision timetable is somehow still hanging on for dear life, the blue tack now hardened to stone.

There goes the knock. Now, the footsteps. Then, the heavy curtain being drawn across, then my mum's loaded sigh. Finally, muffled voices. This is day nine. Every evening at exactly the same time Claus comes. On the hour, his soft knuckles rap the glass.

When Claus caught up with me on my birthday, I was terrified. The look on his face was definitely rage. That unknown man's twisted features, the man I don't want to know. By the time he started the engine, I was trapped inside a full-blown anxiety attack. Perhaps my being vulnerable seemed to trigger the right switch. He killed the engine and sat, head down, hands jiggly about in his lap. By the time I recovered, his posture was visibly softer. 'Get me to my parents, now,' was all I could say. He drove in silence whilst I rested my head on the cold window trying not to think or feel.

Outside my childhood home, I told him. Our marriage is over. I'm done. He begged and he cried, but I got out and walked away.

When she opened the door, my mother took one look at my face, enfolded me in her arms and asked, 'Has he been unfaithful?'

I was able to reassure her, but in the days since I've wondered. I'm no longer sure of what I'm sure of. He goes off on long trips, works long hours. He could easily have a wife in every port. Maybe that's who he speaks with at night in his office bedroom or when he stays on the phone in the car before he comes in. He explains everything away as confidential work he can't discuss.

Each evening since I came home, my mother has dished up a delicious home-cooked meal, apart from on Monday which was fish and chip night. I've hardly been able to touch anything. When we put our cutlery down, dad asks, 'Have I had my supper?' then I thank mum for the meal. Before I retire to Esther's room, mum asks if I'd like to speak to my husband when he knocks. Each night I say, 'I'd rather not.'

The front door closes with a sharper bang than usual. The curtain is put back to keep out the draft, but instead of returning to her armchair as usual, tonight I hear furry slippers padding up the stairs.

Her wedding ring bashes against the wood as her arthritic hand knocks the bedroom door. She hasn't commented on the emptiness of my ring finger. A head in curlers peers through the gap, waiting for the permission I don't want to give.

Mum wheezes in. She moves the school books I'm supposed to be marking from the ancient rocking chair and plonks down with an audible sigh. Pausing to catch her breath, she leans forward to stroke my foot, all she can reach.

Before she can speak, the bedroom door reopens.

'Kezzy, have you done your paper round already?'

'Hi, dad. Yep, everyone has their weekend news.'

He looks to my mum, she's closed her eyes and looks exhausted.

'Marion?'

'Yes, Robert.'

'I can't find my work trousers.'

'No work tomorrow, love.'

'Oh.'

He moves his attention to me, then to mum, unable to find the solution. 'So, I don't need to go to work?'

'No, go back downstairs and put the radio on.'

'OK, but Kezzy should be getting up, Esther is already at school.'

'OK,' Mum says, smiling at me. 'I'll get this lazy girl into her uniform and down stairs.'

With that he goes, leaving the door open. We hear him inching his way downstairs, huffing and muttering.

Then the tears start. First mine, then hers. I think of my dad degenerating, about Esther, and then about my mum. My poor mum losing my sister, then my dad and then having to shoulder the shame of a daughter who leaves her marriage before her first anniversary.

Mum manages to haul herself out of the chair to perch on the side of my bed. She rubs my back whilst I face the wall and cry and cry, my head pounding and nausea swilling in my stomach. I let her ramble on about how hard the early months of marriage are, meals to cook, a house to run and how it all takes time to adjust.

'Marriage is far harder than the wedding mags imply, Keziah.'

I don't tell her about the cleaner, the gardener or the fact Claus does all the cooking. I also don't tell her I think I want to leave for good.

I let her solve the wrong problems whilst I drift off. Is it possible to miss someone so badly yet not want to be in the relationship? The psychologist I saw at university said loss will always trigger a catastrophic reaction for me. Is that what this is? More grief for Esther? Or am I grieving my happy ever after?

When the final curtain swallowed her coffin, I promised I'd change. I promised I would be like her, self-sacrificing, thoughtful, the daughter my parents need. I promised I would climb the career ladder. I promised I would find a solid man in a suit with whom I could create three clever grandchildren. I promised I would stop taking risks, being impulsive or doing things to cause my parents worry. Stop biking. Stop doing the things I loved.

How then do I tell mum I've fallen at the first hurdle?

The creak of the door stops mum in her chatter tracks.

'Marion?'

'Yes, Robert.'

'I can't find my work trousers.'

'No work today, love.'

'Oh.'

‘Go back downstairs and put the radio on.’

My dad turns around, the obedient child my mum deserves.

Mum kisses my head like I’m five and follows him down.

The door closes and I’m alone.

Splashing my blotchy face with cold water, I promise myself I’ll sort things out by the end of the week. I’ll talk to Ameena tomorrow. So what if she was right all along? Maybe I did rush in. Then I’ll tell my mum and then face Claus to sort out collecting my things. If dad was more himself he’d say, ‘Mooching about like a filthy teenager won’t help anyone.’

The lesson plan unfinished on the desk is the Christmas story, at least that’s one that won’t take long to prepare. Esther’s revision plan clinging for dear life on a cork board chunks study into one-hour blocks. I’ll do an hour, then watch a film and have an early night.

Before going any further, I flick through my school planner to check my assembly dates. Please tell me it’s not my turn tomorrow.

The scruffy asterisk marked in felt tip jumps out. The date must be wrong. My hand shakes as I swipe through page after page, counting each day. Surely not. This can’t be. I’ve somehow lost two weeks. I sit down. Standing it’s harder to focus, to control my panic.

I peel the pages back more slowly, one at a time starting on the first day of the calendar month. The symbol says 23rd November. I look for other symbols, to see if it’s a mistake. I’ve occasionally done that before or marked something else with a pencilled star and got muddled. But, no, there’s just that one symbol, etched clearly, no doubt, a bright red multi line star to indicate my predictable twenty-eight days due date. My last period was the 30th October. So how can it be the 12th December? My period is nearly two weeks late.

11

A New Chapter

Nicky

At the top of the volcano, the cold air smells fresh. Nicky is breathing hard and fast. His face is bright red. Spinning around with his arms out wide, he pretends he could fly. He could fly away from this high point, hover over the hills, the green fields and the high trees. He knows he would feel laughter if he could fly.

In all the world, this is his favourite place. He can't believe his mum agreed to come. This morning, when she woke him with shiny hair and a fancy flicky fringe he knew this would be a good Saturday, but he didn't know it would be a great Saturday. He's supposed to be at his dad's but he's got work so he's going tomorrow.

When he heard her open his bedroom door, his clock shouted 8am. He held his breath. She's never up this early. Then, she walked gently and whispered in his ear, 'Wakey, wakey, rise and shine,' as she tickled him and giggled. The house smelt of bacon.

They ate a massive England breakfast and he remembered their family trip to Disney. Every morning they had breakfast on their own table with four chairs, when they were a normal family, when he had a mum and a dad who loved each other and when it was his dad's job to keep everyone safe.

In the middle of the dining room was loads and loads of food, basically anything you could eat was on that table. Dad had bacon and eggs. Mum had toast. She let him put the bread in the machine. It was so cool, the bread went in a hot hole and then rolled down and popped out the bottom, splat. Every day Nicky had pancakes with maple syrup and his dad didn't mention the syrup.

'Look at me,' Nicky shouts to his mum, from the concrete seat that everyone in his village calls the volcano.

'Smile. Wow, hold it there.' His mum keeps pointing her phone and taking photos.

Nicky leans against the grey stone monument watching her climb the hill.

When she reaches the top, she's all smiles as she reaches in her bag and retrieves a huge bag of chocolate eclairs, his absolute favourite. She catches her breath as he chews on his sweet and watches the birds. He's glad of his new winter clothes his mum bought online as it's freezing, especially at the top of this hill.

'Starlings,' Nicky tells his mum pointing to two medium size birds in between a robin and a blackbird.

'Get you,' she says, elbowing him affectionately.

Mr P gave him a thick book with a different bird on every page, it tells you what they look like and how they sing. Nicky thinks he might be a bird watcher when he grows up. At the moment, Mr P is teaching him about finches. Sometimes they sit on the bench at the bottom of the garden and his wife brings scones with jam. Nicky hasn't mentioned this to his mum because she thinks Mrs P's a silly cow.

Nicky keeps taking sneaky sideways looks at his mum. She looks so lovely when she's done up nice. He knows it'll be alright when his dad sees her like this. He'll remember how much he liked her pretty lips and the smell of her perfume. He squeezes his mum's hand and she does the same.

Yes. He repeats to himself. It will soon all go back to normal. His dad will come home. His mum will learn to cook. His grandparents will come for visits and once again he'll have clean clothes and the right length trousers so the boys at school will like him.

His mum unwraps a toffee and pops it into his mouth before taking one for herself.

'Come on,' she says, pulling him up and into a tight hug. 'Time to go home for bangers and mash.'

As they run down the steep hill with their arms spread wide like flying birds, he can't believe it. He can't see himself but he knows he's smiling. He thinks it might take a while before his laughter comes back but he knows this is a good step in the right direction. In his mind he conjures up the face of the teacher he loves. He pictures her asking him again, 'What makes you laugh?' Soon he'll have some answers. He'll say, I laugh when my dad tickles me in bed, I laugh when we mess about in our own deep pool, when it's blue and full of splashing. I laugh when the three of us cuddle up to read a funny story.

The sound of voices interrupts his head movie. Nicky realises they are almost home. His mum has promised supper, ice cream and then a film. She's not fancied that for ages.

It's the couple who own the corner shop. They must be going home as the man is carrying two carrier bags of shopping and an umbrella is hooked over his wrist. Nicky doesn't know the man's name which upsets him as he likes to know people's names.

'Hello Nicky, hello Lisa,' his wife says.

'Hello, Vi,' his mum replies. Nicky didn't know that was her name.

'I'm glad I bumped into you, a delivery van was asking for your house.'

'Oh, that's coz the sign dropped off, I need to get it fixed,' his mum explains.

Nicky taps his head so that he'll remember to ask his dad to help with the sign.

'Don't worry, I pointed them in the right direction, hurry up and you'll meet them, they've not long gone. Proper handsome pair.' Vi laughs but licks her lips at the same time which Nicky finds disgusting.

He can't wait to get home. He knows what it is. They ordered a wooden climbing frame with a rope hanging in the middle. They picked it together from the Argos catalogue.

It was in the sale as it's winter, Nicky hopes he might have more friends by the summer as Mr P struggles with his arthritis these days.

His mum is excited too as she's almost running. As they turn the corner, Nicky spots the white van outside their house. They've parked on his curb which he's not altogether comfortable with. The van might topple over. What if it did and crushed Bella or Mr P, or even him, or his mum.

A man is leaning against the side, smoking a fat brown cigarette. Nicky can smell it even though they're not even close.

'Brad,' his mum shouts. 'How are you?'

She let's go of Nicky's hand and races ahead to greet the delivery driver. How does she know his name too?

'Not bad,' the man says and gives her a kiss on her cheek after he's taken the brown smoker out. 'And this must be little Nick,' he says to Nicky, rubbing his head. Everyone knows not to do that now he's older.

Nicky goes around the back of the van leaving his mum tangled inside the man's arms. He can hear a deep voice and rustling.

Two massive doors are open, it's like his wardrobe.

The floor of the van is covered with boxes and in the middle is a long parcel covered in black plastic. Bending over the parcel is a man. He has a big head and a long bushy black beard like a pirate. He could also be a mighty warrior, it's hard to tell.

Nicky is staring at the massive sausage parcel, trying to work out what is going on, and where his slide is, when Brad joins him.

'Blimey, Tom, what on earth's in there?' Brad shouts to the man in the back.

'A dead body,' he laughs.

Then he notices Nicky, wide-eyed and curious. 'Alright,' Tom says without looking at him.

Nicky realises his mum is standing next to him as well. She's laughing too. Everyone is laughing. Nicky can't think why they are laughing. He feels awfully sick. How can it be funny that someone's dead? Why have they brought the body here? Is he working for Grendel? Nicky doesn't like this man one little bit.

The pirate jumps from the van like a great lump and his mum opens her arms for a hug. Pirate warrior lifts his mum off the ground. His muscles are bulging and he has tattoos on both arms. One is a fire breathing dragon but Nicky doesn't know what the other picture is.

Whilst the men and his mum are chatting and laughing, Nicky can't resist another look inside the van. He moves closer. There is definitely no sign of his slide. He counts five boxes. He has never liked odd numbers. He sees a guitar, a suitcase and then the body.

Tom jumps back into the van and grabs one end of the body. Brad grabs the other end and they lift it out and start walking towards his house.

They start singing, ‘Hi, ho, hi, ho, it’s off to work we go.’

Nicky looks up at his mum but she’s too busy laughing with the men. She presses the control to open the gates. Nicky wishes the gates would close, crushing these villains before it’s too late. He wonders if he could fight them to the ground. But he’s too scared. Instead he stands open mouthed as they carry the body down the drive towards his house.

His mum grabs his hand to follow them in like a funeral parade. When they get to the porch, the parcel drops to the ground and the plastic splits. He grabs for his mum’s arm to stop himself from passing out, and shuts his eyes before he sees the dead body tumbles to the ground.

His head is spinning and he thinks he’s going to be sick again.

He opens his eyes.

It’s just a red carpet.

‘Aren’t they just the best fun?’ his mum says, grinning.

‘Why are they here?’ Nicky asks.

‘Sorry, mate, did I not mention Tom’s coming to stay. Just for a few weeks?’ With that, she follows the men into the house.

Whilst the three adults enjoy a bottle of wine to help them with the unpacking, Nicky opens each cupboard to see what he can make for his tea. He finds some Jacobs crackers. The butter is too hard to spread but he’ll make do. The adults don't notice when he slopes off to his room with a plate of crackers, a chunk of cheese and a bottle of coke tucked under his arm.

His mouth is dry which makes it hard to swallow but he's determined not to cry. He tries not to imagine his bangers and mash and the rich gravy she makes on a good day.

He can't help feeling disappointed. He really thought today was going to be the Saturday when she noticed him all day.

Keziah

Tonight's the night. I can't tolerate the uncertainty any longer, and I'm driving my mother insane. Of course, she's not telling me that.

'Take as long as you need, darling,' she keeps saying even though the circles under her eyes get darker with each day I'm here.

I was so sure, sure I was done, willing to admit I'd failed. I've spent endless evenings googling for other couples who split within the year. One girl left her bloke before they came home from honeymoon. My mind was made up but if I'm pregnant that changes everything. Then it's not just about me. I can't deprive a child of its father. I can't be the reason for another incomplete family. There's a little boy at school. He's developed an obsession with me. Every time I'm on lunch duty, he runs up and grabs my hand and won't let go. Ameena said he's one of hers and his parents are divorcing.

I'll do the pregnancy test. If it's positive, I'm resigned to going back to Claus, to making things work; surely it's a sign, a sign from the universe, from Esther. If the test is negative, I'll stick to plan A: leave, start again.

This evening, I came straight home from school instead of laying out the displays for next week's topic. Usually I can't enjoy a weekend if I don't get that done before I leave on a Friday. But I need to face up to the situation, for everyone's sake.

For the last few nights, I've watched Claus from the window as he ambles back to his car. He sits there for up to an hour. I've no idea what he does. But this evening I'm going out.

In my hand, I twirl a stick wrapped in white paper. I turn it between my fingers, over and over, this way and back. A majorette practising a new routine. How can such a small item create such confusion?

I'm fifteen days late. The only time my periods went crazy was after Esther died. I missed two but the doctor said stress can do that.

Could the stress of breaking up, the fear of telling my parents, Ameena, that we've separated after less than six months, be sufficient to mess with my rhythms?

Maybe, but I feel gut wrenchingly sick all the time.

Ten minutes to go. I've dreamed for so long about the family, two parents and at least three kids but not now, not when I'm frightened, not when I'm thriving at work.

On the other hand, I can't survive another traumatic loss. What if I couldn't ever get pregnant again, what if my parents lose all hope of a grandchild?

I check the mirror. My swollen eyes look obvious and the top I'm wearing is unflattering. Perhaps Claus will take one look and recoil with revulsion. That'll solve one of my major issues of the moment.

I have no idea what small talk my mum makes on the doorstep but it always lasts at least five minutes. So I'll have time to hurriedly pee on a stick and let destiny decide. I'll wait for mum to close the door, then make a run for it. If she knows we're talking, she'll be arms folded, waiting with bated breath, will they, won't they. I'm not ready for that.

At two minutes to six, the knock comes, louder than usual. Mum groans as she struggles to get up. I give her time to make the front door. Without looking, I grab the ugly stick of doom and brush past dad, oblivious to it all, and escape out the back door.

I stand and wait just inside the side gate. I want mum to be back in the sitting room and Claus to be reclined on his heated seat.

When I open his passenger door, the look on his face makes me want to laugh out loud. But I don't. I sit down on the cream leather, uninvited.

'How are you?' he asks studying his exceptionally clean hands. He twiddles his wedding ring but doesn't comment on the absence of mine.

'Not so good.' I confess. 'You?'

'Not so good,' he answers.

'What shall we do?' he asks, staring out the front windscreen. The car has his aroma, a comforting combination of fabric conditioner and fine aftershave.

He pauses. Panic is chomping at the bit. When he's here, I'm back to our first date, desperate to catch him, hold on, rescue that passionate-though-vulnerable teenager. But the coldness, the lists, his room, his intensity, his secrets. I can't.

There are tears bubbling onto his cheeks. I must remember the other man, the unrepentant, secretive one with the cold eyes. That one scares me.

'Claus, we have a problem.' The sound of my voice, louder than I intend, jolts us both.

His head snaps around to look at me. 'What?' He stares, frozen, searching for clues.

'My period is late,' I blurt out.

His body tenses. 'Are you pregnant?' he asks unconsciously looking at my stomach but then catching himself and lifting his gaze to my face. I can't read him.

'I don't know. I'm not sure about us, but I've done a test and if it's positive I'll come home, but only if you agree to some changes.'

I allow him to see the pencil of plastic wrapped in toilet roll. I don't want to know. I twist it around in my hands without unwrapping. How can something so small and inoffensive create such turmoil? What do I want it to say?

Claus stays quiet, I can see his head trying to catch up, struggling to know how to respond when we're already in such a mess.

Then, he lifts his hand and moves it quickly over to mine. Gently, one by one he unfolds my fingers until the test is exposed. Fortunately, it's arrogant window of prediction is on the underside. Claus looks at me and I nod for him to go ahead. He turns over the crystal ball so we can both see our future.

12

Starting Again

Nicky

Nicky is relieved when his dad pulls up; he hasn't seen him for ages. He goes on lots of work trips these days. Nicky's rucksack is heavier than usual, as if he's going for a long weekend. This will be the longest he's stayed. When he's carrying a bag, he likes to lean against the gates rather than wait on the curb. When he hears Neil Diamond singing, he knows his dad is fourteen and a half seconds away but he looks at his watch anyway. Tom gave him a grown-up watch and a cheap mobile phone for when he and his mum go out in the evenings. The watch has an orange second hand which makes it easier to see. Tom has been doing weights with him, they use his new watch to count their repeats. In the car, Nicky wonders if his dad will notice his muscles are bigger. Tom says there is no need for him to be so weak.

The car turns into Granchester Road and they stop outside number 44. This is his tenth visit at Nancy's. He writes down what he eats, what he drinks and what he talks to Nancy about.

Before the car has even stopped, Nancy is at the door. Nicky's face still goes red when he sees her because of that first time. Nicky thought he would hate Nancy. But these days he likes her so much, he thinks he might love her. He still loves his real mum the most, obviously, but Nancy's house smells so nice and he sleeps so well.

Nancy doesn't have a drive and there's no big gate to keep out strangers. Nancy says everyone is welcome. She did reassure Nicky that didn't include monsters and pirates.

It takes him six strides to get from her gate to the black front door. The top section has two glass windows that make him think of number eleven. Nancy knows he doesn't like odd numbers. She told him to stare at the letter box until the door looks like a smiley face and not an odd number. Nicky now sees the knocker as a nose.

Nan, as Nicky now calls her, is wiping her hands on her messy apron. He runs into her arms and he can smell butter and chocolate.

'Well, hello, boys. In ya come,' she says, helping Nicky take off his coat. His dad gives her a peck on her cheek.

'And how's my favourite fella?' Nancy asks, following Nicky into her sitting room.

Here, he knows where everything is. Nancy's place is small and every room is named after what you do in it. He sits in the sitting room and puts on his slippers. Nancy got them from the market; they have Power Rangers on both feet.

Then off he goes to use the upstairs toilet. On his first visit his dad explained that like the flat, there is only a communal bathroom here.

All the way up the stairs are pictures of Ava. Ava is Nancy's girl. She goes to see her dad at weekends so Nicky hasn't met her yet. But she's coming today. There are four chairs around the kitchen table and Ava's dad is dropping her sometime soon. Using the novelty of a bannister, Nicky pulls his body up each stair. He nods and smiles at each picture. Ava on her first day at school, wearing a smart blazer and a straw hat. Ava on a paddle board. Ava dressed as a pirate. At the top of the stairs is his favourite – Ava in her bridesmaid dress, holding some coloured flowers.

He likes her ever-so red lips and her long black hair. He thinks she looks a lot like Disney's Pocahontas. He loves that film even though the boys at school said it was for girls.

Whilst his pee is pouring, he tries not to see the toothbrushes. There's dad's one, his one, Ava's one and then Nancy's one. Now that he loves her, he feels awful about what he did with her pink one. No one noticed it went missing.

Sometimes he knows he's the monster.

Grandma says you judge a house by how clean the bathroom is. Nancy's bathroom is very clean. So is her oven, which is the other sign Grandma uses. Nicky's knows his bathroom is disgusting so it's a good thing grandma can't visit.

There are toys in the bath, which Nicky feels is a bit childish. He has a sneaky peek in Nancy's room. He thinks it's funny she has two dressing gowns hanging on the back of the door. A pink one and also a navy one with a hood, just like his dad's. There's a lovely picture of Ava in a gold frame.

Ava's room is where he sleeps, and Nancy says when he's here it's the children's den. The carpet is purple, the curtains are purple and Ava's bed covers are purple. In her bed, there are about a million teddies. He would like some of them. Nancy has put his rucksack on the top bunk. She's got him a duvet to match his slippers.

'Nicky,' dad is shouting from downstairs. 'She's outside, come see.'

His dad pulls back the curtain so they have a triangle to see through. A fantastic grey car with orange bits on the spoilers.

'Nice car,' his dad says.

Then the passenger door opens and a dark-haired mermaid steps out. Her hair is as long as her bottom and falls over her denim skirt. She has a white T-shirt and a black jacket and a furry handbag. Nicky's tummy lurches in a way he's never felt before. The car screeches away and Nancy huffs. His dad opens the door and they watch Ava walk up the path. Nicky thinks she is the most beautiful creature he has ever seen. He knows. This is the girl he loves. This is the girl who he'll keep safe. This is the girl who will bring him laughter.

She gives him a megawatt smile. He rewards her with an awkward grin.

Then she sees his dad. His dad sees her. Nicky sees them seeing each other. When she opens her arms wide, he knows. When his dad opens his arms, he knows for sure. When she runs into his father's arms and he lifts her high, and twirls her in the air, and her hair floats in the sky, then he knows for sure that this is the girl. This is the girl he hates.

Keziah

The woman sitting opposite me is surely a model. She crosses her legs provocatively before checking her phone. Her legs are longer than my entire body and just above her red-painted toes she has a dragon tattoo twisting right up her ankle. For goodness sake, it's January, put some woolly tights on.

She's flicking though a fashion mag but her arm is looped through her partner's as if he's about to run; maybe he is. If they weren't sitting so close, I'd think he was her father. A perfectly formed beach ball is stuffed up her designer dress.

We were promised there would be a maximum of three couples in the waiting room but it's just us and them. The receptionist acknowledged our entrance with a polite nod, discreetly checking my name and birth date but since there's been an uncomfortable silence.

Claus, though, appears to be quite chilled apart from his relentless finger tapping on the back of my chair. I am far from relaxed. My stomach thinks it's going for an interview. Over the last six weeks I've tasted every emotion on the human buffet table. Currently, I alternate between disbelief and terror, mostly terror.

I feel a final hand tap near my shoulder and then Claus springs up to get coffee. He strolls across the room with the poise of Dr C. Doerkson. Only this place could have a lounge bigger than your average semi. The lush velvet chairs wouldn't be out of place in a grand hotel. I catch Mrs Perfect glancing at Claus and feel a stab of jealously. Even in casual clothes, Claus looks like a professional. He has a uniquely straight posture, an attention-grabbing presence.

As the machine drips his espresso into a tiny host cup, Claus's phone vibrates gently against the cushion next to me. NW flashes up as the caller. When it stops, I notice five missed calls from the same person.

Before I can pick up his phone for a closer look, he's placing a decaf latte on the conveniently angled side table. A coffee machine and bone china seem an odd combo.

'You've missed a call,' I inform him as tear open the individually wrapped biscuit.

There is a definite pause. Then he quickly puts it on silent and shoves it in his inside pocket.

'A persistent patient,' he explains, picking a thread off his chair. 'They'll have to wait.'

Typically, as soon as I take my first coffee slurp, the white door opens. Out walks a tiny lady with a neat bob wearing inappropriately high heels.

'Mr and Mrs Doerkson,' she raises her eyebrows to ask. We follow her navy suit into the dark cave.

'Mrs Doerkson, would you like to lie here,' she says, patting a couch. I do as I'm told and Claus takes the chair close to my head.

I'm never ill, so clinics and couches are an alien concept. Looking down at my flabby thighs I'm disappointed. In our friendship group, I was the fit one. There wasn't a gym class I hadn't tried and that was on top of at least one run a week. These days I seem to do nothing but work and stay home. Claus grabs my hand, giving me a great big grin as the doctor turns on her screen.

'OK, Mrs Doerkson, can you pop up your T-shirt for me, please.'

She tucks what looks like an old-fashioned nappy under the edge of my clothes. I smile inwardly to think of Mrs

Fancy Pants from the waiting room having to remove her entire outfit to show that ball.

A miniature Christmas tree hides on the windowsill. Someone will be in trouble; surely at these prices, an employee has been tasked with removing the decorations for the new year. No way Claus would've left ours beyond the customary twelve days.

We had a fabulous Christmas, truly perfect. My parents came on Christmas Eve, I wanted them there when I woke up. One of the many concessions Claus agreed when I went back to him.

Given he's such a fan of dotting the i's and crossing the t's, I made him sign my terms and conditions. He tells me his obsession with lists and note making is a family thing. Apparently, both his father and grandfather carried a notebook and fountain pen. We signed my demands with a school biro.

My reasonable requests include being allowed to see my friends without comment, receiving less texts during the day unless there are extenuating circumstances, no illegal tracking devices, no discussions about men and for him to stay in our bedroom even when he's not feeling great.

I text him when leaving and arriving. He is not allowed to question me about past dates and in the same spirit I will respect his privacy.

The contract lives within a crisp envelope in the kitchen drawer; it hasn't been mentioned or needed since. Claus took three weeks leave to match my school holidays so we've had three weeks of love, laughter and planning for the future.

So here we are in a private clinic. Only the best will be good enough for junior Doerkson. I'm glad my father isn't quite in his right mind. A labour supporter all his life and a staunch advocate of the NHS, he'd be less than impressed to find out we've spent a year's wages on unnecessary scans and coffee, when paper towels and a urine test would suffice.

Dr Wan sits on a stall with a screen turned on.

'So, we're doing a dating scan?' she says, putting an instrument loaded with cold gel on my belly.

'Yes, please.' Claus takes his gaze away from the screen for a second to answer. I need to stop watching his every gesture for a flip out. He's taken everything in his stride, a professional dad who seems to have all the answers. I, on the other hand, feel completely out of my depth and mostly terrified.

My eyes cloud over as I consider my own dad, yelling at the finish line of every race. Downhill biking was his idea. I wasn't in with a great crowd, I was desperate to hang around street corners having a cheeky fag. Esther was the good girl, always with her head in a book. Having fun and meeting boys were the main objectives of my early teens. Dad had been a keen cyclist as a young man and I guess they thought it would keep me out of trouble.

The coach was immediately interested and not long after I joined the club, he suggested I went for sponsorship. It surprised everyone as I had always been a bit clumsy and impatient. Esther was the graceful and persistent one.

'So,' the doctor says, pointing at the white fuzzy bean, and bringing me back to reality, 'there's the heartbeat, nice and strong.' Claus squeezes my hand. He gets out his hanky and wipes his eye.

'So your baby is nine weeks, I believe. Does that match your idea?'

'I think so,' I confirm, though frankly I have no idea.

How on earth did I get pregnant anyway? I'm so religious about taking my pills. On our honeymoon, I was teasing Claus that contraception shouldn't be only my responsibility.

As a joke he took the packet, popped out the pill, and presented it to me on a serviette. Laughing, he commented, 'See, joint responsibility.'

Without fail, Claus brings me my pill, a glass of water and tea before I sleep, even if he's sleeping in his own room.

'We're looking at the last week in July for your due date,' the doctor adds, studying a coloured table on her computer.

'Perfect timing for the school holidays,' Claus observes.

I feel a frisson of worry. What on earth am I going to tell my colleagues? I've only just accepted a promotion.

Back in his car, for once I'm glad for the odd sensation of a heated seat. I love this car. When I first met him and he said he liked nice cars, I desperately hoped it wouldn't be a flash red thing with a personalised plate. I was so relieved when he pulled into the school carpark in this matt grey beauty with a regular number plate. I can't wait until the sun comes out and we can slide back the roof.

But right now, it's freezing. Claus slips his arm around me and rubs my shoulder until I stop shivering. Together we gaze at the first photograph of our baby. For the first time, I really believe in a happy ending for everybody, the two of us and my parents. This is the ultimate fulfilment of the promise I made to Esther. Sure, a bit earlier than I planned, but lots of teachers work part time.

We are still trying to make sense of the blurry bits when Claus's phone vibrates.

He whips back his arm and scrambles to try and turn it off in his pocket but the call connects to the car speaker. A peculiar robot voice speaks from the black mesh at the front of the car. Someone has gone to great lengths to disguise their voice. It sounds like the voice changers we have in the school dress up box, the kids love play acting Dr Who.

'You should've followed through. You're running out of chances. You will not get away with it,' the automated voice cackles.

Claus tries to stop his phone but the message keeps going.

'We will never give up.'

The call ends, and I turn to look at Claus. The colour has drained from his face.

'Who on earth was that?' I demand, a shiver running down my back.

Claus takes a deep breath and wraps his arm back around me. 'It's just an unsatisfied customer, please don't worry. Don't let them ruin this moment, sweetheart.'

We both gaze back in awe at our little bean. Can this small collection of cells be the cement we need, the blank canvas we can hang over all the darkness that's been before? A new masterpiece created by us.

13

Competition

Nicky

Nicky's weekend is not going well.

'Hey Nick, Nick.' Tom is on his back on his special mat lifting a massive bar over his head. Nicky hates it when Tom calls him Nick. Nick means to steal. He hates it even more when Tom repeats his name like he's special, but not in a good way.

'You wanna beat your target, big man?' Tom shouts, blowing out his cheeks. Nicky thinks about tickling his feet so he drops the weight and dies.

Nicky doesn't like lifting the blue weights, they hurt his belly. Tom says it'll make him strong so he won't get bullied at secondary.

She and Tom go out, but Mr P says monsters don't come around their way. If he sees Nicky's home alone, he and Bella come around for a cup of tea and a Disney film. Nicky sometimes has a spoon full of sugar in his tea. Tom is much better than Paul but usually they come back drunk. Then Nicky has to cook for them and watch both their breathing all night.

Nicky hears his dad's engine two streets away. He checks his watch and listens to hear what album his dad is playing.

The music that's playing is new. Dad swings open the passenger door. Nicky throws his bag in the back seat and pulls his seat belt across. His dad clicks it in.

'Where's Neil Diamond?'

'Hello to you too!'

'Hello. Who is this singing?'

Dad passes me a CD cover, the man on the front has black glasses.

'Stevie Wonder,' he says. 'What do you think?'

'Dunno.'

'One of Nancy's favourites.' He turns it up louder.

Nicky doesn't know the words. It's not so fun with Stevie.

'Can we have Neil now?'

'Sure, change the CD, the others are in the glove box there.'

Arriving in the car park, the roller coaster is going. If it's too windy they stop it. Nicky hopes it gets windier. Today, he and his dad are meeting Nancy and Ava at the beach for their first family day out. He thinks it's a stupid idea. It's freezing and he's got a lot on his mind. But Nancy told him 'happy families compromise'. After the beach they are going to the arcade for him. Ava likes the sea, she likes skimming stones across the water.

All the way along the motorway Nicky has been thinking. Thinking about how Tom says Nicky can call him dad. Nicky will never call anyone dad, he has only one dad and he's keeping him. Thinking about how he wishes he could live with his dad for secondary. Nancy works at a school and she says they do really cool stuff like marching and cricket. His dad says they'll think about it nearer the time, depending on the situation.

Most of all, he's been thinking how he needs to know who he loves and who he hates. It's just not very clear anymore. He knows he hates the boys at school, they throw his apples and punch his back. He knows he hates Paul and hopes he stays in prison until forever. He loves his mum, his dad, Mr P and Bella and probably Nancy.

But he's very confused about Ava. He has a picture of her under his mattress. He took that without asking before he met her. When he kisses her photo goodnight he thinks he loves her again. He thinks about her hair and her mouth and when he can't sleep he thinks about how she let him choose the film when he stayed over for the first time.

Then, she plonks herself on his dad's lap and twiddles his hair where it meets the back of his collar. When she does that or leans into his dad watching the film, Nicky knows he hates her. In fact, he wants to kill her. He's growing stronger and his fingers are long. When Ava is snuggled up to her dad, Nicky imagines putting his man-of-the-house hands around her pale white neck and squeezing tight. Paul used to do that to his mum. When he stopped she would splutter and cry. Paul told her the next time, he'd hold longer and she'd be snuffed out.

Nicky really loves Ava but sometimes he wants to snuff her out.

'Look, Nicky, the people at the top are waving, we'll go up there after lunch.' His dad looks up at the idiots on the top of the roller coaster.

'Let's go find the girls,' his dad says, grabbing his son's hand. Nicky thinks it's stupid that his dad calls them the girls. Nancy calls him and his dad 'the boys'. He thinks that's stupid as well.

The wind is blowing hard, it's not a very good day to be at the beach, which is exactly what Nicky told them when Ava suggested it. Nicky wants to curl up on the sofa at Nancy's, with his slippers and new dressing gown. Nancy would be cooking whatever he demanded. She calls him the food boss.

'There they are.' His dad points to the only two people on the beach. They are next to a stripy windbreaker he knows came from his shed. Ava is gripping on to her duffle hood, the picnic basket is by her feet. He thinks she looks like red riding hood and wonders if he's the wolf.

'Hey Nicky, over here,' Ava shouts and waves so her hood flies back letting her hair go mad. Nicky has never seen her hair do that before. He thinks it's like a girl from Disney.

Nicky narrows his eyes as his dad moves close and puts his hands on Ava's shoulders.

'Hey, how's my favourite girl?'

She looks at Nicky and he looks at her. She is the prettiest girl he's ever seen in real life. Ava pulls her hair up using a scrunchie from her pocket. It's blue with lemons on it. It looks like a horse tail.

Nancy and his dad lay out a tartan blanket but it's hard as it keeps blowing up like a kite. She stops it with her bottom on one corner. His dad finds it hard to put himself on the floor and stretch out his legs, but manages to secure the other end of the blanket.

'I'm not as young as I was,' his dad laughs and Nancy giggles

'Come on kids, sit down here,' Nancy says, patting the space in between.

Ava rushes forward and pushes herself up against his dad. His dad puts his arm around her and makes a shivery sound.

'I'm not hungry,' Nicky says and walks to the sea. He picks some smooth stones and skims them into the water.

'Good one,' his dad calls when one travels for miles across the surface of the sea.

Nicky kicks the stones under his feet creating a puff of dust that gets in his throat and makes him cough. He looks back at Ava, she has her hand in a packet of crisps. Nicky is quite close to them now.

'Do you want your food?' Nancy calls to him.

'No,' Nicky says with his back to them. Dad starts a sentence but then Nancy speaks quietly, but Nicky can still hear her.

'Leave it,' she says. Nicky imagines she is reaching across Ava and touching his dad's arm. How dare they keep touching and kissing his dad. Why doesn't Ava stick with her own one? Her own dad, with his flashy car and fancy suits. Ava says he's a clean freak and she isn't allowed to eat crisps on his sofa. Nancy just laughs and says, 'Quite right too,' even though they all eat crisps and chocolate on her sofa. Ava says she hates her dad. Now she's trying to steal his so she gets a new one and he'll be left with stupid Tom.

Nicky chooses a bigger rock. He pulls back his arm to show off his growing muscles and chucks the rock hard into the water. It creates just the right amount of splash.

'Hey Nicky, not so big, its splashing us.' His dad sounds cross but he's not shouting.

'Come and get some food,' Nancy calls.

Nicky ignores her.

Just as he finds an even bigger rock, he hears footsteps crunching behind him. Before he can let it go, his dad grabs his arm and takes his stone.

Nicky's dad puts his hands on Nicky's shoulders but not in a lovely way like he did with Ava.

His dad looks cross as he puts his finger under Nicky's chin and lifts his head.

'You've got five minutes to find my good lad,' Dad says, staring down. Nicky wipes some snot from his nose with the back of his hand. His dad gives him a screwed-up hanky with oil on the corner.

With his dad still standing there, Nicky lets himself look back up the beach. Nancy is climbing up the stony slope with the rolled wind shield, tucked under her arm. Ava has the basket and a Sainsbury's carrier bag; she turns back and smiles at Nicky.

His dad forces his head back to look at him, a large hand on each ear.

'Nancy is taking Ava to get jumpers from the car. We're going to the arcade. If you don't start behaving, I'll drop you back to your mother's.'

Nicky doesn't want to go home and, anyway, his mum will be out. He heaves the biggest rock in his eyeline and chucks it into the shallow water splashing his dad's trousers. His father stays silent, watching him. He holds his hand out and Nicky ignores it.

His dad gives up. With a big sigh, he turns and marches up the stones, big strides, rushing to catch up with the girls.

Nancy and Ava are waiting at the top, the things are in the car. He spots Ava's freckles for the first time. She is looking down at her wellies but when Nicky reaches the top, she looks up, smiles. Her endless smiling is so irritating.

Nancy grabs his dad's hand and they walk on ahead. Nicky tucks down his chin and follows behind, slower. He leaves Ava standing by herself, abandoned, left behind.

Nicky walks close enough to hear his dad speaking to Nancy. She is holding tight to his arm like she wants to pull him back.

'I'm so sorry,' his dad says.

His dad is sorry he has a son, Nicky's sure. He's here, making trouble again, being irresponsible and rude like his mother. He know his dad wants to be a dad to Ava but not to Nicky. His mum said he wanted a girl, she told him how they had both wanted a girl, a pretty girl, with freckles, a girl who was kind and smiley, polite and friendly.

'Don't worry, Nicky will come around, it's the green-eyed monster inside of him that's the problem,' Nancy laughs.

Nicky's ashamed that he's the monster. Bad boys come from bad mums. He knows that. He looks at the water, then the cars, he thinks it would be better if he wasn't here. Ava would put herself between her mum and her new dad. They would walk along holding hands, three happy people, a happy family.

Then, the tears come. All he wants in life is some laughing. But all he feels is sadness and hurt and disappointment and fear and he's fed up with it. He's always known he is a bad kid. His parents wanted a pretty kind girl like Ava but instead they got a bad selfish monster.

I didn't put my bike away.

My dad left because I'm bad.

I put Paul in prison, my mum said I did, but when she calmed down, she said I didn't.

I can't keep my mum safe

Sometimes I hate her.

Sometimes I hate Ava.

Sometimes I hate Dad.

I'm a monster and make bad things happen.

Bad kids have bad mothers who find bad men.

He's about to run off, run back to the car or his house or somewhere no one can find him. After all, no one would care anyway.

But, before he can get going, before his tears of desperation reach his chin, he feels something. He feels something touching his hand. Something soft and warm. He looks down and sees white fingers and pink nails. He watches as a skinny hand slips inside of his. It feels so nice, so warm and so soft. It is simply the nicest feeling he's ever had.

Keziah

Registration, assembly followed by literacy, morning break, craft and numeracy. The predictable routine is like a balm to my soul.

'Yes, Ellie?'

'Put that back, Billie.'

'Oscar. Get down.'

I have a definite tummy curve now, but Claus doesn't want me to tell anyone until after the next scan. Claus doesn't want my parents to get excited and then be devastated if I miscarry. He never mentions telling his mum.

Ameena has been badgering me with her trademark investigative asking. 'You OK, you're a bit pale? . . . Where's the old Kezzy? . . . Is there anything you're not telling me?'

I feel awful for deceiving her. My old self was transparent, heart on my sleeve; everyone knew my business. I'm sure Claus is right, though; best to keep it our little secret until the right time.

Today is Wednesday, my favourite teaching day. I have a prep slot and no after school clubs. After lunch, my kids get to do gym at the leisure centre which leaves an hour for me to slope off for much needed food and fresh air. Since white bean came on board I can't skip meals. It makes my head spin and the nausea becomes too evident.

I'm just scrabbling about looking for my purse, ready to leave, when a female voice interrupts my thoughts. 'Keziah?'

Looking up, I'm confronted with a familiar face I just can't place. She's young, dressed in baggy dungarees and a tie-dye cardigan. Is she a teaching student? I do hope I've not forgotten a visit.

'I hoped I might catch you, the office manager said you'd most likely be here.' She looks around the room. 'I love that,' the familiar stranger enthuses at the newly decorated wall. Each child has completed a rocket using different mediums for this term's topic. I must remember to take down the Valentine's Day collage.

'Hattie, how are you?' I say with more confidence than I feel. Was she the one still in training or the qualified one?

'Very well, thank you, although so glad that's over.'

'Oh dear, what have you been up to?' I ask, not wanting to be rude but wishing she'd go away so I can escape.

'Training on the junior site,' she replies, her eyes still on the hanging mobiles.

'Ah right, what's the topic?'

'Functional contextualism.'

I have no clue what that means but she doesn't seem to pick up on my blank face.

There's another long pause whilst she studies the topic board.

'Tell me, is this the one-off training?' I say, grabbing my bag. I distract myself with images of greasy comfort food from 'The Plaice', my favourite chip shop on the corner. Claus will never know.

'Just a one-off. I was only helping this morning, so I'm all done.' She smiles, still studying the display, pointing to her favourite aspect of the space artwork. 'And I'm thankful for that, I feel such an idiot standing up in front of experienced teachers like I know this stuff.'

'Don't beat yourself up, it was you guys who introduced me to imposter syndrome. None of us really know what we're doing.' I laugh but head for the door, keys jangling in my hand. 'Sorry to dash off like this, I've got a craving for chips,' I say, regretting my choice of words. I don't want her guessing I'm pregnant, and definitely not telling Claus I'm off my nutrition plan; that could cost our baby ten intelligence points if he's to be believed.

'I'm starving, can I stalk you to the chippie? I was sad you had to rush off that evening.'

'Sure.'

Any other day I would be glad of the company but I don't need an energetic puppy at my heels, especially one who shares the same master, it all feels a bit odd. But then I remember: it was her. She was the one who seemed to know all about Claus's upset in Oxford. Instantly I realise I've been given a gift horse.

As we cut across the park, the hope of Spring is here. Even though its freezing, there are glimmers of yellow in the grass, newly flowered, waiting to be mown down by a football. The ice cream kiosk is open but a young girl wrapped in a jumper is filing her nails. On a damp bench, a couple of mothers watch their kids cycle, chatting whilst clinging to coffee in plastic cups.

As Hattie chatters, seemingly undeterred by my silence, I internally rehearse what questions I can ask without revealing my ignorance about my husband's past. The pregnancy has pushed a lot to the back of my mind. Claus has been away so much there's not been the opportunities to interrogate him. Perhaps there's also a part of me that would rather not know.

'What brought you to the area?' I ask when she takes a short pause from her monologue for breath. Her enthusiasm and intelligence are exhausting. Was I this keen in my twenties? Right now, all I can think is that I wish I'd worn an extra jumper and some gloves.

‘Clinical training, we get no choice where we do our placements.’

‘I see. A good department, though? I know Claus was chuffed to see an opening there when he was thinking of relocating.’

‘It’s a superb placement, he’s so patient, amazing, given all he’s been through. If I was him I wouldn’t have had the courage to return to work.’

Hoorah, she’s given the opening I need.

‘Ah, bless him.’ I point to a toddler who has fallen. I need thinking time without losing control of the conversation. This may be my only opportunity to pump a source for info.

‘I think Claus needed work as a distraction,’ I offer, hoping the catch in my voice isn’t obvious. I need her to believe we’re the closest couple ever, that there’s nothing he hasn’t shared.

‘I’m sure, and then meeting you was the icing on the cake, he describes you as his saviour all the time, it’s super cute.’ She grins like an idiotic Cheshire cat.

‘Yes, he’s very supportive and kind.’

I decide not to add *most of the time*. We had a small blip yesterday when he refused to talk about some more messages from that abusive client. I want to go to the police but he snapped back that it’s none of my business. Then he stomped off to sulk and disappeared into the bathroom, silent behind a locked door. He did apologise this morning though, probably because he’s away for the next few days visiting another out-of-county kid. He seems to get dumped with all the out-of-area referrals.

I wait. Surely Miss Chatterbox won’t resist adding more gossip.

‘I know you’ve made a massive difference. Mike has known Claus for years and he said that after Jenny, Claus was a broken man. Apparently, he didn’t leave the house for weeks. Mike thought it might be the end of his career when it went on and on.’

How do I ask why some kid called Jenny led to some sort of personal breakdown? I’m guessing he missed something or somehow made mistakes with the level of risk. What went on and on, some sort of investigation?

Instead, I say nothing. We buy chips and lean inside a bus shelter to eat.

‘I’m so sorry, Keziah, it must be awful me talking about her death without acknowledging your pain in it all, so clumsy of me.’

I’m shocked, and completely stumped. Who was Jenny? And why would his devastation about something at work hurt me when it was before we met? My brain goes into overdrive. Was it misconduct? Then I catch myself. Keziah, this is Claus, what on earth are you thinking?

‘It must’ve been so awful, especially when the inquest didn’t confirm one way or another. I mean it’s bad enough someone dying but when the media uses words like ‘suspicious’, ‘unexplained’, it adds so many layers. I mean, as if he wouldn’t have blamed himself whatever their stupid verdict.’

Hattie goes on and on with no apparent need to make this a two-way process. I shouldn’t have worried about being subtle. She’s a young gossip, enjoying the second-hand juicy nuggets she’s collected from the office floor.

‘Yes, awful, I can’t imagine,’ is all I can muster.

As if responding to my accelerated heart rate and over breathing, my chest tightens and I’m certain little bean does the promised wiggle I've been craving. Oh, my goodness, there it is again. My baby really is in there.

Hattie has stopped chattering and is staring. No doubt she's diagnosing me. Lost to myself, glazed eyes, an inane smile on my face. Yep, she'll say to her colleagues. That wife of the boss, she's definitely unhinged. Total nutter.

'Keziah, I feel really bad but I need to get back to work. If I don't go soon, I'll be late for my next meeting,' she says, like I've delayed her with *my* questions. She retrieves her rucksack from our feet. Was she really hungry or was she seeking me out? She turns to go, then pauses to chuck her chip paper in the bin. I watch her head off.

Do I want to know? Probably not. I fasten my top button, snuggle deeper into my coat ready to stomp back. But, my feet don't follow. I spin around just in time to call after her.

'Hattie?'

She turns around, frowning. What now?

'Who was Jenny?' I ask.

She pauses, walks a bit closer.

'Pardon?' she replies. I know she heard.

'Who was the girl who died, who was Jen?'

She speaks very slowly as if I'm stupid, deaf, or perhaps an unhinged client.

'Jenny – Jenny Doerkson was Claus's first wife.

14

Home Alone

Nicky

Nicky counts as he skips along the pavement. Dad and the boys at school say skipping is for girls, but he loves the soothe of a bounce. He's far enough away from school to enjoy a skip.

In the last couple of weeks his life has got much better.

When Ava held his hand at the beach, she didn't let go for the rest of the day. Apart from when they went to the toilet.

She asked him why he was crying and for the first time ever, he told. He told her about his bike, and his dad, and Paul. He told her about history day and how he screwed up. He told her about the carpet and Tom, and how he's terrified in his big house when mum goes. He even told her about the police and the wardrobe and that secretly Disney films are his favourite. The only two things he didn't tell her are that he wets himself and he wishes Nancy was his mum.

She listened carefully. She listened with her head on one side with her fingers twisting and twirling her luscious hair. He wanted to stop talking and thrust his fingers into her hair and kiss her smack on the lips like a Disney prince. When he finished talking, she didn't laugh or run away in disgust. In fact, after he stopped talking she bent down and kissed him on his cheek, just a quick one but a definite kiss, with her lips and everything. No one was looking but he couldn't believe an older girl would hold his hand and love him.

Then this morning, his life got even better.

When he was packing his lunchbox and washing last night's glasses, Brad arrived. Then Tom came out of his parent's room carrying the black gym bag. Together, he and Brad rolled up his grandmother's red carpet and heaved the trunk back into the van. Nicky carried two boxes all by himself.

He heard Tom say to Brad, 'Get me outta here.'

His mum said, 'Good riddance to bad rot.'

Tom waved out of the window and Brad honked the horn as they left. Nicky gave them a cheerful wave and sauntered towards school.

As she kissed him goodbye, his mum was OK, she wasn't crying like when Paul went. She said, 'Hey you,' and ruffled his hair. 'You're the only man I need.'

As he skips nearer and nearer, he remembers he is the main man again, in charge. Now he's older, and has a woman in his life he hopes he'll do better, not let mum down, like when he was nine and a little stupid. He thinks about how when Paul was choking her, he wanted to be strong, he wanted to save her but couldn't. He feels terrible about that. Instead of rescuing her, he went back to the wardrobe and put a pillow over his face.

He so wants to be a good man, to keep mum safe but inside he knows he's a terrible boy because he has terrible, evil thoughts. He knows how terrible he is, and never shares his bad thoughts with anyone, not his best teacher, not Ava and definitely not his dad.

He knows if he told someone his very worst thought, they would lock him away or maybe even kill him because he is a bad monster. He knows that thought makes him so bad but somehow it just pops into his head without his permission. Sometimes the thought comes when he's in bed and even though he counts, and rocks and bangs, it stays in his head. Sometimes it comes when he's in class, or even when he's gripping onto his teachers' hand when they walk around the playground. He's tried everything but he can't get rid of his evil, monstrous, bad thought.

He's so glad that no one knows that sometimes he secretly hopes his mum could disappear. Obviously, he doesn't want her to be hurt, after all it's his job to protect her. But sometimes he just wants to be normal with a mum like Nancy who waits at the door, who tucks him in, who cooks and cleans so their children can just be boys. On days like today, he wishes he could arrive home and find his mum gone. Just like that, in a puff of smoke like the pumpkin carriage in Disney's Cinderella.

The best thing about his life is Nancy's house. She says they are a happy unit, two boys, two girls. They argued for ages about a family song, but only in a good way where you laugh in the middle. In the end they agreed it could be Nicky's favourite – Sweet Caroline. That's what Ava calls him now. Caroline. When he comes in, she shouts, 'Hello Caroline.' He knows it's a girl's name but he doesn't even mind.

When he gets closer to home, he stops skipping. He's not sure what mum would think about skipping now he's ten, especially with him being the man and everything.

Nicky strides sensibly into Castlegate. Passing Chantry view on the corner, he peeps in the gap between the trees and the tall black gates. It's very quiet so the people must be at work.

He bashes in his gate code as fast as he can. As soon as the gates slide apart, he can see the front door is open. He wonders if she might have baked a cake and have a flowery pinny tied on her waist. His dad always liked her like that.

He throws his bag down in the entrance hall. There is something to smell. His nose twitches like a rabbit. This smell is definitely not cake. This smell is disgusting and makes him want to turn around and shut the door behind him.

'Mum,' he shouts, 'it's me, I'm home.'

Two bottles lie by her chair and a half empty one by the sink. The two from the floor clink as he holds them together. He empties the third one down the plug hole and takes all three out to the recycling. He's glad he remembered the bin this morning. Mrs P says the bins must be retrieved on the same day they're emptied.

'Silly cow,' Nicky mutters, without being sure who he's referring to.

'Mum,' he bellows down the hall. Sometimes she takes an afternoon nap to get her strength up for the evening. No answer. He knows she'll be the shops or at work. He can't remember where she goes on Thursdays. She often forgets to lock up when she's drinking. It used to drive his dad mad, and now he's the man of the house, he can understand why. It's getting dark and even though he's ten, he still thinks about Grendel.

An empty dish is on the kitchen table. At least she's eaten lunch, sometimes she doesn't eat all day. He doesn't like seeing the bones on her shoulders. Nicky sniffs the bowl as he carries it to the sink. It's Weetabix. He wonders if she got up late and had breakfast or had breakfast for lunch. He feels bad he didn't make toast.

Nicky wipes the table and empties his school bag. Ava said he needs to do his homework as education is important.

She says if he doesn't study, he'll end up as the stop/go man by the traffic lights. Ava is going to university to study medicine like her aunt. He promised he'd try harder.

Going back down the hall to get his highlighter pens he sees his mum's bedroom door is half open. He didn't notice that before. The bad smell is coming from her room.

He pushes the door and looks in. Her duvet is made. The room is tidy. Usually her room is messy like his. He still can't understand why it smells so bad; it's like when he had a tummy bug. Maybe it's the drains. He decides to open the small window in the ensuite, that way it'll take the smell out but not make her room cold.

He stops in the doorway. There is water in the bath but no one is there. The towels are in a crumpled heap on the mat. As he bends down to hang them up, he sees her. His mum is completely naked and it looks like she might have fallen off the toilet. Her skinny body is wrapped around the bottom of the toilet. She is the smell. There is sick everywhere, on the toilet seat, down the sides and all around her. Nicky tries not to breathe; his throat makes a horrid noise and he thinks he's going to chuck. He counts back in threes.

His mum is completely still. Even though the sick is revolting, he puts his ear to her mouth. She's not breathing and her face is a strange colour.

The green uniformed men carry the stretcher and put her in the back of their van. Mr P comes up behind him.

Nicky closes his eyes. He knows this is his fault. As he rocks back and forth against Mr P's chest, he chants to a familiar rhythm and knows for sure that he's a bad, bad, bad, monster boy. Such a bad monster that his evil thought has killed his own mother.

Keziah

There was no way I could teach a class after what Hattie revealed. So with my woollen hat still on from my park walk, I ran to the school office to make my excuses. I gabbled out the symptoms of a stomach bug, turned and left.

Thank goodness Claus is away. I drove home, changed into my PJs and haven't moved for over twenty-four hours.

Who can I tell I'm the second Mrs Doerkson? All the lies he told about never loving anyone else, me being his true first love, his saviour, his soul mate.

Soil mate, that's what he is. All my hopes and dreams are soiled, dirty. What about our relationship is real? Who is this baby's father? Do I know anything at all about him?

Alone, and lost in my thoughts, the boxing match is fierce, the gloves are off. This is street fighting, spitting, viscous, fast, spiteful.

The first fighter in the ring shouts, Give him a chance, ask him.

A viscous punch lands from a more agile opponent: Your husband is a liar, a ruthless, deliberate liar and you are passing on his DNA.

Desperate to stop my thoughts spiralling out of control, I do my usual and grab my iPad, a handful of ginger biscuits and search YouTube for the life that should've been mine.

Mindless watching of the best downhill mountain bikers is still my best medicine. I watch Rachel Atherton, current female champion, bumping down the slopes with elegance.

I insert my Apple air pods; one of my stocking fillers from Claus. I want the realistic sound as well as the visuals.

My body does it with her, lift up there, bum down now, grip, go, hard, push down, go, go, go.

My chest throbs with exhilaration from the race but I'm still here, lying on a leather couch, in a house that hardly feels like mine. Reflected back to me from an over-polished TV screen, I see a face I don't recognise. I see a sallow face that's miserable, a face that's deflated and a face that's defeated.

I should be travelling the world. Maybe not riding competitively but at least coaching. Maybe even scouting the youth clubs, spotting the kids just like me, transparent, optimistic, making their plans with no expectation of disaster. I shouldn't be dressed in teacher clothes or this glorious white dressing gown. If I was out of Lycra I'd be wearing a scruffy stained onesie and roughing it at a youth hostel.

I'd call Esther and she'd smile and ask, 'What are you like?'

She'd ask, 'when are you going to settle down, buy a house, have some kids, find Mr Right, get a proper job?'

I would throw back by head and roar with affectionate laughter, 'When I'm ready, big sister.'

I took one day off school after she died. I wasn't a swot. Lessons for me were the fillers between the fun and chat of breaks. As soon as the day ended, I'd race off. By the time some of my friends had ambled home. I'd be on my bike, helmet on, plastered with all-weather sun cream and half way to the club house. Dad would collect me after work, often arriving early to chat with my coach or catch me out on the hills. We were a team. Esther would be at home studying for A levels, mum would be chopping and peeling. They were a team. On the dot of seven, dad and I would barge in the door expectant of a home-cooked feast and we'd join together, one perfect happy family, two and two made four.

The last day I rode was a week after Esther died. My coach was nagging, understanding but insisting it would help. I couldn't waste time if I was still planning to compete in the juniors at the end of the summer.

So I convinced myself all was well, Esther sitting at her desk, mum in the kitchen, dad at work. I packed my kit, including a snack and my map and sat on my bike.

After a week of utter despair, and overwhelming physical grief, the saddle felt like my resting place. Even my pain settled for a moment as I felt the familiarity. My hands, arms, legs and body knew exactly what they had to do. My coach was right, biking would heal me.

But then there was a weekend race, and my parents were at home when I wheeled my bike to the back door. They came out to find me, my mum carrying a cup of tea thinking she'd find me crying on the back step. My dad just behind him, the Sunday paper in his hand. I saw their faces as they looked from me, to the bike and back to me. My dad tried to smile but my mum couldn't. She was ashen, she wobbled and for a moment I thought she was going to faint. The fear in her eyes was transparent as my dad steadied her from behind, his hands on her shoulders, his gaze unable to meet mine.

What on earth was I thinking? My poor, poor parents were broken and their only daughter was about to ride into the sunset and risk her life for fun.

Instantly, I jumped down, yanked off my helmet and said, 'I've resigned from the club. I don't enjoy biking now. Need to focus on school. I'm polishing my bike ready to sell.'

Relief flooded my mum's entire body. In that moment, I made a silent promise to my sister. See, I can do it, I can be you. Loyal. selfless, careful.

By now Esther would be a top surgeon. She wanted two kids by the time she was thirty-five so now she'd be expecting number one. She would be living on a hill married to a consultant and loving every minute.

Sitting here in my fancy house, on a fancy hill, in my fancy nightwear, I'm living her life. But I've ended up losing myself in a life that's hers not mine.

With renewed vigour, I search my playlist for an old favourite and press play. Familiar lyrics make my spirit soar in a way that feels unfamiliar.

For so long, at every junction, I've asked myself, 'What would Esther do?' I know now the question is, 'What would Kezzy do?'

Kezzy, that strong optimistic girl who believed she could make it to the top, the girl who wouldn't be bullied, who was resilient and unstoppable, what would that girl do?

Before I scoff the rest of the biscuits, I text Ameena, 'Hey bestie, I need you, and I need you now.'

15

Near Death Experience

Nicky

Mr P left Nicky alone at the hospital because the silly cow called him home for his diabetes. Nicky has been waiting for four hours, thirty-three minutes and twelve seconds.

Outside, it's very black.

A nurse with a deep voice told him to sit when he set off for his seventeenth corridor circuit. Nineteen gets Mr P safely home. He completed the extra two when she went off shift.

Be a good boy, Nicky, good boy, good boy, be a good boy, Nicky, be a good boy, good boy.

'Hey, it's OK, wake up.' A hand comes on his shoulder, he startles awake. The new nurse has a hole in her tights, he can see her leg through it. She hands him an orange carton and a kit Kat.

'I'm Rose, you were dreaming kiddo, whispering and nodding your head.'

'Sorry.'

'Ah no, you're OK, you've been waiting a long time, shall I help you get the straw in the juice?'

She shoves the straw in and orange liquid dribbles down the side. Nicky gulps his drink and rips off the chocolate wrapper.

'Gosh, you must've been hungry. Here you go, sunshine, some pencils to make your drawing more colourful. Why don't you add some flowers and trees in that graveyard?'

She gives him five childish crayons. Five is not a good number so he drops one and uses green and black to add vultures in trees.

Nicky rests his head on mum's belly to feel her breathing. He can't sleep in case she dies.

Good boy, Nicky, keep her safe. Don't leave, don't sleep, don't be late. You're the man, Nicky. Be a good man, not a bad man, not a monster, Nicky.

A crash and a waft of air makes him jump. Nancy rushes through the automatic doors so fast his dad gets stuck in the middle. Nicky doesn't check his dad is OK, he can't wait. He leaps up and rushes into Nancy's tight embrace. Nicky inhales her smell; his breathing slows for the first time since he arrived.

'Steady on, you'll knock her flying.' His dad smiles. giving his son a gentle pat on the arm. So safe and warm as he snuggles into Nancy's soft tummy. She keeps her arms around him, he never wants her to let go.

Snuggled up to Nancy, from the corner of his eye, he watches the hospital bed with its white sheets and knitted blanket up to mum's nose. Then, to his horror, her eyes ping open.

Mum doesn't know Nancy and he's being cuddled. Nicky doesn't know what to do. His mum needs him but he wants to stay put. He untangles himself and sits back in his watching chair.

'Hello, you must be Lisa. I'm Nancy.' Nancy puts her hand towards his mum but lets it drop. Mum can't get hers out from the blanket. She's crying but he left the tissues in Mr P's car. He always messes up. Mum looks at dad and then Nancy and then Nicky.

He knows it's his fault.

'We've come to get Nicky,' Nancy tells his mum.

I'm a good boy. Good boys do not leave their mums. Good boys keep their mums safe.

'Thank you,' mum mumbles without looking at him.

'No!'

Nicky's shout is loud; Nurse Rose runs back. Nancy says everything is fine but it isn't fine. It really isn't fine. Nicky throws his body onto his mum. She puts her arms around him. She still smells of sick even though the grumpy nurse washed her.

My mum doesn't know what she's saying cos she doesn't know she's sick, she's been in an ambulance. She doesn't know she's in hospital. She doesn't know Rose checks her every ten minutes, she needs her ear checks. She needs her arm measuring. Poppa says she doesn't know what's good for her. I know what's good for her. I'm the man of the house. Only I know what she needs. She needs to wake up, she needs her coffee first, but not too hot. if her hands are shaky it spills. She needs her toast with only butter. She doesn't like jam, it makes her sick in the morning. If she's wobbly, she needs to lean on me or she falls and wets her pyjamas. She can't get any more bruises.

'Come on, Nicky, it's OK, it's OK.' Both his dad and Nancy are trying to lift him off mum. She is struggling to breath and Rose can't check her. Nicky won't let go, he hangs on to the sides of the bed as the three adults attempt to lift him off his mum.

Then he feels hands pushing under him, his mum is speaking louder, pushing him away.

'Nicky, go, just go.'

He can't stop his feet slipping. She is pushing and they are pulling. Nancy's hand is over her mouth. Her eyes are wide and she's gasping oh no, oh no. Nicky catches Rose staring. She is disgusted with the monster boy who abandons his mummy and lets her die.

Rose is weeping whilst cuddling poor Nancy who has to take the bad, bad, boy. The boy who made daddy leave and tried to kill his own mother.

Keziah

Within an hour of my cry for help, Ameena is banging the door with her fists. I can't get the door open quick enough. She slams the door with her bum because her arms are overflowing with a rainbow of packets.

'I didn't bring beer, as you're obviously pregnant,' she says, carefully transferring her food baby to me. I cradle a large bar of Cadbury's fruit and nut, two family packs of Walker's crisps and a six pack of Diet Coke.

My closest friend, unchanged, disarms me. The supplies remain in a heap on the hall floor as she steers me into our cosiest room and onto the lengthy sofa; there she gently strokes my hair whilst I cry and cry.

All the pent-up emotion and craziness of the last weeks haemorrhage out, a tsunami of mixed emotions. Stupidity for trusting him, guilt for shutting out good friends, a sadness, anger and an anxiety I can't articulate. I've made a dreadful mistake. I should've listened to my mum, to my friends. They told me I couldn't know enough about a man in just a few months, that no one is that perfect; but I refused to hear. I so wanted the happily-ever-after that I closed my ears to the black smudges that ruined the rose-coloured specs.

When my tears finally pause, she says, 'Wait there,' leaning me back against the settee like a rag doll and disappearing to retrieve the much-needed junk fest from the hall.

Alone, Claus smiles down at me from a photograph taken on our honeymoon. Taken at the end of a perfect day at our favourite restaurant, he'd presented me with a bespoke bracelet he'd sourced on the island. The jeweller had repeated the inscription of my wedding bracelet, 'Forever mine'. I'd been content to accept the implicit apology.

Ameena chucks a bag of salt and vinegar from behind and shuffles herself into the opposite corner of the sofa to me. We both sit with our legs splayed on the attached foot stalls, each with our favourite crisps.

It's a good job Claus can't see her, shoes on, food on the couch.

Chucking my crisps in at speed, I'm strangely ravenous. I didn't eat my chips, distracted by Hattie's big reveal, so I've eaten nothing in the last twenty-four hours.

'So,' she says, screwing up her crisp packet, aiming for the fire grate.

Without hesitation, I tell her the whole miserable tale. About Jenny. About leaving. About his moods, and the desperation for order that borders on OCD.

'Why on earth didn't you tell me?' she says

'Because I was ashamed, because you were right, because I wanted you to like him.'

'I warned you he was too good to be true,' she says.

'Ameena, I can't deal with that. I promise there's so much to like about him. When you walk in, he clams up and becomes his worst version. I know what you think, too tricky, too serious, too old fashioned and, yeah, he's different to Mark, different to my exes but I like that. I love him.'

I've not mentioned the wedding night fiasco or the boyfriend list.

'So,' I say with more confidence than I feel, 'I want us to be a team, the goal is proving I can trust him. I need you to want that too, if you can't promise that, I'll do this on my own.'

She pauses. Then, tentatively raises her hand. We do a childish high five, a gesture we repeated endlessly through teacher training. I manage a giggle, something I do less often these days.

'Right,' she says, a new determination in her voice. 'Where is project "Prove Claus" going to start?'

'You look downstairs, the study, the garage, the out-shed and the library.'

She raises her eyebrows but wisely resists the urge to comment.

'Okeydokey, what you going to do, put your feet up?'

I chuck a cushion at her. It's so good to be mates again, to feel less alone.

'Nope, I'm doing upstairs, bedrooms and second study.'

Two hours later, Ameena comes into my bedroom with tea. Her ironed T-shirt is looking tired and her fringe damp with sweat.

'Thanks,' I say, cupping the steaming mug. 'I hadn't realised we've been at it for so long, sorry.'

'No worries.' She plonks herself on Claus's side of the bed, next to me and slings an arm around my shoulder. I'm glad he's taken his old man slippers with him. The trendy ones I got him for Christmas are still in a box.

'Found anything interesting?'

'Nothing I didn't know about,' I say, removing his pile of textbooks from my lap and onto his pillow.

'You?'

'Not a thing, although that's what feels odd, Kez. I'm sorry, I'm doing what you asked, presuming innocence, but to have a massive house like this with no old photos, no souvenirs, ornaments, piles of old coats even?'

‘He hates clutter,’ I explain.

‘Yeah, I get that, but this is a whole different level.’

‘Look in my dressing room and you’ll be reassured,’ I laugh. We’ve shared a room over many years. She knows what I’m like.

I don’t tell her that the room I’m most interested in, the guest room, the room Claus sometimes sleeps in, always gets dressed in, is locked. I don’t have a key. I’ve seen in there often enough, through the door at least. It’s the same as this; white and clean.

Cup still in hand, Ameena wonders over to stare out the window.

‘It’s so beautiful here,’ she says without a hint of jealousy.

I so wish I’d trusted her before. It would’ve been lovely having company when Claus is away.

‘All I found is . . .’ she says, turning around. My heart skips a beat but then she laughs. ‘Five boxes of the *Guardian* in chronological order.’

‘Aaah, yes I know about those. He likes to keep track of the news.’

She comes back and shuffles so close, our thighs touch, her breathing is a rhythmic comfort. Leaning my head on her shoulder, I enjoy her familiar scent, Chanel number 5, hidden beneath the smell of hard work.

‘Come on,’ Ameena says, pulling me up.

As I move, my shirt shifts to reveal my midriff. I’m already hefty and not yet four months.

‘Crikey.’ Ameena pulls my clothes up higher for another look. I press my fingers into the base of my spine and thrust my belly forward for full effect.

She hugs me tight.

'Congratulations.'

We stand for a few seconds, taking in my belly, giggling at it's funny shape in the mirror. She wipes away unexpected tears.

'Let's order a Chinese and after we've eaten we'll search the internet. Can I stay over?' She giggles like we're teenagers. Her lightness is rubbing off on me and I feel better, not resolved but better.

'Sure, Claus isn't back until tomorrow evening so no hurry to run away.'

I do as I'm told, eat my Chinese and stick to two glasses of wine. Claus would prefer no alcohol or a half glass but, hey I'd prefer to be his first wife.

She types 'Jennifer Doerkson' into google. The top hit is a midwife from Essex county in the US and a global outreach doctor who's been training dogs since 2001.

I suggest she adds 'England' after her name. That just brings up heaps of LinkedIn and Facebook profiles. We get the same when we try 'Jenny' or 'Jen'.

Ameena leans back against the couch, expressing a loud, frustrated sigh. I snatch the screen as an idea jumps into my head. I type 'Jenny Doerkson dies, death and Claus Doerkson'. Bingo! Ameena claps her hands, then stops. This isn't really a cause for celebration.

Ameena, loving the drama, takes back her device and reads like she is Charlotte White on BBC news.

'Friends paid tribute to an Oxfordshire woman who died over the weekend. Jennifer Doerkson suffered fatal injuries after falling in Spitfield Road, Portsmouth, on 9 March. She was hit by a heavy goods vehicle. The driver Ben Harvey — a local man— was treated for shock.

"I have no idea what happened, one minute the road was clear, then she was under the wheel."

Friends paid tribute to Jen on social media and a card left at the scene, which read: "She was a kind-hearted lady with a great sense of humour and a heart of gold." Jennifer died from her injuries at Southampton General Hospital after being treated at the scene. She was on a short break with her husband. Police are appealing for witnesses.'

Seeing it in black and white is awful. An accident, a first wife, and Claus there at the same time. No wonder everyone at the psychology party was speaking in hushed tones. But something about the location rings a bell, though I've never been that far south. I'd remember if I'd been to Portsmouth, or even Hampshire, surely.

Spitfield sounds so familiar. I'm sure I've seen it somewhere before, I remember thinking what a bizarre name for a road, and recalling how a boy I fancied at school used to spit when he was kicking a ball on the field.

I don't say anything, just let Ameena keep scrolling through the Google hits. I'm beginning to feel overwhelmed, so I'm relieved when she finally gives in and slopes off to the second guest room.

The birds outside usually soothe me to sleep but tonight they appear to be involved in a family scrap. Their noise is irritating, scratchy. My back is giving me grief and I can't get comfortable despite the stupidly expensive memory foam. Rolling over to Claus's side in an attempt to relieve the ache in my spine doesn't work either.

Just as my eyelids start to settle, I'm startled back to high alert by the sight of his bedtime reads. Energised by a fleeting memory, I drag myself to the floor and lift the heavy books onto my lap one at a time.

I take off the top one and see the title of the scruffy hardback. Then I know I'm right. Tucked just where I left it, hidden within the text about coping with guilt, I find the slim column of writing. Turning over the small scrap of paper there it is, in plain sight.

Yesterday whilst out walking with her family, an eleven-year-old girl was hit by a car on the Spitfield Road. Hampshire police are asking any witnesses to come forward.

There's no way I'm sharing this with Ameena. Two deaths, in the same road, decades apart and somehow my husband is linked to both.

16

Home Again

Nicky

Dad's head nods forward, then jerks back, then nods onto the window, bang, he jerks back. Next to him, Nancy is driving fast along big wide roads, away from his mum, and hospitals, and Mr P and Bella.

Nicky knows they are moving closer to Pompey. From the back seat he sees The Spinnaker Tower in the distance, white ladders on a pole. Ava says the tower has a magic glass floor, Nicky disbelieves her but it's an exciting idea. The massive brown signs list the activities in Ava's scrap book about Portsmouth where she lives. The historic dockyard. Gunwharf Quays. Charles Dickens' house.

Nicky closes his eyes and remembers a film he watched with his grandparents. The children stepped into an ordinary wardrobe, just like his with the clothes and the doors and the fear. But then there was magic. The magic of another world with happy feelings, and hope and a happy ending.

The motorway comes to an end, blue signs turn green, then narrow roads with shops that lead to Nancy's haven of hope and warmth. Usually by now he would be wondering what's for supper, what film they'd watch as a family. But today everything feels different. Today, the closer he gets to his second home, the harder he hurts. His counting head is pushing in, he feels sick, worried.

'Home sweet home,' Nancy whispers, unlocking the front door with one finger on her lips. 'Shhh, we mustn't wake Ava.'

The babysitter packs her knitting in a plastic bag and groans as she pulls herself off the chair and shuffles out. Nicky doesn't know why a girl two years older than him needs a sitter. Dad mutters to the sitter in the hall. Nicky knows he's telling her what Nicky did, how he made Nancy and Rose cry. Nicky's terrified someone will find out it was him, that hours before his mum almost died, her monster son wished her gone. Even he knows that makes him a disgusting boy.

Nancy leads him upstairs, tugging his hand all the way.

'Here you go,' Nancy says with his orange pyjama top in one hand and the wrong bottoms in another.

'I put them on the radiator so they're nice and warm.'

Nicky snatches them. At home he sleeps in pants and socks. You never know when there'll be a night emergency and he despises the pain of bare feet on the gravel.

There's Ava's hump in the top bunk; her breathing in and out calms his tight chest. Ava's room is twenty steps across. Patterns are very important and must be completed. Start at the lamp, touch every furniture piece, walk to the light switch, do five taps, walk back to the lamp. Stay safe, momma, stay safe. These patterns must be completed before sleep. The patterns must be completed in the exact same order and patterns are crucial even when your body is weak and desperate for a cosy bed.

He studies his watch and notes the time. If he doesn't finish his rituals with sufficient speed, his mum will die.

Nancy won't want a murdering boy in her house, near her and her girl.

His feet are sore and his body aches but he must finish the patterns. Three more to go and then he can sleep. Then no one will ever know what he thought, what he did. A thud. For a moment he freezes, musical statues with no soundtrack. He waits and listens. He hears rustling, but can't locate the noise. Is his dad outside? Maybe Nancy is showering.

Finally he sees. A wild animal caught in headlights. He sees two purple legs, like two skinny ropes hanging down. He follows the legs and sees more purple, a purple body with a pink elephant on the front. Then he sees her. Ava sits with her legs dangling over her bed fence.

'It's OK.' She smiles. 'I can wait until you've finished.'

As he accelerates forward, just one more circuit to do, he's horrified, ashamed, embarrassed. He knows his face is red and his pyjamas are sticky. He so wishes he could stop, that it wouldn't matter, that he could be a normal boy.

At last he collapses on his bed. It's done. His mum will live. He releases a long-held sigh and watches as purple PJs descend a wobbly ladder.

The two of them sit. Backs against the wall. Legs across the bed, hers longer than his. His woollen socks gathered at his ankles. Nicky's hand wants to stroke her silky trousers.

Ava's hair is tied in a great fat plait that she's pulled around the front and twiddles as she speaks. He so wants to wrap his fingers around her hand. An unfamiliar feeling pounces. There are no numbers, rituals or patterns associated with this one. He doesn't know what this feeling is. He just knows it comes when fear and sadness and shame go away.

'So,' she says, 'you're my brother now.'

'No, you weirdo.' Nicky gives her leg a gentle shove.

She leans over the end of his bed and heaves a plastic box onto her lap. As she moves the smell of her shampoo wafts to Nicky's nostrils and he feels immense pleasure despite his fear of being caught chatting at night.

'Have you seen these? They belong to my uncle Theo. My mum has been trying to find stuff to make you feel welcome. She really wants you to live here.'

This strikes Nicky as a truly marvellous idea. But then he remembers his mum and that with Tom gone, he's back on man duty.

'Your mum doesn't look after you very well, does she?' Ava says, leaning close to his face.

'My mum does fine,' he snaps.

'My mum has cocoa pops for the morning. I'm not allowed sugar but she says you're having a miserable time.'

'No, I'm not.'

'My mum says you are, she says your mum is a drunk and you do all the work. My mum thinks it's disgusting. I heard her shouting at your dad last week. She said he's being a turkey, with his head in the sand and he should look.'

'Look at what,' Nicky asks feeling an increasing urge to pee.

'I dunno. I was sitting on the top of the stairs but they closed the door. If they shout it's easier to hear what they're saying. I'll show you tomorrow.'

'I know how to listen, stupid.'

'Don't call me stupid, that's really rude, my mum says you're a nice boy.'

Nicky can't think of anything but the drip emerging on his pyjama bottoms. He remembers the last time he wet his pants like a baby. Paul from the phone went mad. 'It stinks,' he had shouted, 'you're too old to pee your pants.'

Paul had stood over him, shouting whilst he made him strip the bed and change the duvet. His mum stood behind mouthing, 'Sorry.' Her voice stayed quiet.

When Nicky comes back from the toilet, Ava is back on the top bunk but chatting as if he's been there all along.

'I know how you feel Nicky, I have a rubbish parent too. My dad doesn't visit, he doesn't care, all he cares about is work and cars. Sometimes I hate him, and sometimes I don't. Once when I was seven . . .'

Nicky stays silent, clutching his alarm clock close to his chest, it's the only thing he has from home, a comfort. He never gets to know what happened when Ava was seven because he falls asleep.

Keziah

Drip. Drip, drip, drip. Drip. The only communication in the whitewashed house is a frustrated sound from the hot water tap. The rhythm matches the pounding thud of my heartbeat. An obedient Cath Kidston case sits at my feet, bulging at the seams. I'm waiting for Claus. Ameena is waiting for me.

Rage woke me in the middle of the night. How dare he humiliate me like this? I imagined him lying in his hotel room, missing me, knowing the next day he'd be home, his stupid, naïve, passive bride waiting to suck up his lies without question. I imagined him next to me, breathing. In through his nose, chest rising, out through his mouth, chest falling. His bare chest, freshly waxed under pristine sheets, freshly ironed. The anger in me was terrifying, months of suppressed bubbling fear. If he had been next to me, I was sufficiently enraged to have woken him, screamed in his face and punched his beautiful blue eyes until they turned black.

So, at 2 am, when everyone else on this prestigious estate was asleep, I peeled my hefty frame from sweat drenched sheets. Then I frantically gathered every piece of me, from this soulless hole and stuffed it in my holiday luggage.

Sitting bolt upright at the kitchen table, I'm poised for attack. My back is throbbing. I've got so big even my maternity jeans are tight. I wish I could blame it on the baby but the amount of Easter eggs I have scoffed is obscene, I seem unable to stop eating for comfort. Even the cheap eggs without filling got shoved down without conscious thought. Yet still I feel as empty as those hollow eggs. If I can't move or sleep at under six months pregnant, I have no idea how I'm going to work for another two.

I've thought endlessly about other ways to play this but this is the only way. If I leave without one last try, I'll regret it as time moves forward. If I say nothing, I'll make a resentful mother. So, with Ameena's help, I devised this plan. Claus doesn't know it, but he has exactly thirty minutes from the second the door opens. I crave the happy ending for me, my baby and my parents, but I can't live with a man I don't trust.

I know what he'll do. He'll come in with his peaceful face, time away will have made his heart grow fonder, he'll be attentive, his best self. I can't read, watch a screen or listen to music. I have to keep my focus on the plan or he'll win me over and before I know it he'll be rehanging my clothes in the wardrobe.

When he walks in, I won't give him a minute to gather his defence. I'll fire questions at him before he can rush upstairs to unlock his private room and secure his very important brown case with its confidential combination lock. I'll have the upper hand before he can take off his very important suit, and shower off the very important details he's digested whilst working away.

Since he's been away, since finding out I'm the second one, I've rediscovered Keziah. I didn't even know she was lost. She disappeared when Esther died and never returned. When Claus walks in, he'll be speaking to the voice of an undefeated bike champ. Keziah is back, and she's a fighter. I'm Keziah, not Claus's wife or Esther's legacy, not even my parent's daughter.

I know how the next hour will play out. His inability to be consistent for more than a few weeks is the problem. I can't live with a man I don't know, who can't openly weep with me, who can't tell me his secrets, even if I don't like them. I want be optimistic but I know in my heart he'll miss his chance. My assertive demeanour will either make him close down and scuttle off or he'll become the professional psychologist, give me some therapeutic wisdom and scuttle off. Sadly, what he doesn't know is whilst he's creeping about upstairs I'll go, I'll go for good. Ameena is waiting in her car a mile away for the thumbs-up.

The internal buzzer pings me back to the present. The gates close and I note the time. He now has twenty-nine minutes so if he has an urgent call to finish, he's blown it already.

Today, he's quick. The car door slams and in he strides. A sharp intake of breath makes me feel light-headed. Why does he have to look so good?

In his exquisite blue suit, his case is in one hand and in the other the most beautiful bouquet of flowers. An expert florist has selected two-tone pink and whites to create an enormous floral display.

Claus rushes in, all smiles, but stops a few paces away.

His eyes drop to my case. Which way is he going to turn, pathetic or professional? Before I finish speaking my truth, his eyes will darken, his shoulders will rise and his back will flip around. Before I close my mouth, he'll be up those stairs. If he doesn't look, he doesn't have to see. If he doesn't see, it's not happening.

But then the most extraordinary thing happens. Of all my predictions, this wasn't one of them.

My husband falls to his knees as if he's been struck by God.

'No, no, no,' he sobs. 'Don't leave me, please don't leave me.'

He doesn't wait for a response but instead grabs at my ankles begging me not to leave.

His cries are wails, a wounded animal, someone is killing him from the inside. The noise is awful. I can't bear it. What on earth do I do?

I gently push his head up.

'Stop it, stop it Claus,' I say, almost shouting, disciplining. He rocks back into a begging position but hides his face in his hands. I have never seen someone like this. It's scary, more so than his bully.

Eventually he allows me to pull his hands from his face. His complexion is drained of colour, his eyes are swollen and his face smeared with dirty tears. A broken man, a grieving man. I support him into the other room and onto the settee. Twenty-four hours ago, I was here, weeping on my friend.

Eventually he speaks. 'Please, don't leave me. I'll do anything, anything.'

Watching him, I want to cry with him but I will not let go of my determination to see this through. My phone is continually vibrating. I know it's Ameena. Shall I come, what's happened, have you done it yet? Have you told him?

Side by side, easier than face to face, I wait whilst Claus brushes his trousers and loosens his tie. Without looking at me, he blurts out, 'Whatever you've found out, I'll explain. It's not what you think, just don't leave.'

Talking to my drink, I say, 'Claus you were married before.'

'Yes,' he says, finally looking up, meeting my eyes. I hold his gaze and speak.

'I want to know who you are and why you've lied for so long.'

I'm shocked by how calm I sound. In my head I'm reprimanding Liam, I simply want an explanation. He won't be allowed out to play until I get what I want. And he knows it.

Claus doesn't reach out. His hands remain in his lap, his head stays down. He retrieves a neatly folded handkerchief from his bag and frantically dabs at his eyes.

'I'm so sorry, I've wanted to tell you all along. When you told me about Esther, on our very first date, I felt so sad for you because I know what it feels like to suffer loss. So much of your story resonated with my own. We are two people who've been hurt through no fault of our own. But then you told me what happened, your part in her death, your unresolved guilt and shame and it was about you. It was your story, not mine. I felt it would be inappropriate, selfish to talk about me, to compare your story to my pain.'

I open my mouth ready to jump in, unwilling to let his raw honesty touch me.

'So, you thought you'd stay quiet, not seek an opportunity on our fifth or sixth date when we were speaking of something else, to mention you had been married. You thought it was OK to propose but yet still not say? To marry me and not mention that lawful impediment?'

'I'm not still married, there's nothing unlawful about our marriage,' Claus interrupts my rapid fire, sitting up, brushing the dust off his trousers.

'Maybe I'm not the second or third. How do I know what's true and what isn't? What other wardrobe skeletons are ready to crash out and knock me over next time you're away?'

'I'm sorry. It wasn't my intention. Everything is true. I haven't lied.' His tone is flat, hopeless. My good intentions are wavering.

'I think omitting to tell me you had a wife is lying.'

'Yes, I believe you're right,' Claus answers.

I don't respond. He continues.

'I planned to tell you on the second date but we had such fun. Then the third and the fourth came. I shouldn't have been having dates at all. My intention was to stay single. It really was. I hadn't had a single date since Jen and didn't want one. But then you came. I was your knight, a hero. I wanted to be that person. I wanted to make it all better, be your happy ending, for you, your parents. I wanted to make up, but most of all for the first time, I was in love and it was terrifying.'

I'm silent for a while, before saying, 'All the trust I had – all the trust we've regained since last year – has gone.'

'I have no excuse, I'm so sorry. By the time we'd been seeing each other for a few months, you kept saying how right we were together, how my anchoring stabilised you, how a man like me is what you need. I was too scared to say. I thought you would leave if you found out I wasn't as perfect as you hoped, that I wasn't the consummate professional you needed.'

'Tell me about Jen? Who was she? How can I be the only woman you've fallen for? Didn't you love *her*?' I demand.

My phone continues to bleep, text after text from Ameena. Sometimes she's as relentless as Claus. Claus doesn't ask who is messaging me but waits patiently for me to finish checking the screen. I switch off my phone and refocus.

'No, I didn't. It was a terrible mistake. She was years older than me but desperate for children. I wanted that package. I had a big house, plenty of money but I was lonely. I had the consultant job and wanted the family photo on my desk.'

I stay quiet

'She was training to be a nurse, she seemed straightforward, optimistic, if a little unoriginal — dull perhaps. She made me feel strong, adequate. I confused that with love.'

He pauses.

'Go on,' I say, back in teacher mode.

Claus takes a breath, speaks very quietly, emphasising his words. I lean in to hear. 'Very quickly it went sour. I realised almost immediately I'd made a mistake. She became very dependent, troubled. She spent more time in bed, was self-harming, yelling at the neighbours. I tried to get help but she wouldn't accept it. It feels terrible to say but she became a terrible burden.' He pauses, swallows. 'And then she died.'

'But if you didn't love her, why were you so gutted? You took months off work.' I know I sound harsh, but I need answers.

'If I'm honest, it was grief for me, not for her, but grief for the man I imagined myself to be. What psychologist lets his wife get into that state. I'd failed.'

As if Claus can read my thoughts, he says, 'I'll make it up, I promise.'

His gaze shifts to my belly. My hand instinctively goes to little bean, who is growing every day, growing towards an entry into this mess. Is being born to a father who is a liar better than living with a single parent in a cramped flat; a mother who is always stressed and exhausted?

'Can I?' Claus asks. His voice is gentle, his eyes are clear. I can see him. He isn't the liar, the monster I've told myself he is; told Ameena he is.

I nod. He moves closer. His breath is still rapid. He puts his hand over mine so together we touch this tiny person inside of me, our baby.

As he looks up, our eyes meet and I realise we can work this out. I don't have to compromise my own identity just because I'm a wife and mother. We've got plenty of money, after the baby when I'm working part time I can get back on my bike. Claus isn't stopping me, I am.

‘Let’s see your parents first thing, tell them the good news, their dreams have come true, their first grandbaby is coming. I bet even your dad will understand if we take the scan picture, show him the evidence.’

Claus slips his hand into mine and pulls me gently upstairs, helps me into my pyjamas and pulls up the duvet. Then, he returns with my case and a mug of hot chocolate. He’s unable to suppress a grin as he leans forward to pop a kiss on my belly.

I switch my phone back on. Five missed calls and a text bleep from Ameena. ‘You coming or what?’

I text back, ‘All fine, you can go to bed.’ I add a smiley face emoji and tell myself that I got what I wanted. I got the answers I needed, the happy ending.

When I look up, Claus is carefully unfolding each item from my suitcase and rehanging my clothes in colour order.

He’s about to hang the last skirt but I can’t let it drop, not quite yet, not having got so far. I catch him off guard, distracted.

‘So how did Jen die?’ I flush knowing the answer.

Without turning, he replies.

‘She took her own life.’

17

New Directions

Nicky

Nicky elbows Nancy and Ava out of his head as the car approaches Castlegate. He tries to forget about breakfast parties, and shabby dressing gowns warmed on the radiator. He tries really hard to forget Ava's stupid chatting and the smell of bacon from downstairs. But however hard he shakes his head, those happy memories boomerang back.

His overflowing bag is in the boot. Ava sat on the top whilst Nancy tugged at the zip. In the end they left it open. He has a football water bottle for school, like the other boys, and three spare pairs of pyjamas. Nancy says he must take off his socks at night or he'll get Athlete's foot. She has packed food to keep in his wardrobe, for emergencies. Nicky didn't ask what she meant by non-perishables.

Mum stands outside their gate in the velvet dress his dad likes.

'Hey, my big boy, come here, I've missed you sooooo much.' Mum opens her arms and waits. She's even wearing shoes.

He needs to step up. Sometimes his mum says, 'Not everything is about you, Nicky.' But today he's very tired.

Unfortunately, Ava's teddy topples out when Dad throws the bag over his shoulder. Nicky rushes to brush the dust of its cheek. It's Ava's favourite, only a lend, to keep him company at night when he's afraid; she kept his shark T-shirt, the one with the big hole near the neck.

'Bit old for that, don't you think?' his mum says to his dad.

Nicky remembers he's the man here. Whilst she and his dad stand, looking at each other, he opens the boot and hides the bear under a tartan blanket. He hopes Ava doesn't find out.

Nicky has spent so long wanting this, wanting his dad to see his mum in her velvet dress, with her lipstick on and smelling of flowers. Wanting dad to look into his mum's eyes and fall back in love. But, now he wants to squash dad behind the steering wheel and send him back to Nancy so they can squabble over the soundtrack whilst cooking lasagne.

When dad speeds too fast out of their close, Nicky tries not to cry. Now, it's him who doesn't want to be here, treading on eggshells and clearing up all the time.

The house is different. Everything is clean like it used to be. The table is clear of magazines and clothes. The floor tiles are white with no stains. The blinds are all raised. It's just like when dad lived here and grandma and Poppa drank tea at the table and stayed for lemon sponge.

The range oven is on and there is food cooking. The light is fixed. Nicky can see a cake tin in the fan oven and a big white dish on the top shelf of the other. It smells delicious.

Nicky can't quite believe it. He grins at his mum and she smiles back.

'What you smiling about?' she asks.

Before he can think of a good answer, she jumps in.

‘Macaroni cheese with bacon and chocolate brownies alright for you?’

‘Yes, please!’ Nicky shrieks as he runs down the endless hall dragging his bag behind him. Perhaps it will be OK this time.

His room is similarly transformed. His bed is made and smells of washing and his pyjamas are ironed and in a pile on his pillow. He scrabbles in the bottom of his bag to dig out his non-perishables; Crisps, chocolate biscuits and ten packs of super noodles. He didn’t want to hurt Nancy’s feelings but he doesn’t like the chicken flavour. All the food goes in a shoe box in his wardrobe. Holding the door open, he tries not to think about hiding or being frightened. He locks it with the tiny key and buries it under his mattress with the spare door keys.

At supper, they have napkins rolled inside silver rings. Grandma left those with lots of posh cutlery with flowers on the handles. His mum drinks one glass of wine, which is OK. He has blackcurrant in a wine goblet so they’re both the same.

‘Cheers,’ his mum says as they clink their glasses. ‘Sorry, I got ill,’ she whispers, kissing his ear.

‘No problem,’ Nicky assures her.

‘It’s going to be good again,’ she promises.

After supper, he puts on *The Lion King* as he knows that makes her happy. When the film ends, his mum jumps up and folds up the blanket. Then she sends him off towards the hall, her firm hands on his shoulders, steering his body like a car.

He knows she is exhausted in the evenings.

‘Right, I’ll tell you what . . .’ she says with a smile so big he can see her fillings.

Nicky stands in front of her, expectant.

‘Special treat, first night back, you get to use my ensuite.’

Nicky can’t believe it. He loves that. His parents’ bathroom has a jacuzzi that blows bubbles and a bidet to squirt water up your bum. At Christmas they all squeeze into the round bath. Nicky chooses a bath bomb and they scoff mince pies, not caring about crumbs in the water.

Tonight, he stays in the bubbles until his fingers are wrinkled. Whilst perching on the bath edge, his fluffiest towel tucked up to his chin, Nicky’s world comes to a dramatic stop.

Hidden right behind the pipes of the toilet he spots something that tightens his chest so he can hardly breathe. He stares at a tiny item. It’s so repellent that his skinny legs start to violently shake. He swallows hard, hoping he won’t be sick.

His newly washed towel falls off as he scrambles to the floor and lies face down on the stone tiles. The cold goes unnoticed. For a moment he lies still, paralysed with fear, not wanting to lift his head. If it’s true, from this angle he’ll be able to see it clearly. Please, please don’t let it be true, please, please let it be a lost screw.

He counts fast, out loud whilst scrunching his eyes so tight they produce tears. He doesn’t want to look. He turns his head to one side, looking away, an ear to the ground, listening to the purr of the cold floor. He can’t work out why the tiles aren’t warm like they should be.

He opens his eyes, wanting to be brave but makes patterns from the lines on the walls. Patterns must include a three. Three repeats, one, two, three and it will be gone. Threes make the wrong things right. It worked at the hospital, it worked to get the police, it worked to make the bullies stop.

Thirty times he repeats his threes, best be sure. Better to be safe than sorry, Grandma says. Then he slowly twists his head and stretches out his hand, palm flat, feeling around to catch the offending item. His fingers find it and then he knows for sure.

He closes his hand into a fist whilst he builds up the courage to take a proper look. Keeping his eyes closed, he sits up. Leaning against the bath, the smell of bubbles still obvious, he watches his chest go fast, in and out.

He opens his fist; his fingers are pickled pink from the bath and he sees what he doesn't want to see. He sees a rough metal skull and pushes his finger into the sharp pin. A bright red drip escapes onto the tile.

Pictures flash in his head, a jumble of images on fast forward, pictures he hates. Pictures he's been trying to lose. He sees a hand with dirty nails, two thumbs squeezing around his mum's throat. From behind a closed door, an ugly gorilla replays in his mind. Above that thick neck, below disgusting greasy hair is an ear. The pale flappy bit at the bottom glistens with silver.

Clutching the sharp object, he runs from her bathroom to the respite of his room. He ignores the music, the drunken laughter and the crash as he slams his bedroom door so hard the handle wobbles. It's dark and he can't find his wardrobe key so he climbs onto his windowsill instead. He used to hide here when his mum came screeching. He yanks the curtains together so they hide him but he can't close the window as the clunk will give him away. He shivers and pricks his thumb over and over with the pin of the silver earring.

He is praying Nancy won't mind about the blood on his new pyjamas when a door outside makes a crash. Huddled into a small ball, he shivers. The footsteps are getting closer. They are marching towards his window. Heavy footsteps getting closer and closer to his open window. He's not stupid, he's ten now, he knows that if Paul comes in his bedroom from the inside, he's well hidden behind the curtains. From the outside, with the window open and no curtains to cover, he knows his small naked body will be seen and captured however tight he curls. A voice. A man's rough voice is calling. He's been spotted and he knows what's coming.

The window is tugged wider from the garden. A deep voice calls his name. A tall outline towers so close the man's breathing blows on Nicky's neck. An arm reaches in and grabs from behind. Before he can react, his body is stolen from the room, his legs scrape the windowsill and the earring escapes to the floor. Nicky is wrenched out towards the patio; his feet follow in a deformed backwards summersault.

There's a crash in the darkness, the man falls backwards, the limp body of a child has nowhere to go. Silence.

Keziah

Claus has wangled an extra scan and a day off work as my blood pressure is sky high. Fortunately, we're winding down for the May half term so it's easier to leave the TA in charge for a few hours. She's going to do an extra P.E session as I can't do any physical activities now.

This morning, Claus was whistling before he reached the shower. He left the door open and was jigging about to songs whilst he shaved and moisturised. He's so excited about the baby.

It's been a couple of weeks since Claus told me about Jen. I've not mentioned her since. Once he told me it was suicide I couldn't think how to follow it up. I don't know much about mental illness, that's his thing. I don't want to upset him and put him in a bad mood, but I would like to ask more. Why does the internet say it was a road accident, why were they on holiday if she was so ill?

For a while I thought I'd reconnected with some of my old values: courage, curiosity and assertiveness. Maybe it's the hormones but right now I keep changing my mind. One minute, I think I'm ready to challenge his account of her death. Leave it, Keziah, my mum would say, let sleeping dogs lie. Other times, with a rapidly growing bump, I just can't be bothered to deal with anything I can easily avoid. He has history. So what? I have history and I'm ten years younger. It was stupid to get Ameena involved, though, she won't let it drop.

'So that's it, is it?' she demanded at school yesterday.

Even when I ignore her she rants on. 'I mean, his story and the press don't quite add up, do they? I mean, was it an accident or did she kill herself? Surely there'd be follow-up articles? What questions did they ask him about it? You need to ask him. I've looked and can't find a thing. Keziah, you can't just push it out of your mind, lock it away, not think about it.'

So now I avoid her.

Ameena is wrong. So wrong. I lock things away, because that's how I survive. In my brain, I have a huge room of metal compartments. Hundreds of unopened safe boxes. Boxes to stash my unwanted memories, one tiny key for each box. A room with thick metal walls guarded by well-trained staff. Each box has something I don't want to hear, or see, or believe. Thankfully, all the keys are missing.

Several boxes contain Esther, the accident, my guilt, what I haven't told anyone. Another box contains grandma's dying weeks and her funeral. There's the box of dad; his diminishing self, grief for the daddy I'm losing. There's a whole row for my marriage; the wedding night, the bizarre behaviour, night calls, midnight walks and his room with a locked door.

Two boxes now sit on the highest row, two kept out of reach, double locked; these ones can only be reached with help from security. One contains Jen and her death The last one is hidden in the far corner of that high shelf. That box holds a child dying on a main road. Obviously the child I've imagined is a perfect child, with golden hair, long and mermaid-like but smeared with sticky blood, her legs entangled with Jen's whilst Claus stands by, a passive observer.

'Kez!'

'Oh gosh, what?'

Claus has parked the car. His face is close to mine and he looks concerned, anxious.

‘We’re here, you OK? I called your name but you didn’t answer, for a horrid moment I thought you’d passed out.’

Whilst Claus gets my bag out of the boot, I ask myself, am I OK? No, probably not. I’m terrified my belly will be empty or worse. Maybe, as a punishment for my deceit and all the stress, this baby will be ill. I dreamt I had an emergency caesarean and when they lifted the baby above the screen, it was slimy and green. My sleep ended before I found out whether it was a frog or an alien.

For the last couple of weeks, I’ve woken in the middle of the night, panic stampeding over me so I can’t breathe or think.

In the chilly waiting room with its metal chairs and hushed whispering, Claus slips his arm across the back of my shoulders. He pulls me closer and attempts to turn my cheek to him. At least he agreed to return to the NHS.

‘It will be fine,’ he says.

It will be fine. it will be fine. it will be fine. I’ve taken his mantra for myself. I repeat it over and over when I lie awake. I repeat it when the little boy with the funny ears and awkward smile begs me for a hug. I repeat it when I ignore Ameena’s invitation to a girls’ night out or when Claus takes what he calls a break night in his room.

A young woman in a pink uniform skips over, a big grin on her face. The look of optimism, expectation, a fun weekend in sight. ‘Follow me,’ she says. Her pace is fast, hands in front pockets. I’m sure she can’t be eighteen.

‘This is my first third trimester scan, I can’t wait,’ she admits just before we go into a darkened room.

‘Mine too,’ I quip. *I can wait.* A man in turquoise slacks and a T- shirt sits on the other side of a couch looking less excited than his able assistant. ‘Hello Mr and Mrs –’ he glances at his clip board '– Doerkson. I'm Dan, one of the radiographers.' He leans over to shake my hand. Claus strides over to the professional side and offers a firm handshake.

'Please have a seat.' Dan gestures to a wheeled stool on the customer side of the bed. Claus bends his legs to perch but he's far too tall. When Dan turns his back to flick through my file, Claus catches my eye and smiles.

'If you'd like to jump up on the couch, Mrs Doerkson, I'll check your baby.'

Dan rolls up my T-shirt; I watch Clause flinch, look away. Surely, he won't accuse me of flirting with a medic. The ice-cold gel prompts a sharp intake of breath. I stare expectantly at the computer screen, desperately hoping my baby is okay.

Claus is leaning in, peering into the screen, the most fascinating film he's ever switched on. He squeezes my hand. 'Look sweetheart, please look.'

Dan has started a running commentary. 'Here is the heart beating, two legs, two arms. So, remind me, do you know the gender?'

'No,' I say. 'At the last scan our baby was being very coy, kept his or her legs crossed the whole time.'

Dan laughs. 'Often the little blighters don't cooperate but your baby is very happy to reveal today so would you like to know now?'

'Yes,' we say like we've synchronised our response.

'Well,' Dan says.

I look at Claus, tears in his eyes as he waits for the verdict.

'Look, she's waving. Hello mummy and daddy, your little girl is saying,' Dan says in a helium-fuelled voice. I think he's impersonating a female but it sounds more like something from a Halloween movie.

Twenty minutes later, four scan images tucked in his briefcase, Claus links his arm through mine and chatters like a school boy as we amble along the characterless corridors.

'Your mum is going to love this, and I thought Ameena might enjoy a copy. She needs to start an attachment if she's to be the godmother. Shall we frame it? First picture of our creation?'

Back in the car, with my coat wrapped around me as tightly as my bump will allow, I let slip my plan.

'I'll return to work after October half term,' I say with more confidence than I feel.

Claus stays attentive, the listening face he uses at work.

'I'm not sure I'll thrive if I stay home all day?'

'Don't worry, sweetheart, I've been thinking about that same topic.'

'Have you? That's great, I was worried you'd want me to take longer.'

'Knowing you, you'll enjoy it when you get in the swing. Just think you can watch an inordinate number of box sets, text your friends all day, spend more time with your parents and perhaps even do supper when I'm working late?'

'That'll be great for my maternity leave but I need the structure and purpose of work.'

'I knew that's what you've been worrying about. In fact, I was chatting to Carole last week when I was in for an assessment.'

'My Carole?'

'Well, yes, if you think of your headteacher like that — 'your Carol!'. I did some training for the local heads last week.'

'Did you?'

‘Yes, I’m sure I said. Anyway, I told her about the extra scan and your high blood pressure. She said she went back too soon and was consequently stressed at work and home. I assured her you wouldn’t need to do that, given our finances are so stable.’

I resist the temptation to snap. I hate the idea of being spoken about as a child they’re caring for, planning a joint intervention.

Claus continues in the face of my silence.

‘She said structure and routine were the key.’

As he finishes his sentence he reaches in his back pocket.

‘As soon as she said that I knew the answer. I couldn’t believe I’d never suggested it before. So, when you were in the bath last night, I did this.’

He retrieves his fountain pen from his top pocket and uses it to point, like a teacher with a troubled child.

The paper is divided into three columns. In the first column is times, the next one has a line of description and the final column is blank.

‘I thought showing you this might help you feel less anxious. We can use this before the birth, and tweak it when the baby arrives.’ He uses his pen to show me. The first line reads, ‘8:30 am: Get up, bath or shower.’

He continues with his rationale. ‘You don’t want to stay in bed too long, that won’t do you any good.’ Without waiting for input he continues. ‘9:30 am: Eat breakfast for fuel.’

And so it goes on, to include snacks, relaxation time, admin and calls, social afternoon after nutritious lunch.

‘Then,’ he adds, as if a real treat is coming, like extra play for being a good girl – in my school we call that golden time, it can be earned but also taken away; is that where this is going? – 'how about you take charge of the cleaning?' He looks at my face, and adds, 'And supper two days a week?'

He leans back for a stretch; long arms reach up to the ceiling revealing a tanned and toned stomach to be proud of.

When his limbs return to base, he gives me such a delighted smile, a small boy taking a bow at the end of a star performance. He pushes the paper towards me as if what is being offered is the promotion of my dreams.

'What do you think?' he asks, genuinely interested.

18

Sad Departures

Nicky

The sun is rising but no one has slept in Heathfield House, Castlegate.

Snuggled inside an oversized woollen cardigan, Nicky sits in a high-backed armchair clutching a mug of Horlicks. He feels too sick to eat the toffees on his lap. He can hear Mrs Pinkney looking after her husband in the bathroom.

'You silly old fool, you could've killed yourself *and* the boy.'

'I know.'

Nicky was terrified when he got stolen from his bedroom window but as soon as the arms reached in, he knew the voice and the smell was Mr P. They both fell backwards in slow motion, Nicky was convinced he was going to die, that he'd never get to say goodbye to Ava, Nancy or dad.

But, Mr P's belly was soft and the overgrown grass by the window made a soft landing. Nicky brushed himself off but the older man stayed silent in the weeds. His mouth was gaping open and blood was oozing from his nose. Nicky was certain he had killed his kindly neighbour and that it was punishment for the monstrous thoughts that kept coming. He was about to run when his only friend opened one eye and groaned. Together they waddled around the swimming pool as if competing in a three-legged race. Nicky clambered over the low fence and held out his hand so Mr P could do the same.

Next door, at Nevern house, the patio doors were ajar, which was lucky.

'Shhh,' Mr P said as they pushed the glass panels wide. When Nicky saw Mrs P's horrified face, he thought she was staring at the boy who was shamefully naked. He tried to cover his private parts with his hands but then clocked she was freaking out at the sight of her damaged husband. Her skin went a funny colour and she grabbed the sides of the chair. Her boney feet poked out of a floaty nightie. She looked like a ghost with duck feet but Nicky kept that to himself.

'I'm calling an ambulance,' she said. '*and* the police,' she went on before Mr P could speak.

'Hang on, it's worse than it looks,' Mr P said, holding his hanky to his head; the blood was leaking all over it. Nicky had to look away because he felt sick. He knew the mess was his fault and he could go to prison if Mr P died.

Mrs P came back with a whiskey for her husband and a hot drink for Nicky. He couldn't take his mug as he was using a cushion to cover himself. Mrs P smiled and gave him her cardigan. She said she'd seen it all before. Nicky knew she hadn't seen his naked body before.

Nicky wasn't enjoying the taste of the brown hot drink, but the warmth had calmed him down. He listened to Mr and Mrs P arguing in the other room whilst he flicked through a boring magazine.

'What on earth got into you?' Mrs Pinkney shrieked.

'I just saw red. Yesterday, I saw her. She was all tarted up like a dog's dinner, promising a new leaf! But I told her, I told her if she put that kid in danger again, she'd have me to answer to!'

'Well, that clearly worked.' Nicky hears Mrs P cackle.

'Exactly, and enough is enough. What's wrong with the woman? I watched his car drive in not two hours after Nicky arrived. I mean, who returns to a bloke who has given you two black eyes and threatens your child.'

'And what father leaves his boy with an alcoholic he can't manage?' Mrs P says, before adding, 'but why didn't you just call the police like a normal person?'

'I was going to. The social worker gave me her card at the hospital but it was late. I wouldn't forgive myself . . .'

Nicky strains to listen but the tap is noisy. Nicky wants to go and see, he wants to check Mr P is OK and to say how sorry he is..

'Then I saw him, curled up on the windowsill like a scared rabbit ready to be skinned. Something took over. Before I thought, one leg was over the fence.'

The tap starts again, harder this time. The magazine is full of adverts for old women, hairnets, scooters and even plastic pants. Nicky chucks it on the floor and studies the small holes in his thumb.

As soon as he spotted the earring he knew it was Paul's.

His grandma said you shouldn't wish anyone dead, but Poppa said there are exceptions. He truly hates Paul and wishes him dead. His dad promised him Paul wouldn't come back.

'You OK, pet?' Mrs P says, rubbing the back of Nicky's hand.

He can hear Mr P speaking on the phone.

'Hello, Nancy dear, I'm sorry it's so early. I'm afraid it's bad news.'

Nicky panics when he hears that. What bad news does Nancy need to know. Has Paul killed his mum? Are the police here again? Will he be put in care like the awkward kid in Maple class?

A hard knock on the front door startles him. His mum is screaming.

'Who do you think you are? I'll have you charged with abduction.' Nicky puts his cup down and runs to the noise.

Mr Pinkney stops him, pushing him back so he can't get near the crack in the door, can't see his mum. This happened before. His dad went, now his mum is going.

'Give me back my son, or I'm calling the police,' she shouts.

'Go call them, Lisa,' Mr P says, closing the door in her face.

She doesn't give up, she bangs and shouts. The letterbox flies open. Her lipstick is smudged. She has black lines running down her face. She's a mess, their family is a mess. He can only see her mouth moving. It looks like a clown puppet moving with no hand. Nicky is so ashamed. Ashamed for her, ashamed for him, ashamed for his dad.

Before he can protest, Mr P lifts Nicky and carries him away from the letterbox, caries him, still kicking, into the other room.

But his mum is there. She's gone around the back. Her face is squashed up to the glass. She's waving and talking but he can't hear her. Using his elbows, Nicky shoves aside Mr P to join her at the window, mirror images. Her flat hands on the outside and his on the inside. Nicky watches the sobs that attack her entire body. Helpless he stands frozen, trapped. From this glass cage he is unable to move, unable to save her. She crumbles to her knees, her head in her hands.

Staring at his crumpled mummy on the floor, her pretty dress covered in stains and her face messed up, he remembers the evil wish he made. He wished her gone. He was supposed to keep her safe. He was supposed to be the man.

Keziah

The sky is grey, more like November than early June but thankfully it's warm enough to sit on the doorstep. I was hoping to make it to the end of the school year. I was also hoping Ameena could be on time today of all days. She's been begging to spend time with me, to go out, have a proper catch-up, and I no longer have the energy to fight. I know my plans and I will action them when I see fit in a way that's right for me, us. My compromise is a lift on my last teaching day. If I wait out here, she won't nip to the loo or make comments about Claus's new wine cabinet and make me even later.

I can't believe today ends summer term for me, the start of at least a four-month break, that's how I'm thinking it – a break. No need to describe it as maternity leave, no need to say it's my final day before birth.

This time last year I was yearning to be married, desperate to be labelled as 'wife' not as 'singleton looking for love'. Would I go back if I knew my mum was right, if I knew marriage was hard work, if I knew by now I'd be heavily pregnant and about to leave work?

Hearing the low purr of an engine, I gather up four carrier bags; chocolates for the kids, blu tack remover, and loads of craft stuff my colleagues will need whilst I'm off. I aim the remote to open the gates, but instead of her old banger, a sizeable van pulls into the drive. It's Derrick, Claus's odd job man. Apparently, all the neighbours use him.

The heavy door swings open and he jumps to the ground with an agility I envy. He can't be far off retirement. He puts his hand up in greeting but goes straight to the back of his van, keen to get on.

‘Hello, you’re looking well young lady,’ Derek offers with a cheeky wink when he reappears.

‘Thank you, what are you up to today?’

‘Claus wanted the CCTV and video doorbell installed before you’re home alone. Think he overestimates the crime rate up here,’ he laughs.

‘Oh yes, I remember now,’ I lie.

Before I can ask Derrick exactly where he’s fitting cameras, Ameena arrives. We’re already running late. I’ll put ‘thoughts of CCTV’ into metal box 43 and focus on the day ahead. I want to soak up every last minute and make it one to remember for the kids.

However clean the school hall is, there’s always a musty PE smell in the air; cheesy feet and stale sweat. The orchestra strikes up, prompting a wobble in my bottom lip. I swallow and force my head high to lead my kids to the square mapped out for us. I take my place at the edge on what Liam calls Mrs D’s throne. It’s actually a tired felt chair, only teachers are allowed to sit off the floor.

I keep my beady eyes on the tricky ones as they each collapse quietly into their cross-legged posture at my feet. Even Liam has made progress, at the start he’d get detention every week for misbehaving in assembly.

Three hundred children wait for their open assembly, the once a month opportunity to show off to their parents. Empty chairs at the back are full of eager parents, the ones from our neck of the woods, who do lunch and hair, nothing better to do. That’s not for me. Fortunately, Claus took it extremely well when I screwed his homemaker schedule into a ball and lobbed it in the fire.

At my feet, Liam is craning around to spot his dad. Apparently, he promised he'd be here. I want to say, 'No chance, sunshine,' but I smile as he catches me looking.

'No, Liam,' I say firmly as he shuffles back towards the scruffy haired boy, the one who keeps me awake at night. A bit too quiet, walks instead of running. Mum has nicely cut hair and designer outfits but something isn't right. He often gravitates towards me on playground duty. We've had a few brief chats but he doesn't give much away, seems content to just follow me around. I hated telling him this week was my last. Occasionally, his mum is there to collect him at end of day but mostly he leaves by himself. I've never seen him engaged in physical play, as if he has too much on his mind to show interest in Pokémon cards or football. I'll remind Ameena before I leave, ask her to keep a special eye.

Ameena is the last teacher in, a rabble of children follow her, elbowing each other and messing about. Despite her chaotic style, she would be picked from a line-up as the senior teacher. She clip-clops her kids into the red square with shoes I couldn't manage on an evening out. Elegantly she folds the skirt of her suit to sit down; her neat figure fits perfectly on her throne unlike my elephant backside hanging off the sides.

I briefly close my eyes to enjoy the low-level noise of impatient whispers and the recorders warming up. There is a burst of giggles from the popular girl group. No doubt it'll be the same group dating all the boys in senior school. I can already see Emily Underwood as Prom queen.

Carole Marston stands up to create an instant hush. I wonder if that will ever be me.

The orchestra plays 'All Things Bright and Beautiful'. Mr Smart, the music teacher, plays his clarinet on the front row; an overgrown pupil on a seat too small.

I catch Ameena's eye and we both suppress a snigger. Gosh I'll miss this place.

The kids applaud as the final writing award is announced. But after twenty-five prizes, the claps are weak and fizzle out before the winner reaches the stage.

'And finally, we have a sad thing to announce, 'Mrs M says, looking directly at me. Ameena makes a small imperceptible nod in my direction.

'I'm very sorry to say Mrs Doerkson is leaving and won't be back next half term. She's going to have a baby.'

Children turn to stare at my stomach, some are wondering how it got there, others fearing how it'll get out.

'We'll miss her but know she'll make a great mum to her own little girl.'

I spot Mrs Turner holding a bouquet and wrapped presents in a bag decorated with cartoon storks.

'So, Mrs Doerkson would you like to join me on stage'

No, no, I really wouldn't. I stand as the Head told me and make my way on stage to meet the two chosen children, bringing to mind naughty kids, late-night lesson planning and staff meetings so I don't cry in public.

'Thank you so much,' I gush to the children. Billy is more interested in his elevated view. I have to wrench the flowers out of his distracted grip.

On the dot of three the bell rings.

Usually I relish the end of day – by now I've had enough — seven hours on my feet is plenty – but today I didn't want that bell to sound.

A muddle of chubby hands push to get their coats. They have lots to take, sports kit to wash, craft projects to hang and lost property to reclaim. Some parents gather by the classroom door, some look happier than others. Will I enjoy time with my children or be desperate to get the kids out of the house? My mum never made us feel a nuisance.

'Bye, Miss!' Emily and her friends rush off without a backward glance. Emily's mum whispers something to her daughter. She comes running back and hugs my legs, her curly hair ruffling against the bottom of my belly. I wave to her mum as they walk off, hand in hand, mummy and daughter. I wonder what my girl will be like. I allow myself a last look at everything I love; the crazy artwork on the walls, the end of day mess, the lost coat hanging unclaimed and an untidy pile of Lego discarded as soon as the bell sounded.

As I walk through the playground I let the tears roll down my cheeks as if I'm one of the children. Before I can wipe them away, a grubby hand pushes a tissue into mine.

Embarrassed I look down; it's him, my favourite fella. I grab his hand for a reassuring squeeze, unsure who is reassuring who.

Together we walk out into a noisy sea of adults and kids. As I wave off most of my class with a raised hand, he clings tighter to my other, the warmth of his body infusing my leg and thigh.

The playground is almost empty but no one has arrived to collect him. I know what I need to do, what I always do. I need to peel his hand from mine, and give him a gentle push. Off you go, sunshine, back home, my shift is done.

But instead, I grasp his shoulder and pull him closer. He looks up at me, his eyebrows squeeze more closely together, wide eyes search mine.

I'm unsure if he's puzzled, or glad. He makes no attempt to move away. I don't want him to go and by the way he flings both arms above my bump, he feels much the same.

Without warning, he starts to cry. Heart wrenching body jerks move him against me as he sobs and sobs. Huge gasping noises escape as he forces his face into the side of my body. My arms tighten around him and tears fall down my face. This isn't the professional, senior teacher impression I wanted to leave but most people have gone and I no longer care.

This frail boy's tears show no sign of drying up. Relentless tears cascade down my cheeks, collecting in random dark blobs on my blouse.

'I know, I know, Simon, it's alright,' I tell him, over and over. 'I know.'

National Hospital of Neurology

Nine-month Review

NHS number: 485 777 3496 Gender: *female*

Current diagnosis:

- Conscious
- Tetraplegic

Injuries sustained:

- Severe and complex neurological and physical injuries
- Broken vertebrae in lower spine – no movement from mid chest down
- Skull Fracture above right ear and occipital region

Progress to date:

- Patient increasingly aware and frustrated
- Frequent fits of physical aggression

Family situation:

Family intelligent and supportive, mother continues to visit daily and would like daughter to go home. I've advised this would be unwise given high care needs

Frequent male visitor but not a relative – make sure visitors book is used please

Plan:

- Sedated at night
- Putney hospital no longer appropriate
- Referred to social worker to seek long term residential placement
- Social worker – Annaliese Edgington

Signed:

Dr.A. Lutte-Elliott

CONSULTANT IN NEUROREHABILITATION

19

Hushed Tones

Nicky

Mr P drove Nicky back to Nancy's. He arrived too late for supper so she cooked him pizza from the freezer whilst his dad and Ava finished off their moussaka. Ava gave him the end of her garlic baguette and laughed as oil dripped down his chin. Nancy told her not to be silly but Ava stuck her tongue out, behind her mum's back. Nicky thought Ava was fun but also extremely naughty and irresponsible.

'Right, you two terrors, up those stairs,' Nancy laughed, whipping them with her tea towel.

Ava raced to the top. Out of breath she turned around to heave Nicky up the last few steps. But Nicky was still at the bottom.

Ava waited patiently. Nicky had to say hello to each photo on the wall as he climbed the stairs. His rituals could not be broken. He knew other people don't realise it's him who keeps them safe.

Nearly at the summit, Nicky spots a wedding photograph he hasn't seen before. It's much higher than the others. Nancy is wearing a short white dress which surprises Nicky as he thought wedding ones had to be long.

‘Is that your dad?’ Nicky puts his finger over the man’s face.

‘Yeah.’

‘Where is he?’ Nicky asks, wishing Ava would stand still when she’s near stairs.

‘Most of the time I dunno.’

‘Did he leave?’

‘Yeah, when I was five.’

‘What did you do to make him leave?’

‘I dunno.’

‘Does he come to this house?’

‘No, he’s not allowed.’

‘Why?’

‘Because he is volatile.’ Ava articulates the last word very slowly as if she isn’t sure she’s saying it right

‘What does that mean?’ Nicky asks, grasping her hand for the last step.

‘I dunno.’

Ava gives him a quick peck on the cheek when he finally arrives on the landing.

Four skinny legs lean against the sink to brush teeth and wash faces. Before they get out of the bathroom Nicky hears Nancy and dad coming up.

‘Well done,’ Nancy says when she sees they’re done. Nancy says ‘well done’ all the time. She says it if he reads a sentence, if he puts his plate in the sink, even if he doesn’t wash it up. She says it if he makes himself a drink. If he makes Ava one too, she makes such a fuss, anyone would think he wasn’t the man in his other house.

Nancy bends down to give Nicky a hug, then straightens up to do the same for Ava because she's almost as tall as her mum. Then Nancy moves back as it's his dad's turn.

Nicky's dad pats his son on the shoulder and scruffles his hair like he always does. Nicky waits with his hands behind his back to watch his dad do the same for Ava.

But Ava doesn't wait for her pat. She takes a few steps back so she has a run up, then she dashes forward, throws her arms around his neck and piggy backs onto his front. His dad doesn't stop her, he puts his hands around her waist and lets Ava cuddle into his beard. Nicky is truly repulsed. He thinks he's going to be sick.

'Night night, daddy,' she giggles as she snuggles into *his* dad's body.

Nicky has never known feelings this big. A howling rage overtakes his small frame; he knows the monster is bursting out and that he's actually going to kill her. His body moves without him. He knows he can't stop. He knows he's out of control as he punches. He punches with clenched fists on every part of her body. His dad spins around holding onto Ava with one hand and pushing Nicky away, holding him far from his body to stop him hurting his little girl, the girl he has always wanted.

'Nicky, oh Nicky, no, stop.' Nancy pulls him but Nicky turns on her, he grabs her hair and yanks it, so her head jerks downwards. She lets go. Nicky returns to his dad who has pushed Ava in their bedroom and is keeping guard outside the door. His arms are folded like a bodyguard. Nicky flies at him, energised by further frustration. He kicks him hard in the shin. Then he prepares to give a hard punch in his dad's soft gut just like Paul gave him the second time he wet his pants. Ava opens the bedroom door. She's covering her eyes and crying. Nancy is crying and his dad is crying.

Exhausted and defeated, Nicky leans against the wall; his body slides down to the floor where he sits with his head between his legs, his arms shielding his face. He hates himself so much, he wishes he could die.

Nicky peeps out through a small gap in his hands and looks up. He sees Nancy give dad a gentle push on his arm. 'Go,' she says, 'I'll deal with this.'

He knows he deserves what's coming.

Maybe she'll call the police. Maybe she'll push him down the stairs or let Ava kick and punch whilst she holds him still.

'That'll teach you,' Paul used to shout.

Nicky holds his breath. Nancy is talking to Ava in the bedroom but he can't hear what they are saying. He never wants to look at Ava again. Already he knows he doesn't hate her. He wishes he did.

Then Nancy comes back to the hall. She closes Ava's bedroom door and turns off the light.

Then she sits next to Nicky so close he can smell the garlic on her hands. She puts her arm around him and draws him to her chest. Then she wraps both arms around him and holds him while he rocks and sobs.

'There, there sweetie,' she says. 'I'm so sorry you're hurting. Ava shouldn't have done that. He's your daddy, only your daddy.'

He can't understand why Nancy isn't cross, why she isn't hurting him.

When he finally closes his eyes, she gives him a gentle poke and helps him into his bunk.

'Night then.' Nancy closes the bedroom door very slowly. Nicky waits. There is a lot left to do, he has more counting, and patterns to walk than usual after what he did. Then he needs to scrub his hands until the badness goes. But before he stands, Ava's legs climb down.

'Nicky,' she whispers.

He doesn't want to look at her. Her lashes are long. Nicky hopes men won't hurt her when she's older.

'Sorry,' he says, speaking to his toes.

'It's OK, mum said you were sad.'

'I'm not.'

'OK. But, anyway, he's not my dad. I was just joking.'

Then Ava tugs his arm and takes him to the door. She giggles and puts her finger on her lips. She whispers in his ear, it tickles.

'I'll show you how to listen.'

She keeps his hand as they slowly descend the stairs, one quiet step at a time. When they get four steps from the bottom, Ava sits and pulls Nicky next to her. She shuffles her bottom closer until he can feel her breathing.

'Don't be so tough on him,' Nancy says

'He deserves to be punished, it was outrageous. I'm so ashamed.'

'Think about it. He's jealous. Think about how grumpy you were when I insisted my wedding photo went up for Ava.'

Nicky knows they're talking about him. He knows his dad is ashamed to be the dad of a monster and not a beautiful girl.

'He's so confused,' Nancy says. 'What else do you need to happen before you take responsibility? You need to go back to the social worker and tell her you've changed your mind. Tell her we want residential custody.'

'We can't, his mum needs him,' his dad says.

Nancy's voice is getting louder. Nicky wonders if she's standing up.

'He needs parenting, he is not the adult, you are.'

'I can only do my best.'

'Well, that's not good enough. If you won't step up, I'll apply and you can go,' she shouts.

At that, there's movement, a door slams. Ava yanks him so hard he thinks his arm might come off. They dive in to their room and collapse on Nicky's bed laughing until their sides hurt.

Keziah

On our third date, Claus swung open the door to his mansion with immense pride. This spiral staircase took my breath away. The light oak matches the wooden floor and the twisty construction transports you smoothly to the second floor. 'Creative but functional,' Claus laughed.

But today, gripping the polished banister and taking tentative steps, this staircase is an intimidating climbing wall. My loaded rucksack doesn't help, especially with such a cumbersome body. My heart is racing. How on earth did I become so unfit and, more importantly, how on earth am I going to kill eight hours with no purpose?

Reaching the summit, I gasp for air and plonk down my heavy bag, before glancing down the stairs. For one dark moment I imagine Claus returning after my first maternity day to find a broken heap at the bottom of his arty masterpiece. I shiver at the thought.

Claus was shuffling about this morning before he left for work. The cupboards were opening and closing at speed as he sourced nutritional snacks for my lunch. He just can't help himself. When he finally reached the front door, I thought I might've got away with it. But then I heard the jar, and finally the ominous rattle as each coin fell onto the windowsill.

When the sun is out and the lights are on I believe my husband's truth. Whatever others might think, I see the hurt in his eyes after a difficult day or when an uninvited memory flashes back. I know in my heart he's a good man.

Night times are harder. In the darkness when the house is quiet, a small persistent voice whispers in my ear. That voice asks questions, questions I don't want to answer. Questions I should ask but don't. Questions about locked rooms, night walks and work trips.

As my maternity leave creeps closer, the quiet voice became more insistent, more frightening. In the early hours of this morning, that small hesitant voice, the voice that was normally suppressed by routine and structure, lesson plans and parental visits could not be silenced. It was no longer whispering but shouting, bellowing, it was ransacking my mind and wrenching open long-closed boxes. Before daybreak it was screaming questions I could no longer ignore. Terrifying questions to which my daughter deserves answers.

Who is NW?

How did Jen come to her end?

What really happened in Spitfield Road?

Carrying my rucksack across the spacious landing I scurry into the box room. I take a furtive glance behind me and rush to close the curtains.

This room is dark, a musty smell hovers in the air. It's the room that remains neglected, undecorated and cluttered with old fashioned furniture. To me, this the only room in the entire house that feels comforting, cosy, like my family home. When Claus is away I frequently retreat to this room to read or watch biking videos.

Despite what Ameena thinks, I'm not stupid. So just before I left work I cajoled Adam the geeky IT bloke into giving me a tech chat. Since Trackergate,, Claus has known details I haven't told him. Nothing important – one time, he knew about my return-to-work date and another, he seemed to know I was planning a cinema trip. He claimed he heard me mention it to mum on the phone but I hadn't. When I next used my iPad it was on cinema searches. It seemed too much of a coincidence. Adam explained if we share an iCloud account he can see all my searches and know what postcodes I've looked at, everything.

Reaching down the back of this chest of drawers is not easy with a volcanic lump in the way. But that's where I've been keeping the ancient tablet I took from my dad's desk.

I cradle the tablet to my chest like it'll save my life, as I lean against the door and slide to a sitting position. For a few minutes I watch my vast belly move as my breathing rises and falls.

Item by item I empty my leather bag, its colour is fading and the wrinkles reveal decades of use. It was Esther's study bag and not a day goes past when I don't dream of returning it to her.

I take out a thick spiral notebook, my phone, a print-off of the two articles about Jen's death and a map of Hampshire. Right at the bottom of the bag is a photo of me as a teenager. I'm red in the face with a medal hanging around my neck on a multicoloured ribbon. My dad is holding my hand in the air with a beaming smile. It was my first gold medal. The same framed photo sits in mum's sewing room; my old bedroom. I shove the photo back in the zip pocket but hope its presence will reconnect me with that courageous girl. *Whatever you find out, Keziah, you've got this*, I tell myself over and over.

I've hunted for the text book with the old newspaper article but it's gone. The book is not in our room or in the library. I presume he's taken it to work. I've searched the internet but without a date I have no starting place and with the minor details, nothing relevant came up.

In comparison to up-to-date iPad's, this tablet is an old grandma. This connection is slow, the graphics are poor but the password is mine and it'll do just fine. I type in the familiar words Kajagoogoo123.

I start with the British Psychological Society website to check my husband's employment as a psychologist. First I find out he is a psychologist and he completed his first degree in Cambridge; his clinical doctorate was acquired in Birmingham. He then worked briefly in London before taking the Oxford post. There's a nine-month gap after Jen died and then the job here. This all checks with what he's told me. What am I doing? Why can't I trust my husband?

I push those feelings aside, see it as an academic project. When it's done, you'll know once and for all.

I read the accounts of Jennifer's death. There's two on the Internet, and they're exactly the same as the previous twenty times I've read them. There is the one giving details of the accident and a further paragraph recording a coroner's verdict of accidental death.

Whatever combinations of names, dates or key words I type, nothing more is revealed. I turn my attention to the other accident in Spitfield Road, the one that's miraculously disappeared.

I'm certain it was 1988. Using the keywords I search over and over with different combinations but there's nothing, just nothing on the internet. I do the maths: I wasn't even conceived; Claus would've been in school. Two accidents in the same road but decades apart. How is my husband connected? Is this one of his traumatised families? Perhaps he worked with this child's parents, her brother? But it was thirty years ago. Surely people don't harbour trauma for that long and then seek help?

Could such a coincidence happen? He sees a family who are somehow involved in an accident where his wife is killed: was she murdered? If that was the case, it would account for the discrepancy in cause of death. Did he think knowing his first wife died at the hands of a patient might frighten me? Is NW something to do with this, threatening to come for him

– for me? I know he's had at least three calls in as many weeks.

If that's true then maybe I need to be frightened, but at least it would explain his behaviours, the intense need to keep me safe, for privacy, tracking, cameras.

Three hours I've been in here, ruminating, trying to complete a puzzle with only half the pieces. My back aches, I'm starving but I still have nothing concrete. I slam my notebook closed in disgust. However much I think, I can't make sense.

I'll do one more thing then call it quits for today. Google Earth is marvellous. I often google random locations from childhood, places I travelled to compete, holiday destinations, Scarborough, Blackpool, places Esther and I played on the beach, watched Punch and Judy, ate fish and chips.

In the Google Earth search, I type. Spitfield Road, Portsmouth.

Maybe what I'm looking for will become obvious when I spot it.

It's a long road, wide. I can see what looks like a car-cleaning area. Tarmac filled with cars and price tags, some sort of dodgy dealer no doubt. A couple walking, her arm linked through his, a bloke up a ladder, two kids on scooters. There is a line of bars and what looks like a club. The name of the club is possibly 'Chaos', though it's not quite visible. Light up letters that are no longer doing their job. Opposite is a pay-and-display carpark, just two cars parked next to each other. A bus stop.

The middle looks residential. There are several blocks of high-rise flats, ice cream coloured balconies. Further along, bungalows, unremarkable semis. Moving my finger further, I see an ordinary supermarket. Trolleys to the side. Next door a few more shops. At the end of the road is a landmark. A globe in glorious gold. Comparing it with my paper map, it's labelled as a Sikh temple. Apart from the religious building, there is nothing on this road that would mark it out from any other. I zoom in, trying to find an important detail, a eureka moment but everything is mundane, perfectly normal. A big, city road the same as any other.

In a childish temper I kick away all the information. I'm not the teacher anymore. I breathe out, calm down, slow down, don't give yourself a blood pressure crisis. I stretch my legs to relax and mesh my fingers together over my child.

Before the baby answers, my phone vibrates against the desk leg. My body responds as if someone has smashed unannounced though the window.

'Kez, what are you doing?' He doesn't wait for an answer.

Claus is in work mode, impatient. Lots to do. Needs an answer, now. Surely, he can't see me?

'Your mum's at the door. She's been there for five minutes, there's no sign of you? I'm minutes away from an important meeting, see you this evening,' he says. The phone goes dead before I can reply.

I can't help but smile when I catch sight of my mum in my ornate entrance hall. She's a picture in a large floppy hat, clashing rain mac and an umbrella tucked in a Lidl carrier bag. 'What an earth have you got in that bag? Are you moving in?' I laugh.

'I've seen you looking perkier,' she says in reply, eyeing my pyjamas.

Ignoring her, I lead the way to the kettle. She follows, chattering mindlessly about the awful rain when it's June, her friend Betty buying more rubbish, how she had morning sickness with me, what dad has forgotten. Finally, a pause, never a good sign. I wait. A loaded question is coming. It's the voice she used when desperate to interrogate me about a fallout at school. Take a deep breath and launch.

'How come Claus called when I was standing on the step? I didn't tell him I was coming.'

'Oh,' I moderate my voice to sound casual, disinterested, as I pour the milk. 'He has this new gadget, the doorbell goes to his phone, you know what he's like about security.'

'But you're here all the time now?'

I can feel her eyes boring into my back, waiting for an explanation.

'Everyone is getting them and . . . sometimes I miss parcels,' I explain but my sentence runs out of energy and I see her smile sadly as she bustles off to the loo.

She returns holding out her palm. 'Look, find a penny, pick it up and all day long you'll have good luck.'

I snatch the three coins and snap, 'Where have you taken these from?'

Hurt is transparent across her face. 'I found one in the hall and two in the toilet, what on earth is the matter?'

'Nothing,' I mutter, 'just show me exactly where you found them. They need to stay where they were.'

I follow her. In the cloakroom, she places a coin behind the toilet brush and another in the windowsill corner. Patiently, silently, she places each coin back to its same place.

Then, she looks at me. That piercing gaze from childhood. Who took those sweets? Who broke that vase?

But, I can't explain. How do I say, the coins are there to show me where to clean? The coins keep me on track. The coins reassure Claus the house is germ free so, we can enjoy supper, rest together, be a normal couple.

Each day he hides them in different unknown places. Each day I seek them out with a racing exhausted heart, unable to settle until all twenty are back in his jar, to be tipped out and secreted away the following morning. How do I tell that to my mum without making her terrified?

20

The Accident

Nicky

Mrs Hobbs is forgiven for ruining last summer, the last four weeks have been the best summer Nicky has ever had and it's not even the school holidays yet. He tries not to think about his mum. Dad says she's safe, getting help, not to worry.

In the afternoons his dad or Nancy work from home, though mostly Nancy as she's an accountant. Dad is too important to be out of the office too much. In September Nicky will start at Ava's school. She has promised to protect him as she's one of the cool kids and she's far taller.

Today is a big day. This day has been planned for a long time. Their family – Nicky, Nancy, *his* dad and Ava – are going on an adventure. That's what Nancy calls it anyway. Most Saturdays they have a three-person day. Nancy does the chores and Ava and Nicky play at the park or argue over a game of marbles.

Nicky still finds Ava a source of confusion. Sometimes he would give a year's pocket money to marry her and live happily ever after by the sea. She says she'd have to live in a city and hasn't decided if marriage is for her.

'It's not like we've been given good role models, is it?' she says.

But when she touches his dad, he doesn't like his feelings at all. When she sneaks up to tickle him, when she insists on kissing him good night or accidentally calls him daddy, Nicky has frightening ideas. These ideas terrify him and no amount of counting or washing helps.

This morning, the breakfast table at Nancy's reminds Nicky of a special occasion, like when grandma used to come to tea at Louise's house for Kerry's birthday.

There are knives and forks and spoons, all set in a square. On the table mats are three glass jars, a giant one for marmite and strawberry jam and honey for Ava. Toast is always triangles and gets displayed in a metal shelf thing. Nicky prefers it hot from the toaster, then the butter melts. There are four seats, four plates and four cups. In the middle is a giant tea pot like in Alice in Wonderland.

Before Nicky moved here, he'd never had a breakfast party. Each day he and Ava get to take turns choosing who sits where. In this house, everyone wears slippers and dressing gowns until after breakfast and teeth cleaning. Nancy says, 'No one needs clothes smeared with jam and toothpaste.'

It's Ava's job to clear away at breakfast. Nicky does supper. Whilst Ava scrapes the crusts into the bin and empties the milk into the sink, dad rolls out a map across the table. Hampshire is too big so Chichester hangs over the edge.

They are going to plan their Saturday. This is one of their many strange habits. Nancy and Ava love a plan. They plan the route, the food and the time everyone will be back. When the plan is agreed it mustn't change, which Nicky likes.

‘So,’ Nancy says, plopping her bottom onto the chair next to Nicky. He’s sandwiched between two adults which he doesn’t really enjoy. He moves his hands to his lap so he takes up less space. Ava comes up behind and peers over the top. Her hand rests on dad’s neck. She twiddles the curly hairs that grow out of his dressing gown. She hasn’t done her teeth and has beast breath.

‘We’re here and we’re going here,’ Nancy points from home to Gunwharf Quays, a place Ava can’t talk about without jumping up and down. Nicky knows he’ll be disappointed.

‘Woohoo! Dad says excitedly. ‘Can’t wait to get to the top of here!’

He points to a place on the map labelled ‘Spinnaker Tower’.

Nancy unfolds a leaflet so they can see a picture. It’s a tower and it has a souvenir shop and a floor made of glass. Ava has been lots, but Nicky doesn’t fancy it. He stays quiet though as everyone else is excited.

His dad points to a blue area. ‘In there are the big warships; you’ll love it, Nicky. The best one is the Mary Rose, that belonged to Henry the eighth. It’s hundreds of years old.’

‘And after all that,’ Nancy finishes, ‘we’ll get an ice cream and head back home via Spitfield Road.’

She pushes her finger on and on down the long road. ‘Past the beautiful temple where they give out free food on a Friday, past the car washing men, past the dodgy car park . . .’ she says.

Ava giggles. ‘Yeah Nicky, people do kissing in cars there.’

‘Ava!’ his dad shrieks with his mouth wide open.

Nancy laughs. 'She's right, they do.'

'And finally, we'll walk down here and through the alley and hoorah we'll be home.'

Nancy holds her hand above her head to high five Ava and then does the same with Nicky.

Sometimes these people are rather exhausting.

The glass floor was awful. He thought he'd be sick. Nancy held his hand and he held tightly to the rail. Even though his dad promised him a present if he was brave, he couldn't do it. Nicky knows I'm his head that dad would like a son who wasn't a wimp.

Nicky bought three postcards to send. One for Mr P as he sends them to him, one for Bella and one of the tower for his mum. Nicky tries not think about his old life. It gives him a headache.

Walking home, it's not long before Ava is bored, she drops Nancy's hand and dances back to Nicky who is walking a few paces behind everyone. Ava plays hopscotch on her own, he tries not to look. She darts from the hedge on one side of the pavement and then back to the road edge, skipping and laughing. She doesn't care.

Nancy and his dad are ahead with their arms around each other. Every few steps they stop to kiss. Doing that on the street is disgusting in Nicky's opinion.

'Nicky!' Ava shouts from the hedge. He ignores her but she shouts until he lifts his head and looks.

She's leaning against a sign. Behind her is a notice board with rude words sprayed in red paint. Her bottom is against the road name. The white rectangle is on two wooden posts but Nicky can see an S and a T.

‘Come here,’ she says, crooking her finger at him. He gives in and wanders over, his hands stuffed in his front pockets.

She has ice cream on her sparkly T-shirt. A chocolate drip is on the top of her leg. Her hair is in two bunches, one pink scrunchie, one black one. Nicky would prefer it if they matched.

Ava holds her hand up to her mouth and giggles at him over the top. Then she does a revolting thing. She spits in her hand and flicks it on the pavement. Nicky can’t hide his disgust. He looks away.

‘Look, the sign,’ she says, as if that’s a reasonable explanation. He wants to tell tales to Nancy, get her to stop.

Ava moves over and points to the sign. ‘Spitfield Road,’ she says. ‘Spit,’ she repeats, like he can’t read.

Nicky walks away but not in time to miss her wiping her hands on her jeans. He thought it was meant to be boys that were filthy.

Suddenly Ava jumps on him from behind; he doesn’t want her to piggy back him so, he keeps his hands in his pockets until she slips off.

She’s such a pain today.

She wanders nearer the road, pretending she’s drinking a can, pretending she’s drunk. It really isn’t funny.

Nancy and his dad are walking so close together; their hands all tangled together. Dad looks back over his shoulder to check on them. Ava stands to attention and smiles. Dad sees Nicky and winks, or was it at Ava?

Why can’t they see? Why won’t they stop her?

Ava is too close to the road, she’s doing it on purpose, he knows it. His heart is beating fast, his hands are sticky. He hates this feeling.

He watches her. He wants to shout for dad. She's standing with her tippy toes on the edge. He watches her from behind, he's getting closer. The tension inside is building. He knows this feeling.

Her body is thin, if he didn't know her, he'd think she was younger not older. She's not built like the older girls at his school. He inspects his hands to work out if they'd go around her waist. He can see the colours of her stripy heels teetering near the edge.

His eyes are on her back. He can see her shoulders going up and down. He is overwhelmed by a sense he can't express. The adults are oblivious, hidden among others, shopping bags swinging, noise, voices, a siren and then Ava's back to him. The danger, the fear, the hurt, the jealousy.

Ava looks back, their eyes meet. Her bunches follow her head, back to him and then out to the cars.

Cars are rushing past, some so close that sand flies up. Nicky shuts his eyes and pulls her back in his mind. He chants under his breath. *1, close, 2, away, 3, close, 4, away.*

She needs to stay safe. She doesn't know about bad things, monsters or bad men. She laughs when he tries to explain. He can't get the spit out of his mind. Bad, dirty, wrong. *8, closer, 9, away, 10, closer.*

Nicky smells the diesel and sees a bus, a rough rattling sound. *14, away, 15, closer.*

She is leaning forward, leaning back. Nicky ponders the fragility of her bones, her tiny body. He has a bad, bad thought which he can't get rid of however hard he tries.

Out of nowhere, there's a bang, the loudest crash he'll ever hear. Wheels screech to a halt. Nicky covers his ears to stop the sound of screaming.

A rag doll flies, a T-shirt rides up, a body twists and blows in the wind and then falls with a hard thump.

Then the world goes quiet. There’s silence.

Keziah

Each place has a name in gold ink. The cutlery is set for three courses. Pan-fried seabass with new potatoes in a herby butter sauce is ready for the girls.

Claus smiles openly as he places a tray of garlic-laden bread on the Lazy Susan. 'Lazy Keziah' has made no effort towards this evening's procedures, but he doesn't seem to mind.

'Dive in, ladies,' he encourages as he takes his place at the head of the table. He takes a moment, leans back, stretches his arms above his head. He can't hide the pride he feels at dishing up a meal that's above and beyond restaurant standards. Heidi and Ameena don't wait to be asked a second time. Claus watches with his arms folded as they tear the bread, butter dripping off the edges just as he thinks it should.

'Oh!' he said when I asked him how he'd occupy himself tonight. 'I assumed as babies are a joint achievement the baby shower would include me but if . . .'

I didn't wait for him to finish. Seeing his little boy face, all crestfallen, I gave him a hug and told him he could cook.

So, here we all are. Ameena already on her second large glass of red. Flo, the quietly spoken teaching assistant, is listening to offer a kind word, watching to see how she can help. I couldn't have managed last year without her support. She's a marvel.

Heidi is desperately seeking Claus's validation of her parenting.

'Do you think my boys will suffer having only one parent?'

The kitchen is full of silver and pink helium balloons. Claus has hung congratulations bunting across the side wall. 'It's all so exciting, six weeks and we'll meet our daughter,' he beamed as the girls barged into the kitchen, coats discarded in the hall. They got a tour of the downstairs. Upstairs is our private space. They admired the new terrace, perfect for a child, ready for a slide. And now, the room is loud with laughter.

And then there's me. Watching and waiting for an opportunity to get one over my husband. Who have I become?

Claus catches my eye and holds it for a moment. The look that says, it's us, we're the team. I'm glad psychologists can't read minds. If he knew my plan for this evening, he wouldn't be grinning like the proverbial cat.

Whilst he's relaxed, secure, the expert in the room, he's a perfect husband. I can see the look of envy in Heidi's eyes as she hangs on his every word. Flo is obviously admiring the expanse of this house; I have an open plan kitchen that wouldn't be out of place in a magazine. My situation is everyone's dream, surely?

The guilt comes as such an overwhelming pressure in my chest, I can hardly breathe. Whilst everyone is celebrating, joyful. I can think only of one thing.

The room, his room.

For the first time in our marriage, tonight when he got back from work he was distracted, not focused and purposeful like usual. He came in. I followed him upstairs, hovering. He was chatty and clearly excited about hosting. He showered. I changed and lay on our bed, waiting for him to leave his room. I could see into the hall, and his door whilst horizontal. I watched and waited for him to lock the door and pop the keys in his pocket before re-joining me.

But he left it open. I watched him close it but then he saw me and, his hair still wet, he strolled into our room and lay next to me. Without locking the door. I smiled and nodded, but all I could think was, the door is unlocked, he hasn't locked the door.

We went down together, him holding my hand on the curving stairs, telling me to go carefully, to slow down. I waited until he was immersed in his recipe book, then I raced back up to check. Fully expecting it to be my mistake, I looked behind me, before quickly tugging at the door. It was unlocked. I was tempted to rush in then but the girls were minutes away.

'Chop chop,' Claus shouts cheerfully whilst clapping his hands. 'Let's reconvene in the drawing room for coffee.'

I blush. Really, who calls the lounge a drawing room? What century is he living in?

I shuffle behind my friends, remembering what it was like to move with speed and agility but whilst they're larking about, my head shouts, *The mystery room is unlocked!*

I have a plan.

Claus can't resist showing off his knowledge and experience. I need to throw a hook and then I'll do it, I'll run upstairs. By the time the girls leave, the baby will be suitably showered and my fears will be stilled. I'm being ridiculous. He's work mad, privacy mad, and his special room will be nothing more than an OCD space with his clothes in order and a locked filing cabinet.

Claus comes back with a tray of coffee and foil-wrapped mints. I'm perching on the arm of the settee, closest to the door.

Before he's placed it on the oak side table I speak. 'Darling, Ameena was asking about your time at Broadmoor.'

Ameena looks straight at me, raises an eyebrow but doesn't challenge. Claus sits opposite her, crosses his legs and leans forward. He's off.

When he pauses to take another question from the floor. I tap him on the shoulder and whisper in his ear.

'Keep the girls amused, I'm desperate for a power nap.'

'Good plan,' he quips. He's got important issues to debate.

Making sure I put my foot flat on every stair and hold tight to the banister, I pull myself up. I know this is my moment, and I don't have long. Two stairs at a time until the twist at the top.

I pause outside his room. I can hear them interrogating him. Why do people abuse children? How does he cope with watching it? How come these people get to have kids? I hear Ameena say, 'They should be sterilised, no arguments.'

As long as they keep chatting, I'm safe. I check my watch. Don't get distracted, Keziah. I check the handle, please don't let it be locked again.

I'm in!

Five minutes in and I've had a good look. Everything is in its place. There's nothing I don't know about. I let out the air I didn't know I was holding and rub my body, just under my rib cage. I have a sharp pain that won't budge. Hopefully indigestion from all the rich food.

Predictably clean, nothing under the bed, a few baby-related books on his bedside.

Careful not to make a noise, I stand at the end of his king-sized bed and open the wardrobe door.

Six identical blue suits. What did I expect? Even his social clothes are in colour order. Shoes at the bottom, ties on the door. His battered brown case is in its place, carefully balanced in the back corner.

I perch on the edge of his bed. In this lowered position, I catch a glimpse of something behind his clothes, there's a backdrop of plastic that's not obvious from a standing position.

Energised, I drag myself up. Pulling back his jackets like curtains. It's unmissable. There are three sets of drawers hidden behind. The kind of drawers Ameena uses for stashing her school stuff. Craft in one drawer, scissors in another. Nothing Claus would allow into this house.

Small but deep plastic drawers slotted into a matching solid framework glare at me. I hitch up a few sweaters and take the trouser hanger out.

Poking my head outside the door, I can hear that they're all still chatting; I can hear Claus's voice downstairs.

I dive in. I pull out the first drawer. It's full of clothes but the clothes are small, children's clothes. They are not Claus-like at all. They're not folded and there's a smell. Damp? Body odour? I'm not sure. Whatever it is, it's not nice.

Trousers, shorts, a striped jumper, all screwed up and dirty. I chuck it back in, no time to process, and pull the next drawer out. Underwear, but again small, age 9-10, it says on the labels

My mind is racing into horrible places. What is this? Why does my husband have children's clothes hidden in his cupboard? This isn't what I was looking for. Nausea is growing, but I have to see it all.

I move along, on my hands and knees, a teen scrabbling about to find her mum's party dress, forbidden heels and make up.

In the second set, I open the top one. It sticks, I tug. It's harder to see what this is, metal, broken toys, small collectibles, cars, ornaments of animals. This is so odd and creepy. More toys, books and a wooden jigsaw of a tractor in the bottom one.

I'm frantic now, pulling it all out, no time to cover my tracks. What on earth has he been hiding? More clothes, books, gloves and a stray bobble hat. The common factor in this jumble sale is it's messy, smelly and all are the belongings of children.

In the last one there's something I instantly recognise.

My eyes widen with horror as I hear a noise, steps outside, but I can't stop, I just can't. I'm determined to look inside this red document in my hand.

The door bangs open as Claus pushes his way in, the wood crashes into the paintwork.

I see the panic in his face when he sees me, sees what I've done, the mess I've dragged up, the stench I've created. It's on the floor, under my knees, it's everywhere.

He sees the booklet in my hands.

'No, Keziah, no!' he cries. He snatches it away. 'It's not what you think!' he adds, desperation in his voice..

But it's too late. I've seen.. My eyes meet the sad eyes of a small boy in a passport photo. He could be in my class, a vulnerable boy with huge bags under his hollow eyes.

Claus tries to grab me. 'Let me explain.'

'No!' I shout in his face, getting up and pushing past him.

I stand at the top of the stairs, looking down. Clutching my iPhone in my left hand, I use my other to steady myself with the bannister. My head is woozy, the pain in my gut has strengthened. Ameena has come out into the hall below us, her eyes wide as she sees me balancing at the top. The others follow, standing expectantly, an unusual silence from the audience as the drama plays out on the stage.

Claus is behind me, still speaking. 'Keziah please, I'm sorry, I love you. Don't leave, I honestly can't do life without you.'

Inside my belly, the baby is pushing hard and high, I can hardly breathe.

Claus puts a hand on my shoulder, another around my waist.

'Keziah, calm down. This is dangerous, take some breaths.'

'I can't, I'm sorry, let me go.'

My husband won't budge even when I give him a gentle push with both elbows. I breathe in, determined to get free, to go down the stairs, to leave. Ameena starts up the stairs, unable to stand by and watch.

His warm breath is on my neck, I can smell the buttery sourdough. As I turn to tell him to back off, to let me go, my front foot makes an uncertain connection.

One foot dislodges, my phone slips through the gap, a crash forces everyone to stop breathing, just for a second.

'Claus!' Ameena screams with her hand covering her mouth.

A searing pain thunders through my bare foot as it slides over the hard wood. I'm on my back, sledging down, head first, out of control.

It's true. Memories do flash like a slideshow. I see Esther, my parents, the kids at school.

Ameena is striding up two at a time, but the blasted staircase, the highlight of his prestigious home is too long, too precarious.

She stretches forward, her open arms flung forward to catch me. But the void is too great, it's too late. As my head speeds towards the ground, Heidi's contorted mouth produces a sound that pierces my heart.

21

Time Travelling

Nicky

This morning, there is no one to wave him off as he leaves Nancy's for the very last time. There's no picnic to hide and no kisses as the boot is slammed down. Dad watched him pack, saying it really didn't matter that his pencil case was lost under the bed. It mattered to Nicky.

The car is silent, no music on the stereo, no drumming and no man-to-man chat. The windows are sealed, it's like an airless container. Nicky knows he could throw up but there's no point in voicing that fear. Nicky has been told their destination is a very long drive.

He knows there won't be a terrace or an ensuite. He knows there won't be breakfast buffets, lasagne or someone to kiss him goodnight. He knows he'll never again see Ava run upstairs or help him make the final summit.

When the police arrived at the accident, Nicky did what he does best. Absolutely nothing. He found a piece of curb far enough from the commotion and put his head in his hands, right by the roaring road. See no evil, hear no evil.

He didn't move until a sturdy man, smelling of tobacco, yanked him off the pavement by his arm.

'Get up, you'll get yourself killed!' the man shouted. Nicky didn't care if he lived or died.

The policeman took him to a car with the back door open. He sat on his own in that police car for what seemed like several hours. Voices came out of the speaker but no one was listening. In his head he sang 'Sweet Caroline'. He knew Ava would like that. He sang louder and louder, and faster and faster because no one was listening.

He didn't look up when the stretcher went in, or when the doors closed or when the ambulance pulled away. Blue lights flashing everywhere, police car in front and paramedic bike behind. Ava would love all the drama.

Why did he agree to live with them? He tried to tell Nancy he wasn't normal but she refused to listen. He told her about his rage and his patterns and his counting but she refused to send him away. He told her when he went places, bad things happened.

Of course, his dad knew all along.

Nicky watches the trees whizz past, and the Spinnaker Tower get smaller and smaller until it's gone forever.

His coat is inappropriately thick but he still feels cold. His sleeves are down to his fingertips, nails chewed so the tops are bulging and pink.

He catches sight of his face in the wing mirror. His hair is longer than his Poppa likes. He can't see what Ava meant about a handsome face. He sees an ugly disgrace.

After many hours of travelling, Dad wakes him.

'We're here.'

A gigantic building awaits him, looming like a castle. There are gates so wide that his home ones feel small. Between the gates and the huge house, is the longest drive he has ever seen. Above the gates is a name he can't read, a complicated word. Under the word he can't read it says, 'For boys aged 11 to 18'.

He's glad he has long trousers and a smart shirt and tie. He's glad that he's nearly grown up because if there was ever a time to be a man, it is now.

Keziah

Nothing makes sense. A large circular light spinning above my head. This room is airless, I can't breathe. I'm moving my arms, my toes, my mouth, but nothing is changing. Am I dead?

Esther waits on the pavement in the road before school. It's our last day. Her heavy rucksack is by her feet, the front is bulging, misshapen where it's stuffed so tightly with books. Everyone knows she'll get four As and swan off to Cambridge; a foregone conclusion.

She takes my bag so I can roll up my skirt, just a bit shorter, to match my peers. She's a sixth former, can wear what she pleases but her navy trousers and white polo could easily pass for school uniform.

Her eyes are bright, clear skin, never one for spots like me. Her dark hair is in a neat bob but due for a cut, so longer than she likes. So, so alive.

'See you at home this evening,' she promises, a hand in the air. I don't bother to respond. It goes without saying I'll see her at home.

It's Wednesday. Every other day, my dad collects me from the bike club.

But on a Wednesday, I make my own way home so dad can collect Esther from a taster course she's doing at Chester University.

One day a week, Keziah, that's all. The family relocated for my cycling, Esther doesn't complain. Every evening my father collects me, Esther doesn't complain. Every weekend my parents watch me race. Every holiday is organised around my competitions. Our family revolves around me.

But once a week Esther needs an hour from my dad. On a Wednesday, I walk back, it takes only twenty minutes.

The colours are vivid, rain vibrates against the bike club. It's torrential but I have a coat. I have an expensive coat designed to repel the wind and rain. A coat my parents couldn't really afford.

But instead of pulling up my hood like Esther would do, I call my daddy.

'Dad,' I whine, 'it's really wet.'

I hear him chuckle, typical Keziah!

I say, 'Esther won't mind waiting, if you get me first, we'll only be twenty minutes late.'

Dad can't say no to his baby daughter, his bike champ.

'Stop stressing,' I reassure him in the car as he huffs and puffs. The windscreen wipers can't go any faster. Esther won't complain about shivering in a coat that needs updating.

We finally skid to a halt but can't get close to the entrance.

Blue lights everywhere.

'Not another student protest,' Dad tuts, losing patience, tired after work.

I get out, irritated my trousers will get soaked. Why can't he go look? Where is she? She's supposed to be waiting here.

I'm cold, hungry. I run around, searching inside and out. I'm tired, I came last in the trial race tonight. Erin, a younger biker was fast on my heels. If I don't get entered for the championship, my life will be over.

Mum will have dinner ready. Surely Esther can get the bus when she's finished geeking. I give up and head back to tell my dad she's not there. Rushing around the last corner, back onto the main road. I see an ambulance with open doors.

On the floor is a body, one leg bent awkwardly under a slim frame. Blood is forming a puddle near her right arm. My mind denies what I see. Loads of students wear those shoes. All the geeks have bags like that. But then I see the body is drenched despite the waterproof. The flimsy coat wasn't up to a light shower let alone lying in a puddle on the floor.

A man in green steps forward to cover my beautiful, generous, selfless sister. No one is panicking. No one is helping. She's dead.

Before I can rush back to my dad, be sick, sob, scream and collapse, a miracle happens. Today, she sits up. She opens her eyes and smiles. The paramedic stays quiet, they don't push me back.

'Keziah, you came,' she says, dusting off her trousers and retrieving her bag.

We hug; her white musk perfume is delicious. She steps back, holds me gently by the shoulders and looks deep into my soul. 'What if . . . ?' she asks.

There's a pressure on my chest I can't lose. Bright lights alternate with blackness. A hand grasps mine, it takes a minute for my vision to clear.

My mum.

'Oh pet.' She squeezes my hand. 'We thought we'd lost you. You've been crying out for Esther, shouting that she's alive.' Then she starts sobbing. 'My poor, poor girl, what if you'd gone too. I couldn't stand it to lose two.'

The Esther in my dream is still real, just for a moment. Then I'm back. I remember: I sacrificed my amazing, clever, selfless sister because I couldn't be arsed to walk. The hurt of that very first day threatens to overwhelm. The guilt returns; if only I wasn't so stupid, so selfish, Esther wouldn't be dead, I wouldn't be here, my mum wouldn't be heartbroken.

Memories of voices shouting, blue lights and arriving on a stretcher are jumbled up. Was the stretcher at home? I look around for Claus.

In my mind, I see my husband with his head in his hands as I slide away from his fingertips; I see Ameena shouting at Claus, 'What are you doing?'

'Where's Claus?' I ask my mum.

'He's been here, sweetie,' Mum says, stroking my hand, 'but the police . . . they wanted to talk to him about your . . . fall. He had to go down to the station this morning.' She pauses. 'Ameena wasn't sure what happened, she didn't see exactly.' She drops her eyes, withdraws her hands to her lap, straightens her skirt.

'But . . why the police? Claus tried to pull me back . . . I can see him . . . I'm . . .' Before I can coordinate my tongue to speak, my hand goes to my stomach. I remember my baby. I scramble under the blue-knitted blanket. Relief like I've never known when my hands finally rest on a swollen belly. It's only then that the tears flow; gulping, choking emotions that have been barricaded inside.

My dear mum cradles me, her own baby. Finally, there's quiet in the room.

'Sweetheart.' I know this voice and I don't want to listen. She speaks slowly, quieter, not quite her. 'The doctors are concerned about the baby. Dr Garrett has gone in search of another scanner.'

I don't ask who that is or why the scanner. I don't want to see the tears in my mother's yellowing eyes. I want to be calling the register, I want to watch box sets while Claus works, I want to be with Ameena. I want Esther to be alive again. I want her to finish speaking. I want to be anywhere but here, in this clinical room that smells of illness, decay and death.

'Keziah, the machine is here.' My mum's voice is reassuring, just like the day Esther died. When I sobbed and sobbed, confessing I'd killed her, that our lives were permanently ruined, she said these same words, in that same voice, 'There, there, we'll be alright, you'll see.'

But it was never alright again.

Opening my eyes, I see a middle-aged man pushing a trolley.

'I'm Will Garrett. I understand you were very, very lucky, Mrs Doerkson.'

I don't answer.

'May I just lift this up,' he asks, rolling up the hospital gown I don't remember being rolled on. 'This might feel cold.' He squeezes clear gel onto my belly. 'Right, let's see what's what,' he says without looking me in the eye.

For a few moments, no one in the room breathes. I squeeze my eyes shut.

After what feels like an age, Dr Garrett touches my arm and smiles. 'Panic over. This little one is in fine spirits. Strong heart rate, perfect speed. Do you want to look?'

Before I can respond, the door swings open and Claus walks in.

Dr Garrett straightens up like a guard in front of his machine, but it's Claus' face I'm looking at. Fear is flooding his features, that raw primal fear I saw when I was breaking his heart.

'Oh my goodness, surely not!' Dr Garrett exclaims. 'It can't be, can it?'

Dr Garrett grasps my husband's hands in his own. I see that fear again in my husband's eyes. The emotion only I get to see; a frightened boy, not the overbearing, nit-picking monster my friends perceive. Claus averts his eyes. He doesn't want to acknowledge the stocky stranger claiming familiarity, especially not today.

The doctor isn't giving in.

'It is you! When was it, old chap, 1999, 2000?'

He says it in a voice that sounds posher than the one I got; typical consultant tone.

'Perhaps,' Claus gives in.

Doctor Garrett moves to Claus's side, slings his arm around my husband's shoulders and poses as if for a holiday shot, mates together.

'Well, however long, it's great to see you, Nicky – you look so well,' he says, before letting his arm drop.

22

Claus

I wake with my torso awkwardly twisted over my wife's hospital bed, my head has fallen somewhere between her arm and chest. I don't remember giving in to sleep. My entire body aches and the cold metal is pressing hard on my ribs but I don't care because I'm close to Keziah.

Thank God she's alive.

I yearn to open my eyes, let her know I'm awake and ask if she's alright, but I'm terrified I'll break the spell. In this moment all is well. Her delicate fingers are entwined with my hair, something she does at night, when she's fast asleep. I would do anything, give anything, to remain here, with my wife loving me.

What have I done? Why was I so foolish? Why didn't I trust her, let her in? How did I make her so desperate, so afraid, that she jeopardised her own life in order to avoid my embrace?

Keziah fidgets in her sleep. I lift my head and open my eyes but hers are still closed. Her hair is messed up, there's a smudge of blood near her fringe, her cheek is bruised and her lip is swollen and yet, still, she's so beautiful. Besides, the beauty of Keziah is her kind, trusting heart.

From the moment she slipped her soft hand in mine, she trusted me to heal her. That simple trust enabled me to wrongly believe I could be, would be, my healed version with her.

I tried so hard to be that, to be the self I wanted to be, the self that is worthy of her but I failed. Once again, powerless, hopeless Nicky failed to be the man he needed to be. Once again, my attempts to protect have created harm to the person I most want to help.

Keziah startles. She disentangles her fingers from my hair to try to reach for a drink and sees I'm awake.

'Hey,' she says, as if we're back sunbathing in Rome, without a care in the world.

'Hey,' I say, attempting eye contact, trying not to see the way her eyebrow is broken in half by a jagged cut.

It's just the three of us in a silent clinical room. Our family, my future family, the solution to my problem of the past.

'So,' Keziah says, her hand close to mine. 'If you're not Claus, who am I married to?'

'Who knows!' I laugh awkwardly, looking down at the floor with no idea how to begin.

She strokes the side of my face but stays silent. My wife is waiting.

'Nicky, I'm waiting!'my dad frequently used to bawl at me. He was waiting for the right answer, waiting for the reassurance he craved, reassurance that I was OK, that she was OK, reassurance that he was off the hook.

'I'm the same person. It's just a name . . .'

Keziah yelps as she pulls herself up to sitting. I wiggle her pillow and add an extra one until the pain on her face eases. She reaches to take the plastic beaker from my trembling hand.

‘Go on,’ she encourages. Her anxious eyes search my face. I want to make it alright; she deserves an explanation.

‘As you know, my childhood wasn’t great.’

I pause, wanting to say the right thing, to help her understand but not frighten her, to explain but retain my role for her sake.

‘My tenth birthday was the last one I celebrated with either of my parents. Ninety-two days after Ava’s accident, my father died of a fatal myocardial infarction. After depositing me in the finest boarding school in Scotland he took a post in Saudi, and died there alone.

My mother spent most of my school years in and out of rehab. Three days before my fifteenth, she remarried and emigrated. With her in another continent and a dead father, I re-birthed myself. At the end of university, I changed my name, just in time to get a degree certificate inked with my new identity; Claus James Doerkson. For a fleeting moment, I was free, free of history, free of association.’

Keziah opens her mouth to speak before I’ve finished my sentence.

‘But what about the children’s clothes in the house?’

‘Mine.’

My tears refuse to be restrained. This isn’t the man she married. Keziah needs a therapist, a hero, not a disintegrated shell.

She pulls the hanky out of my crumpled suit pocket and gently wipes away my tears.

‘Thank you,’ I say, retrieving my handkerchief. I smile to show I’m OK. The last thing her blood pressure needs is to be worrying about me.

‘When I graduated at eighteen, the other boys were collected whilst I stood about wondering where to go and what to do. The school was almost empty when the headteacher handed me fifty pounds in cash and a key with lock-up 4109 attached on a frayed piece of string,' I explain.

Keziah moves about trying to get comfortable.

'Why don't you rest for a bit and we'll talk later,' I suggest, holding the beaker whilst she takes a few sips.

'I have to know,' she demands as I settle back into the wobbly chair.

Keziah takes my hand and mindlessly picks at my fingernail. My fingers are grubby, the nails uneven. Usually I'd pull back, ashamed, but not today.

I continue. 'I cracked open my trust fund, bought my dream car and found the lock-up. I had no idea what to expect, what secret things had my father left his only son? I fantasised about many options. Would it be the piano my grandmother played, his wedding ring or bank details for money squirreled away in Switzerland?

I don't tell my wife how that naively hopeful eighteen year old still wondered if he'd finally retrieve his childhood bike.

'What was in it?' Keziah asks with renewed energy

'The shelving units you discovered full of dirty stuff my father neglected to sort.'

A nurse bustles in and without comment or apology straps a blood pressure cuff to Keziah's arm.

'I'll go in search of coffee,' I say, rushing out before Keziah can respond.

Even though she's told everyone I didn't push her, the nurses still stare with accusing eyes.

My body responds as if I'm back there, opening that lock-up, hopeful of some sort of legacy, good wishes from the dead. I can smell the stench of all that stuff.

‘You OK?’ an older gentleman in a plastic apron asks as I steady myself on a windowsill.

‘Fine, thank you,’ I say in my professional voice.

Inside the plastic containers were toys inherited from grandparents, pity gifts from Nancy and my passport. There were unwashed clothes and even a dirty cereal bowl. Every item was exactly as I left it that day when we abandoned Nancy’s. That day he drove me to a school hundreds of miles from his visual field. He’d left me to face the stench of my rotten childhood because he couldn’t. He couldn’t face his failure, his cowardice or his neglect. So, he locked it up, ran and threw away the key.

I should have taken it all to the tip straight from the lock up. But I couldn’t face it. Perhaps I’m not so dissimilar to my father. Instead I loaded it into the boot of my brand-new Aston Martin.

When I return to her room, Keziah is tucking in to a cheese sandwich. She drops it back on the paper plate to take the half-filled cup of watery liquid.

‘The best I could do,’ I apologise.

Before I can settle myself in the seat, Keziah’s demeanour changes. She places her food and drink to one side and withdraws her hand from mine to sit up straight. She speaks with an authority, a clarity I don’t recognise.

‘Claus, I know you love me, you couldn’t love me more and I love you. But . . . I can’t come back. You’re suffocating me and I don’t think you can help it.’

I want to put up a fight, tell her these are Ameena’s thoughts not hers. Promise a new start. But I have no defence and she knows my promises are empty.

‘I’ll do anything you ask, just don’t leave me?’ I beg.

Her lip quivers but she replies without hesitation.

‘I was lost and you saved me. You gave me the security to grieve, look back and heal. But this past month I’ve remembered who I am, who I was, who I would’ve become if Esther hadn’t died, and to be honest I don’t think you’ll like the true Keziah too much.’

‘I’ll change, I promise. I’ll back off, stop complaining about Ameena, anything. You have to give me another go. We’re having a baby,’ I plead, clutching her hands in mine.

‘You’ll be an amazing dad and I reckon we’ll make great co-parents.’ She retrieves her hands from my grasp and forces a smile. ‘I can’t live with you any longer. Ameena has found a short-term let and she’s going to stay with me until after the baby comes.’

I don’t know this Keziah so well but she’s made up her mind. I plant a kiss on her forehead and another on her stomach. I close the door as quietly as I can on my way out. I hear her sobbing behind the closed door.

Stumbling away from her room, I push past the afternoon visitors unable to escape the urges dominating my inner core. I burst into the toilets desperately hoping they’re empty. I turn on both taps, and wash and wash until my hands are red and sore. Then I shove open the cubicle door and collapse onto the bleached floor. Finally, an indescribable relief floods my entire system.

As a little boy, each time things got worse, I drew the obvious conclusion: if happiness alluded only me, I was the problem. That’s when the rituals, patterns and routines started. Two degrees in psychology gives me sufficient grasp on my idiosyncrasies. I have accurately diagnosed myself with severe obsessional compulsive disorder, persistent and chronic anxiety and a hint of paranoia at times of intense stress.

For a horrible moment, I feared Keziah was lost forever but here, on this cold floor, soothed by unusual comforts I realise one choice remains. Every part of me says I'll regret it. But I no longer have another choice, there's no plan B. If I don't execute this minuscule amount of control, she'll slip through my fingers forever, and that is not an option. I have to persuade Keziah to trust me once more. I have to get her there, to my place. My only place of sanctuary, the place where my shoulders drop, and my breathing evens out. The only place that will complete the circle. My colleagues call it closure.

Keziah

'Breathe in, breathe out,' Chessy orders in a voice the others seem to find soothing. 'As you breathe in, cradle your baby, caress the curve of your stomach, absorb your new role. Whisper, "It's your mummy here."'

I can hear Ameena sniggering on the mat next to me. She squeezes my hand, a shared understanding that this is way more intense than she'd imagined. Five weeks before my due date seems a bit late to be doing this.

'As you breathe out, let go of your old life, your child-free identity. Say goodbye to the meaningless existence, where nobody depended on you for their next breath.'

My breathing speeds up with each stupid sentence that escapes from Chessy's lips. I open my eyes and look around. Apparently, this flimsy cavern is a yurt and it's where mind and body come together.

'Just what you need,' is how my best friend referred to the glossy leaflet describing the yoga garden. '"You'll find a dedicated haven to rediscover yourself."' Ameena read to me. We'd just moved into the new place. She was full of energy and enthusiasm.

I'm pleased to say I now know exactly who I am and what the future holds. Strangely, I'm beginning to feel pretty excited. So, thanks Cheesy, or whatever your name is, but Keziah has already rediscovered herself.

Claus offered to move out so Ameena and I could go there, but I don't want to look at that staircase. Much to my surprise he accepted my decision, stayed away and resisted the temptation to phone. However, last night he called four times and eventually I gave in.

‘You have five minutes, absolute tops,’ I said, standing to take the call.

‘The problem, Keziah,’ he explained in his consultant tone, ‘is you don’t yet understand.’

‘I think I do,’ I interrupted.

‘But there’s more,’ he insisted. ‘Having put up with me for the last year, you deserve an explanation.’

It did break my heart when he said those stinking clothes were his, his childhood in boxes. But I’m not going back. I can’t pretend to enjoy being a kept woman, who just wants to keep everyone else happy. Esther would hate the vanilla persona I’ve become, a combination of the least attractive aspects of us both.

Last night I spent some of my savings on a new mountain bike, I’m going to start with an electric one. I’m not sure how life will pan out but I’ve decided to explore training as a biking coach, once the baby is a bit older.

Claus says he’ll do anything I ask, but is asking if I might do one thing that feels essential for him. The trouble is he’s being very cagey about what that is. Ameena thinks I should forget about Claus, like the ugly boy I kissed at the end of year nine. Why can’t she see the good? He just wanted to keep me safe, rested, stop bad things happening to me. He’s not a bad man and I’m expecting his daughter.

Ameena is in full drama mode. She reads endless psychological novels and sees shadows in every corner. I know Claus wouldn’t hurt me, he’s not the villain from one of her books but neither is he the heroic prince I created. When we met I needed that knight on horseback to gallop off with me tucked under his arm. I allowed Claus to do that. If we met now, maybe it could’ve worked. But he needs a rescue project as much as I needed to be rescued.

Chessy drones on. 'Notice your breathing, notice your stomach as it gently rises and falls with no conscious effort.'

When I turn to whisper an exit plan, Ameena is dribbling. Her mouth is wide open, her breathing is just how Chessy likes it.

I haven't told Ameena, or anyone for that matter, what Claus is asking but after many hours of thinking, I've agreed. I owe him one last thing. Ameena goes to see Mark for a few days in the middle of each week so she won't see Claus collect me.

I've told him straight, I'll go with him to what he's calling his special place but nothing will change my mind. We'll co-parent our daughter as two single people. He's promised he'll agree without complaint if I just do this one last thing.

I'm not allowed to ask where we're going or why. He is asking me to trust him.

So, when Ameena leaves the house tomorrow, Claus will collect me. He has promised if I go, without telling anyone, I'll get what I deserve. I'll hear his full story and it will all make sense.

I've agreed to trust him so everything will resolve for us both. Only then can I move on.

National Hospital of Neurology

Discharge report

NHS number: 485 777 3496

D.O.B: 28.09.1981

Gender: *female*

Dear Dr Armstrong,

I am so pleased to tell you the above patient has defied all the odds and will be discharged next month into the community. Obviously, she will be starting a new life to the one she has previously enjoyed. She has very little sensation above her mid chest but minimal in her right arm so she could potentially learn to use environmental controls which would give her the independence she craves. She is now more accepting of her tracheostomy and behavioural problems have stopped.

She is fully ventilated with no hope of change so will be cared for under the domiciliary nursing team who will initially visit daily. Can you please organise? Katrina Orchard is aware and will monitor continence.

She and her mother are moving into a rented bungalow. As soon as her medical legal claim is finalised she will be given a long-term adapted solution in the area she used to live. Her mother is against this idea given an unresolved domestic situation. We will see.

They are both refusing psychological support at the moment but please refer her mother to the Guild Care carers group as she is going to need it. I think it might be worth referring the patient to clinical neuropsychology in case she changes her mind.

We will review her here six monthlies.

Kind regards,

Dr A. Lutte-Elliott

CONSULTANT IN NEUROREHABILITATION

CC

Community team leader – Dr Brian Solts

Social worker – Annaliese Edgington

23

Claus

If my fellow consultants could see me now, face down amidst filthy rags, repeating nonsensical childhood mantras, they'd call the specialist police vehicle for removing people at risk to themselves or others. The control centre would receive an alert. One white adult male, still in his work suit, prostrate on the floor, his face smothered in clothes three decades old.

I know my behaviour is abnormal, abhorrent even. Before I reached puberty, my monstrous nature was evident. Watching the neighbours day after day as a scruffy urchin, I made a promise to myself: one day I'd be like them, not a monster like me. I've tried so hard to refurbish myself. The images, urges and dark, dark thoughts are hidden beneath designer suits, clever reports and polished shoes. But despite all my strategies, the valve-releasing calls and visits, I can't stop any of it.

At university and in my twenties I avoided women. I knew they were unsafe in my hands. I hadn't been able to look after my mother; I had destroyed Ava. But then came Jen. Passive, plain, content Jen. Jen, the loving mother I craved. How pathetic, how textbook.

With Jen, my world was predictable, orderly. We married before the end of her training. She didn't graduate. She didn't mind. The cleaner worked around her, I did the shopping and created a different meal each evening. Sharing three course meals was the closest we came to true intimacy.

Thankfully, my passion for her wasn't substantial. Thoughts of her loss didn't destabilise me, hijack me, bind me with uncontrollable fear. We lived in our own way, parallel stumbling. Those first six months were wonderful, dull, mundane. We developed a pacifying rhythm that suited us both. I was as free from fear as I'll ever be.

I really thought the monsters were gone. I had a new name. I was a doctor of psychology with a photo of my wedding on the desk.

Nicky had finally cracked it. He was normal. His inside monsters had emigrated.

Meanwhile, I worked harder, gaining both respect and financial reward. I was destined to be Oxford's head of department by the time I was thirty-five, and Jen seemed delighted to be home alone in an awesome house purchased outright by my trust fund.

Sadly, she was no more normal than me. Of course, she had a long history I didn't know, like I had a long history she didn't know. Jen's death was the inevitable climax to a familiar story. As always, Nicky wasn't enough.

After months of watching her deteriorate, months of desperately trying to save her, I gave up. I didn't expect what happened to trigger such deep feelings of helplessness and rage. I was a mess, unable to work. I was at risk of losing all I had achieved.

I knew I had done wrong – Jen's death was untimely, undeserved. I had failed again. I was as helpless as her.

After that, I committed to staying away from women. I knew in my heart wasn't safe for them.

Then in waltzed Keziah. Beautiful, kind Keziah. The look she gave me that first day was worshipful. For a fleeting moment, the fear diminished. Her need for me was so obvious that it created an inner peace, the thought I might finally get it right. For a while that seemed to be the truth. With Keziah I could thrive, we were not the same, we were two halves of a completed shape. We had such fun; nights out, weekends in, holidays in the sun. I even read a few novels.

Could she break the spell? A decent, caring wife who could create with me a family to erase the pain of my first one. Could she crush that tired stalker once and for all?

I couldn't believe it when she agreed to marry me. I felt ten feet tall. When her father shook my hand and her mum cuddled me tight, I really thought this was it. My happy ending. We made it, I assured Nicky that night, our monsters are locked away, in a secure prison with high walls topped with a barbed-wire swirl. But even then, deep in my subconscious I knew that was a lie. It wasn't safe, not for me, not for her. I have many regrets. But the greatest is exposing Keziah to me.

My plan for our wedding night was for Keziah to feel her happiest, for her to briefly forget Esther, and to know she was now safe, safe from panic, safe from uncertainty and safe from harm.

There was no one more shocked than me at what happened when I saw him pawing her on the dance floor. I certainly didn't expect my internal stalker to be released on parole. Sitting stone cold sober at my own top table, I heard them before I saw them. I heard the noise as they thundered towards me, those monsters had been released without consultation and they were coming for me. What I had never realised is the strength of my monsters is directly proportionate to the strength of my love.

As I wept on the bathroom floor of our honeymoon suite, I was overwhelmed by shame. I couldn't come out. I stayed locked away until Kez was safely downstairs and then swallowed some sleeping tablets to ensure I wouldn't wake on her return.

My plan was to drive her home as soon as she woke up, where she could be properly safe and to then call Ameena to collect her friend. But, then the morning sun broke through the curtains, she opened her eyes, begging to be loved, trusting me to save her. When I looked into the depths of her willing heart, all good intentions flew out that ornate window. I couldn't let her leave.

When she didn't mention my behaviour, I knew we could start again, see it as a one off, a slip. Maybe even something to laugh about when we celebrated our twenty-fifth anniversary.

'Do you remember,' Keziah would say, 'when we were first married, you were so unstable you screamed and shouted at me on our wedding night?'

Now I have another opportunity to do the honourable thing, let her go, to love from a safe distance. So why is it I can't? Why have I persuaded her instead to come to *my* safe place? I need her to understand, even if it's one fleeting moment. A fleeting moment when she really sees me at my worst, but yet my best.

I was flabbergasted when she agreed to come. Obviously, I couldn't tell her where – if I did, she'd never come – but she agreed to trust me. I hope she knows me well enough to keep her promise.

'I'm sorry, my sweetheart,' I whisper. 'I'm so, so sorry.'

I lock my bedroom door even though the house is empty. The house is in darkness, the silence eerie. I gather up the contents of my wardrobe, the clothes, the toys, the photographs and sling them all in dustbin bags. Tomorrow on my final journey, I'll dispose of them in the skip. at the bottom of the hill.

My overnight bag is waiting with expectation, mouth gaping open. I pack a change of clothes, a wash bag and Nicky's ancient passport. Before slipping the battered booklet in my overnight bag, I flick to the photograph. Nine-year-old me stares out, a serious face but full of hope.

'Last chance, Nicky boy,' I tell him giving a gentle kiss on the top of his sweet face, just where the wayward curl meets his eyebrow.

I slip off my jacket and unbutton my shirt; the last button takes too long so I refasten and start all over again. I deposit my entire outfit including under garments on top of the other two shirts. Three identical outfits mock me from the bottom of the wash basket.

Repositioning the wicker container to align perfectly with the dressing table, I leave my room to enjoy a final supper.

Keziah has agreed. The pattern of three will align at my place of resolution.

This time tomorrow, it will all be over.

Keziah

Claus arrives on the dot of eight. Sometimes his obsessive nature works for everyone, he's a man of his word. Before I've even locked the door, he's out of his seat to hold open the passenger door. He carefully lays my screwed-up jacket on the back seat.

'Oooh that's nice,' I say, leaning into the warm leather. 'I haven't slept in days,' I confide. I'm shocked at how much like home he feels. I don't want to feel loved and secure in his company. I don't want to inhale his familiar smell and think of his naked body lying next to me.

'We've got a quite a way to go so put your seat back onto horizontal and you can enjoy a well-deserved sleep,' Claus tells me with a smile. I'm so ready for this baby to come out. I'm so uncomfortable, whether I sit or lie back. My back hurts and I have such an ache in my groin. Thank goodness I've only weeks to go. I'll visit whatever memory lane he desires and then I'll be free to start nesting. I strongly suspect he's taking me to that country resort of our second date. He's told me this place will change my mind, allow me to see him as he really is, as we are, wipe away all the bad memories. But, sadly that time has passed. I want to move forward on my own, create the best life for me and my girl.

I wake with a start. I was dreaming about Esther, back again at the same scene. This time she was dead and no amount of shaking her worked.

'Keziah, Kez, take a breath, you're dreaming,' Claus says in a soothing voice. When we were together he'd rub my back when I couldn't sleep and use that voice to guide me through a mindfulness exercise.

'You OK?' he asks, putting his hand on my knee but then whipping it away. I see him flush.

'Don't worry,' I reassure him. 'It's fine.'

I angle my knees away though. I don't want to give mixed messages.

My belly rumbles and my head hurts, a sure sign my bubba is hungry.

'It's the afternoon?' I squint my eyes to check again on the clock. We've been in the car nearly four hours.

'I know,' Claus says as if that's not unexpected. 'You were sleeping deeply.'

I feel groggy, a bit muddled, but looking out of the window I have a sense of deja vu.

We're not on a motorway, but it's busy, noisy, dirty. Scanning as fast as my mind allows, I see people, market stalls dotted on a pedestrianised side road, large industrial-sized bins, green and blue.

Claus slows down for an old chap to cross. As he creeps over the black and white stripes I see a parking area. A man with a turban is washing a windscreen whilst chatting to a smoking colleague.

I blink several times to gain clarity, puzzle pieces trying to move into place.

'Claus . . .'

I don't get my sentence out because I'm interrupted by his mobile ringing. My chest tightens, my fingers grip the edge of my seat.

That awful muffled voice booms into the car on loud speaker. Claus can't get to it, his face drains of expression as that robot voice crackles through the black felt.

'Last warning, keep your promise – show up with her by close of day, I'm . . .'

The voice fizzles out, the signal is gone and at the same time I see an ominous golden globe in the distance.

I know exactly where I am.

I grab for the door; I have to get out, but I'm sleepy, my legs won't move, my hands miss the handle and then there's a click. The child locks initiated from the steering wheel.

Claus reaches over to pull me from the door.

'Don't be so stupid.' Then he swears. I've never heard him swear in all our time together. 'You could've been killed,' he says as if those threats have not just happened, as if we're not on the road where both Jen and that kid died, as if I'm not a naive lamb being led to the slaughter.

He holds both my hands tight in his left hand as he steers the car with his right hand.

'Just be quiet for five minutes,' he pleads.

My phone is in the back, the doors are locked.

The car slows and Claus indicates to pull in just past a road name. The white rectangle is unusually elongated to fit both words; the letters are so clear, as if the sign has been repainted for my benefit, elevated proudly off the ground on two wooden posts. Spitfield Road shouts at me but I'm too unresponsive to answer.

I lay my head back and close my eyes, resigned.

Finally, the car stops, around the back of garages. Is this where I'm going to be found? I block out the image of mum on the day Esther died, disconnected eyes, hands clasped over her mouth and nose.

Claus releases my hands but doesn't unlock the car. He switches off the engine. My bladder needs relief.

I don't want to see but I open my eyes. Claus twists his body to face my frozen one.

'Trust me,' he demands and leaves the car and goes to the boot. It closes again after a few seconds, a loud uncaring slam.

For a minute I think he's leaving me here, off to get his associates.

But when he opens my door, he's removed his jacket and in his hand is a large bouquet of colourful flowers. Without explanation he helps me from the car. My hefty frame takes longer than usual to shift from sitting to standing, and I wobble, leaning back on the car for support. He waits; unreadable, passive.

Then he grabs my hand, firm but not tight, and strides ahead so fast I have to make little skips to keep up.

'It's nearly over,' is all he says.

We run down an alley between two houses, high walls on either side, the stench of dog muck and cannabis combined. We come out opposite three bungalows. Still silent, he rushes me up the path of the middle one. Standing outside the door, I try hard to compose myself, catch my breath. A neat lawn sits beside a pretty border underneath a window with closed curtains.

Making sure to keep hold of me, Claus juggles the flowers to push one finger on the simple bell.

The door opens just a crack.

I see just the middle portion of an older lady's face, a little older than my mum. Her hair is a stylish short crop, grey but fashionably silver, not elderly blue.

The door widens and a tiny lady in denim dungarees steps back. Is she afraid? First she looks at me, then her gaze travels up to Claus.

At that point, the light comes as if she's seen a miracle.

I have never seen a smile quite so wide or quite so bright.

'Oh, my goodness, she's here,' she gushes, running at Claus and squashing the chrysanthemums as she holds on to him tightly.

She takes the flowers, inhales the pleasing scent, then she remembers me. 'You must be Keziah, we've been waiting a long time.' She steps aside to let me into a spacious hall. 'Each time he's travelled down, I've told him. "Tell her, bring her,"' she says to me, her words fast and hurried.

He comes here? When? Why?

Claus pulls me into a cosy sitting room where tasteful art decorates slate grey walls. A comfy-looking settee calls. My eyes dart around, there's no upstairs. I can see an oven through an extra wide door to the kitchen but nothing else from this angle.

There are no broad-shouldered men in dark suits. I don't sense any threat. In fact, I smell cake.

Claus startles as music starts up in another room. It's loud and coming from the kitchen.

The intro notes blare out and then comes an opening line that is more than familiar.

I see Claus's face light up, tears in his eyes. He squeezes my hand. I hadn't realised he was still holding mine. I have absolutely no idea what's going on but I know this song is close to his heart.

No one speaks as the music continues.

Even I know what's coming next. 'Sweet Caroline'.

And to that soundtrack, in comes a woman, her entrance is so visual and accurately choreographed it could be part of a theatre production, the music, her clothes, the timings.

She is breathtakingly stunning, with long, unnaturally red hair and artistically applied eye makeup around thick black lashes. She stops in the middle of the wooden floor, and looks up at Claus whilst the music progresses.

We all wait for the music to stop; Claus is lolling against the wall, relaxed in a way I've never seen. A small boy, awarded first prize.

When the final chords fade, Claus straightens up. I can see he's composing himself.

'This,' Claus says, letting my hand drop to gesture towards the older lady, 'is Nancy. And this –' he gestures to the younger beauty '– is Ava.'

At that, he reaches forward to kiss her cheek, his tall upper body bent double to reach her face.

She does her best to smile, but one side of her face is slightly lopsided. She pushes her purple-rimmed glasses to their rightful place on her nose.

A plastic tube hangs around her neck with a centre piece that presumably helps her to breathe. Her wheelchair is purple with large black wheels, and a keyboard balances on her lap tray. She taps away then presses a button. 'Hello Caroline,' comes out in a robotic crackly voice. The three of them roar with laughter at a joke that's lost on me.

A whooshing noise begins in my head, the familiar panic rising.

I need to get out.

24

Claus

Nicky, stop, please stop, Nicky. Mr Pinkney is panting and coughing. He can't keep up. The thoughts are chasing me harder. I'll kill him too. Stay away, dear Mr P, please stay away and be saved. My heart is stomping at the same pace, hard against my chest so it vibrates through my head to create a pressure at the back of my skull.

Blinking my eyes several times in an attempt to stop the room spinning, closing in. My legs think they're still nine years old and desperate to escape.

How many times have I had that dream?

To my disgust and horror, I've emptied my bladder on Nancy's clean sheets. I should have told Keziah why I can't always share a bed. There's so much I should have told her but I thought she wanted a professional hero not a bedwetting child who felt more terrified than her.

When terror brings old memories to mind, a black out and a bed wetting accident is often the shameful sequence. My conscious mind gives up. Escapes me. It's too much to bear. I experience a dissociative state.

The first time it happened was when I caught Paul with his hands around my mother's throat.

The key is to get myself back to the present, out of my head, into the now. I sit up and force my gaze outside. I smell bacon, delicious bacon with just the right amount of fat. My heart slows and the panic eases. I tell my body: 'I'm back where all things come right.'

I had no idea Keziah was frightened when I brought her here; I was so sure everything would finally make sense to her that I didn't stop to think how it would feel to be taken to a strange place, to meet people unknown to her. I'm angry with myself for being so selfish and thoughtless. What if the adrenalin had sent her into labour?

Fortunately, after a mug of hot milk and a dash of whisky, courtesy of Nancy, she fell asleep in the guest room. The whole time I could see Ava forming her opinions, judging me, sizing up Keziah, but all I could think was would Keziah ever forgive me? Will she let me love her when she hears the whole saga, the truth? Will she understand when I explain my monstrous behaviour on our wedding night, why my anxiety drives me towards keeping her safe? Will she understand that I just wanted to save her like I wanted to save my mum, Ava and even poor old Jen? Will she be able to respect a man who can only manage three weeks as a functional adult before driving hours to sleep and eat here for a few days? Will she understand that I've done all these things to keep the monsters locked up, to love her as my healer self?

The whirring of Ava's chair moving about next door, the voices of her carers is a beautiful comfort. When abandoned in a boarding school, miles from anywhere, I missed Nancy and Ava. Why on earth didn't I listen to them over the last year? They know me the best. They insisted I wait. They told me to take it slow until I trusted Keziah enough to confess I wet the bed, freak out, had a first wife. I didn't want to listen.

Here, in my white bedroom, Nancy leaves everything in the exact place I left it. She knows the smallest shift will drive me to despair. Oh, how I wish I wasn't like this.

Counting provided me with pace and background noise. It settled the rage that came at adolescence. I now know rage is the seven-foot bodyguard, he's strong and in control. Behind him the terror, anxiety and loneliness cower and tremble.

Patterns are my sanctuary. Same way, same place, same time. Patterns kill anxiety. Patterns kill anxiety for a while. Soon it's not enough. The patterns require more attention. They demand an extra stage, more numbers, a lucky word. I don't know when the patterns took over and stole my life. Nancy spotted it first.

'It's not normal,' she told my dad, 'he needs help.'

'It's just a phase,' my dad replied. My mum's drinking was 'just a phase.' His absence was 'just a phase.' Living in Nancy's house was 'just a phase.' My counting, touching, patterns, compulsions to control the tsunami of negative feelings was sadly not a phase.

When I first met Nancy and Ava it was love at first sight. Terrifyingly positive emotions came in quick succession. Laughter, joy, excitement and happy anticipation had all been missing from my store cupboard. I didn't recognise the labels of these foreign concoctions. At first it felt marvellous, like a warm coat on a cold day, the vital ingredient in a favourite dish. I didn't know then that love ruins the recipe. Love is the problem. When love comes, so does the monster.

A gentle knock calls me back to reality, where I am, what today holds. I hear Keziah, a small whisper.

'I'm coming,' I call back, knowing it'll take at least forty-five minutes to complete the rituals and that's without a shower.

'Tell Nancy I'm on my way but to start without me.'

Keziah

Waking up here, 3A Spitfield Road, an ordinary bungalow, was not what I expected when I climbed into Claus's car. This bungalow is definitely a home. It has been adapted so everything is wider and lower. Most things can be controlled remotely including the lights, doors and windows. But somehow, it's still warm and cosy. The quirky art on the wall is exactly what I'd choose. The sofa invites snuggle rather than perch.

I trudge along the hall feeling awkward. Black-framed photographs cover the walls. Most are pictures of Ava. At school, at a wedding, and later in a wheelchair but on the back of a boat, and finally wearing a mortar board at graduation.

The final frame holds not a photo, but a certificate. A medical report. Calligraphy writing in black ink.

'This certifies Ava Williams rang the golden bell after eleven months in the National Hospital for Neurology.'

Underneath it says, 'Goodbye and good luck.' It's signed by Doctor Ali.

In bed last night I expected relief but despite my exhaustion, it was impossible to sleep. My room is the smallest of four. Nancy had placed clean towels on a patchwork throw. A large seashell was placed on top.

It sounds laughable, but seeing the sign for Spitfield Road I seriously thought I was done for. I imagined my mum being told I was dead. When Claus dragged me to a random door, I expected a crime gang to be waiting, suits and sunglasses. Now in the cold light of day, I feel stupid.

I had made a proper fool of myself, but Nancy was so kind. Whilst they were enjoying the ecstasy of an unexpected family reunion the guest was having a panic attack in the toilet. I was mortified.

The strangest thing about this place is Claus. With these people Claus is different. I've seen the man I fell for. He's gentle and tactile. He walks about in bare feet with no apparent care for the germs he might contract. He laughs with his head back, and lounges in the chair rather than perching on the edge, hypervigilant, ready for action. Nancy fetched him a foot stool to pop his feet up. He was a boy being loved by his mum.

The tender way he relates to Ava is touching, although I don't like the gut-clenching sensation.

Lying awake until the early hours, I've gone over and over old ground. I scribbled down what I know on an envelope. Writing stuff always clears my mind.

The address here is Spitfield Road.

It's *the* road.

Jen was killed somewhere close.

It's the road in the newspaper article.

Did that girl die or was that my presumption?

Could that be Ava? Ava is forty-three, could she be the right age?

If that was her, the child mentioned was Claus, or Nicky.

Why does he feel guilty? He's mentioned being sent away soon after? Did he push her?

Did I imagine an image to accompany the threatening voice, a man in a balaclava, a hanky disguising his usual voice? Could Ava's machine be the voice of NW, but why would she threaten him?

How do I ask this stuff? If I don't ask it, will they tell me?

Hearing Nancy in the kitchen, I remember mum's advice: 'Put on your big girl pants, Kezzy, and speak up.'

My prompt questions are in the back of my maternity jeans. Whilst Claus and I are done, I need reassurance my daughter won't find scary skeletons in her dad's wardrobe.

The smell of a cooked breakfast makes my mouth water.

'Morning, lovely,' Nancy beams. Ava is already sitting at the table.

'Tea?' Nancy asks, pouring from a teapot into a fine china cup.

In between the toast rack, and a hot plate of cooked meats, some photos are laid out, the old-fashioned ones with a white rim.

'We thought you might like to see some childhood piccies,' Nancy explains.

I pick up the first one and stare at 'passport boy' on a swing, he's smiling. Nancy leans over my shoulder to add a plate of fried eggs.

'Oh, Keziah he was the sweetest kid, that scruffy blonde hair and those blue eyes.'

Ava types on her machine at top speed and presses go.

'He was my first love. Sadly, for me he set the bar too high. All those presents and compliments meant no bloke has come close. So, thanks to Claus or whatever he calls himself, I'll die a spinster.'

I smile awkwardly at her; I still have no idea what's going on.

'Spit it out then.' Ava's mechanised voice startles me. 'Go on. Ask. Everyone's got questions, how I poo, sex, whatever's cool, fire away!'

‘Err,’ I stutter unintelligibly. ‘What happened to cause your disability?’ I ask, panicking I’ve not used the right terminology.

‘Got run over, didn’t Nicky tell you?’

‘No, should he have done?’ It’s so strange hearing his name as something else.

‘Well he was there, he remembers more than me.’

‘Does he?’

‘Yeah, his dad and my mum were smooching far ahead.’

Nancy turns around, dries her hands on a souvenir tea cloth.

‘So only Claus saw?’ I ask, aware that sounds loaded.

‘Out of our family, he was. But other people saw.’

I desperately want to ask, What then? What did they see? But I stay quiet.

‘It was horrendous at the time,’ Nancy chips in. ‘We felt all our lives were over, but it was more than thirty years ago. This is the Ava we know, this obnoxious cow who can’t walk not the obnoxious calf who could!’

I laugh. It makes me feel sufficiently courageous to ask, ‘Are you the girl in the newspaper article?’

Ava starts typing but a deeper voice interrupts.

‘How did you know about that?’ Claus asks, sitting down and putting toast on his plate. Nancy hands him the butter dish and then a jar of strawberry jam.

‘I found a clipping in the book by your bed, the text titled *Guilt*.’ I say, not daring to look away from his knife, carefully spreading the jam evenly.

I catch Nancy’s eye. She looks like she’s trying not to laugh; it doesn’t feel very funny.

She sees my face. 'Sorry! just a bit ironic isn't it. Psychologist hides secret in guilt text book.'

Claus doesn't laugh.

'It wasn't deliberate,' he says. 'I didn't know I still had it, I certainly didn't choose a relevant text to preserve it in.'

Everyone waits while Ava types, which gives me some much-needed processing time.

'You're such a pompous git sometimes, do you realise that?' the voice says.

Claus doesn't laugh but he doesn't cry or shout.

Then he swipes the tea towel off Nancy and flicks it on Ava's arm.

Ava cries out without the help of her machine. Claus notices my surprise.

'She can speak, you know, she's just a lazy witch and can't be bothered. She likes the drama of making us wait for her articulations.'

My eyes widen.

'Ignore him,' Nancy smiles, retrieving her towel. 'Ava can speak a little but articulating the sounds takes enormous effort. The machine allows her to keep up.'

Sod it, I think using Claus's only expletive. I'm going to ask.

'So, are you somehow guilty?' I say looking into his eyes.

Ava holds up her palm. I've learnt that means she wants to speak first.

We all wait, no one breathes whilst she types.

'Depends who you ask, if you listen to Nicky you'd believe he pushed me.'

‘I feel guilty too,’ says Nancy. ‘If anyone was to blame it was me, not watching my lively daughter showing off to her new love.’

Ava sticks out her tongue and makes a disgusted face at Claus which he returns, a bizarre sight!

Nancy ignores the feuding children and continues. ‘It was a tragic accident, no one’s fault.’

Ava holds up her hand again. I’m racing to mentally catch up. Surely they’d say if Claus had done something awful, wouldn’t they?

Finally, Ava declares, ‘It was my fault, I was being really stupid, deliberately freaking him out by spitting and carrying on. I could see he was in a state but I didn’t much care. That’s what I was like, admit it, mother!’

‘Yeah, she was a nightmare,’ Nancy confirms. ‘But they were kids and we were adults.’

When I look at Claus, he’s crying. Nancy spots it at the same time. She goes behind him and cuddles him.

‘When will you let it go?’ she asks, a mum to hurting boy.

‘Not sure I can,’ he mumbles, using a piece of kitchen roll to wipe away his tears

Ava pokes him, then types, ‘Man up, Caroline.’

‘That’s what she always called him,’ Nancy translates. ‘He was obsessed with that song.’

‘Still is.’ I’m glad to contribute at last.

‘I am still here.’ Claus is smiling again.

Claus disappears after breakfast, we all know he’s off to do a few rituals.

‘Bless him,’ Nancy says as he leaves. ‘That’s a muddled manboy, he needs the help he dishes out,’ she says, joining me at the table. 'Nick has ruined his life seeking redemption for things nothing to do with him.'

'Whilst he's out can I ask about some other stuff please?'

'Sure,' Ava says with her mouth not a machine.

It's slurred but I get it quick enough.

'Tell me about Jen, he married me without mentioning her.'

Nancy let's out a noisy sigh.

'We told him. We told him she was unsuitable and, then when he met you we told him not to rush – and especially without telling you.'

Ava types, 'He likes giving advice but not taking it.'

'Don't we all,' Nancy rebuffs.

'Jen was clearly unstable. She'd been abused in childhood and had made many attempts to kill herself. She was a nice enough person but not good for our boy.'

Ava flips up her hand and types frantically. 'She was a mental manipulative cow.'

'Ava,'Nancy says, 'that's horrid, the poor woman's dead.'

'So, what, it's still true,' the machine speaks like a petulant child.

'But she died here, on this road?' I'm determined to get the truth.

'Yes,' Nancy says, clearly emotional. 'We persuaded Nick to bring her. He was so devastated when she got herself discharged from the day service, their input reassured him. He called me in tears. He was terrified she'd kill herself whilst he was at work. He has spent his entire life trying to protect broken women and failing. I insisted he came here and let me deal with her whilst he had a break either here or at home.'

Ava types, 'But she hated me.'

'She certainly did,' Nancy confirms without hesitancy. 'From the moment Ava wheeled in, Jen could see how close she was with Nicky, and she loathed us both.'

Ava interrupts with speech but is too stressed and we wait for her to type.

'So the stupid selfish witch killed herself up the road, whilst we enjoyed a Chinese for my birthday.'

'I see you've been updated,' Claus wanders in, hands in pockets, defeated rather than irritated.

'Sorry,' I say, unsure for what. Am I sorry for not trusting him, thinking he was a double murdering child trafficker or just for talking behind his back?

'Don't be,' he says squeezing on to a kitchen stool between me and Ava's chair. 'I drove you here to get the truth. I hope the truth will set us both free. Everything that's good for me is here and yet so much bad has happened here. I thought if we reunited here, it might somehow undo the pattern, complete the good cycle.'

'Yeah,' says Ava. 'Because that makes rational sense.' We all laugh. 'Anything else you wanna know, Keziah?'

'There is,' I say. I copy her dramatic pause before asking, 'Are you the infamous NW?'

Claus smiles. But Ava shakes her head.

'What she means,' Nancy says, 'is yes, at forty-three, I used my mother's phone to make dark stalker calls to my brother because he wouldn't come home.'

We leave early evening. Claus talks openly for hours on the journey home, clutching my hand when he can. He replays the NW messages and they sound way less threatening when I place Ava's face behind them. He fills in more details about what happened with Ava and then Jen and the ominous way they both got hurt in Spitfield Road. At some level he still believes he has internal monsters with independent agency.

Pulling into my drive, I see Ameena behind a twitching curtain. She's worse than my mother. Claud unfastens his belt and takes my hand. 'So, let me get this straight. You knew my wife was killed on that road. You thought I'd killed Ava there. Then you were afraid this was where I sacrifice women in the same place every few years?'

Claus laughs. 'Blimey, Keziah I thought my head was messy.'

Claus unclips my seatbelt and reaches for my bag from the back seat balancing it on his lap as he twists to look at me.

'Keziah, I know I've made such a mess of everything. I'm so glad you've met my real family. Did you see more of who I am there? The real me? Can you accept I'm not the together professional you dreamt about?'

'Yes.' I can.

'Oh Keziah, that's such good news. Can we start over, start again?'

I'm shattered. I want to reach out and reassure him, none of it matters. I want to look into his blue eyes, kiss that wayward piece of hair and tell him, yes, of course. But I can't. I told him I would do his trip and I'm glad I did. I do now understand, I think, as much as anyone can understand another person's story but I'm no longer the girl he rescued. He has healed me, he has saved me so now I don't need a knight, I'm quite happy to sit in the saddle of my horse or – perhaps – mountain bike.

I allow Claus to give me one last kiss despite a bump and an overnight bag.

I lean into his warmth, smell him, feel his arms around me. Now I know who I've married, why he's like he is, I feel sure he'll make a lovely dad.

'Claus, I don't know how to say this. But. No. You need help I can't give. I'm so, so sorry.'

As he weeps, I touch his hand one final time.

'Goodbye, my love,' I say and close the passenger door.

25

Claus

'Hey Dr Doerkson,' Hattie chirps as I push through the double doors.

Sod it! I presumed I'd have the place to myself this evening.

'I didn't expect you to be in,' she says, two of my text books poking out of her bag.

'Clearly not,' I want to say. Instead I smile and say, 'I have some paperwork to collect.'

My office is just as I left it, not even the cleaners have a key. There is a small gold heart left from the day I planned the baby shower. Tears threaten as I remember my frivolous mood.

I fill an overnight bag with final essentials. The photograph of Keziah on our wedding day, my father's paperweight and a few thank you cards from families I've worked with. Have I helped anyone? That's all I wanted to do. I wanted to rescue children like me — the forgotten, the neglected —before they became the adult I am, tortured, ruined and beyond salvation.

Relief has finally arrived. In the early hours, a decision was made. A decision I should've made decades ago. A decision that will liberate us all.

I clear out a few texts book that are mine. *Guilt* is at the bottom. Flicking though the tired pages I find the cruise ship advert. I have no recollection of keeping it. Why on earth didn't she ask me? 'Because you are a vile monster.' My mind knows the truth.

I snap the book shut, too late for regrets. Stay focused, old boy.

Sorting through my large box file, I take all the personal documentation, my insurance paperwork, BPS certificate, HCPC registration card. Academic articles are filed alphabetically. The article I want follows an index card with a sticker.

The article on common suicide methods is on the top, where it was filed. There are advantages for us obsessionals. I unclip the lever arch and remove just the summary page.

Collapsing into my luxurious clinical chair, I enjoy a final view from my office window. Outside, the evening light is disappearing, and the window slowly becomes a mirror in the dark. A haggard old man stares back, I might be mistaken for a retired tramp. '*You* are a very stupid man,' I tell him.

I have no idea why this obvious step has taken me so long. I could've saved so much heartbreak. Three important people deserve explanation. Opening my Macbook, I type.

Dearest Keziah,

Thank you so much for trusting me enough to come to Hampshire. I can't tell you how sorry I am about frightening you. Selfish as I am, I didn't consider how it might be for you. I'm deeply grateful for your gracious decision about our daughter's birth. Having given the matter heartfelt consideration, I won't come. To attend the birth would be too painful. As I promised, I'll leave you alone. I'm so sorry and pray one day you'll forgive me. Please assure your daughter that she was loved by a father who couldn't trust himself. With deepest love,

Claus

Tears cascade down my face.

Enough now, Nicky, enough.

At boarding school, my only visitor was dear Mr P. Without fail, he drove up every month until his health deteriorated, then he came on the train. Even after his wife died and he lost sight in one eye, he sent cards and regularly telephoned. Not much of himself is left but I owe him such a debt.

Dear Kat,

I've transferred a substantial sum of money into the nursing home account. There is enough for his fees until his hundredth birthday. I have added more for luxuries. Please can you make sure my beloved Mr P gets a glass of his favourite tipple each night and anything else he wants. Thank you for the loving care you and your staff have given him over so many years. Transferring him to you was one of my finest decisions.

Kind regards,

Dr C Doerkson

One more email.

Dear Nancy,

What can I say? Thanks so much for the weekend. Keziah of course loved you both. Who wouldn't? Thank you for all you've done. I'm sorry I didn't receive your help with greater wisdom.

I'm going to do what I always should have done. Yours always,

Nicky xx

I abandon the keys on the administrator's desk without explanation and pause for a last glance at my psychology department before running down the stairs, two at a time.

Goodbye, Dr Doerkson.

The front door clicks shut for a final time. It's dark now, so no one can see me. I'm tired of pretending, tired of being afraid. Quite simply, I've had enough.

Coming off the motorway onto quieter roads, the sombre isolation is comforting. Following this course will save others, it's the only way. I open the windows and listen to the gulls, smell the coastal air. The car brushes too close to a bramble bush but I no longer care. It'll stay in the cliff-top car park.

The wind is harsh against my face, the night quiet and empty; not a soul to witness me leaving my disastrous life of rituals and patterns, terror and shame.

'At last,' Nancy would say with a sigh of relief. Her feet on the arm of her chair, a chunk of cake held in her hand.

The image makes me smile as I press the buzzer.

A male nurse presses an entry pad and automatic doors part.

'Claus Doerkson,' I say

The man looks at an iPad mini and shakes my hand.

'Yes, you're on the list, voluntary admission for six-month inpatient programme?'

‘Indeed,’ I say clutching my daughter’s scan picture, my tiny glimmer of hope.

Each time I’ve presented on suicidal risk, I’ve seen the advert for this well-respected unit at the bottom of that article and hoped one day exhausted little Nicky would discover the courage to heal.

Epilogue

A serious little girl, with a straight fringe and brown eyes, gathers her belongings. She says goodbye to her teacher and plods towards the exit. Her first year at big school done and dusted, where did that time go?

She sprints across the tarmac, disinterested in the watching adults. Before school she told her mum three reasons why today was her best ever day. She used her fingers to keep track.

One, it's the last day of school before summer break.

Two, they're taking birthday balloons and cake to someone she loves.

Three, her daddy is coming home forever.

Three good things, she reminded her tired mummy as she had climbed into the car. Her three skinny fingers were still poking up as they drove off.

Still in his suit, her dad is waiting by the school gate. He crouches to her level when she gets close, enveloping her into his arms, before swinging her onto his wide shoulders. The other children look on. But today she doesn't care what they think. Who cares if someone sees her pink spotty knickers?

She perches, gently bouncing as he walks, his hands steadying her legs. She clutches her book bag hoping to read her special story at the party.

Outside the wide gates, the family of three pause so the girl can show off her literacy skills.

Her daddy points at the fancy sign, one word at a time.

'Twilight Lawns – for distressed gentlefolk.'

They wait for the familiar swoosh when Kelly, the matron, presses the high button.

'I'm not sure I want to reach one hundred,' Kelly says to everyone as she opens a door that's painted orange.

On the door is a soldier, it's in black and white, taken in the olden days when he wasn't old.

'Happy birthday to you, happy birthday to you . . .'

They all sing and clap. The little girl presents the blue foil balloon. He's in his usual chair; his eyes are cloudy. They know how little

he can see but he smiles when he hears them singing. Kelly finds his teeth and pops them in his mouth.

The man lets the little girl jump on his knee despite having no idea who she is, or why she's here.

'Remind me of your name,' he asks politely.

She slides off his legs and stands in front of him so he can hear.

'My name is Esther Ava Doerkson,' she shouts whilst performing a curtsy. Then she gestures to her father and introduces him as if he's a fellow actor. 'And this is Nicholas Doerkson and this is Keziah Doerkson.'

Her parents play along, bowing to the birthday boy.

Then, Esther taps her mummy's belly and says, 'In here is Eric Doerkson and you, sir, are Mr Arthur Pinkney.'

She beams her school photograph smile, hands on hips. Mr P Chuckles like he always does when the family visit. After all, he's got no one else now. He leans back in his rocking chair and closes his eyes about to snooze but suddenly he bolts upright again, his hands on his thighs, ready to go.

'Tell me a story'

Esther is prepared, he always asks for one.

There's a story that she's wanted to tell him ever since she could speak. It's the story her daddy tells her. It's changed every few months but he's told her a version of this story, every Friday and Saturday since as long as she can remember.

He always calls it 'The Story of Us'. Every time Mr P asks for a story, she asks her daddy, 'Can I tell him ours?' but her daddy always shakes his head. Today, she is hopeful.

'Can I?' She asks looking at both her parents, from one to the other her face searches their faces. Then just when she thinks she might burst; her mummy grabs her daddy's hand and together they nod.

Esther takes centre stage whilst her mum retreats into the only other chair. Her father leans up against the wall, his arms folded, a megawatt smile on his face. Kelly joins them just in time, with plates and a knife for the cake.

Esther opens her literacy book as if she has a much larger audience and starts to read.

'This –' she pauses for dramatic effect '– this is the story of us, by Esther Ava Doerkson. Once upon a time, there was a sad little boy who lived next door to a very nice man. When the man grew up he fell in love with a heroine who loved to ride her bike. But, bad monsters came and messed it all up. So, he had to go away and finish them off once and for all. The heroine would not allow him home until every single monster was well and truly slayed.'

Esther pretends to use an imaginary sword with more passion than her parents would prefer. Esther lays down her weapon and repositions herself. She inhales such a large breath that everyone else does the same.

She continues reading.

'The man could not risk his family getting hurt. He just couldn't.'

Another dramatic pause to check her audience.

'But after five and a half years, the monsters were dead.'

Kelly gives a surprisingly loud cheer for the hero's win. Mr P wakes up from his snooze for the finale.

'Then the man turns into a prince.'

Esther turns to look at her daddy knowing she made that bit up. He puts up his thumbs, unashamed tears running down his face.

'Then the prince came back and married the biking princess all over again and . . .'

Her parents wait expectantly slightly anxious as to what is coming next.

'Then the Prince zipped baby Eric inside the princess and when he came out, they all lived happily ever after, forever.'

Esther blushes as everyone laughs and takes another bow.

'I added Eric,' she explains, concerned that everyone is crying.

With full attention on his beloved daughter, Nicholas Doerkson throws his head back and laughs and laughs.

Adult Psychology Discharge Report Summary

The Cottage
Inpatient services
The Granary
Old Woking
Gl88 7UN

Dear Dr Fooks, Re: Claus Doerkson.

The above patient admitted himself to our services five years ago. He completed the six-months inpatient programme but continued to attend as a day patient for the following six months. For the last four years he has attended fortnightly for outpatient appointments with our community clinical psychologist who he plans to continue with for less frequent reviews.

He has a complex history of neglect, trauma and severe obsessional compulsive behaviour. He wondered if he might have a personality disorder but from the outset I have reassured him I do not agree. He is a kind and generous man who was let down by both his parents and the community around him.

When he arrived Dr Doerkson's goals were as follows:

1. To better understand the triggers that led to his controlling and obsessional behaviours;

2. To manage jealousy within interpersonal relationships;
3. To return to some sort of meaningful occupation;
4. To learn how to be a successful father.

During his treatment this patient has learnt tools to relate differently to his intrusive thoughts and difficult feelings so he is not driven to behave out of line with his values, e.g. controlling others, safety behaviours and rituals. Regular visits from his baby daughter gave him immense pleasure and increased his motivation to succeed in therapy.

I am so pleased to discharge this patient back to you. Men who have learnt to suppress their anxiety by controlling others are very difficult to treat. Dr Doerkson so wanted to parent his daughter well that his motivation was sky high and his tenacity has paid off.

In the past few months he has been working with a drop-in centre as a volunteer psychologist helping asylum seekers recover from trauma. He is rebuilding a friendship with his estranged wife and has his daughter to stay with him at least two nights each week.

I have every expectation he will continue to stay well.

Yours sincerely,

Dr B. Mumford

MANAGING DIRECTOR OF CLINICAL PSYCHOLOGY SERVICES

THE END

Printed in Great Britain
by Amazon

10348238R00189